MAN IN THE WATER

MAN IN
THE WATER

David Housewright

MINOTAUR
BOOKS
NEW YORK

First published in the United States by Minotaur Books, an imprint of St. Martin's Publishing Group

MAN IN THE WATER. Copyright © 2024 by David Housewright. All rights reserved. Printed in the United States of America. For information, address St. Martin's Publishing Group, 120 Broadway, New York, NY 10271.

www.minotaurbooks.com

Library of Congress Cataloging-in-Publication Data

Names: Housewright, David, 1955– author.
Title: Man in the water / David Housewright.
Description: First edition. I New York : Minotaur Books, 2024. I
    Series: Twin Cities P.I. Mac McKenzie novels ; 21
Identifiers: LCCN 2024005819 I ISBN 9781250863607 (hardcover) I
    ISBN 9781250863614 (ebook)
Subjects: LCSH: McKenzie, Mac (Fictitious character)—Fiction. I
    LCGFT: Detective and mystery fiction. I Novels.
Classification: LCC PS3558.O8668 M36 2024 I DDC 813/.54—
    dc23/eng/20240214
LC record available at https://lccn.loc.gov/2024005819

Our books may be purchased in bulk for promotional, educational, or business use. Please contact your local bookseller or the Macmillan Corporate and Premium Sales Department at 1-800-221-7945, extension 5442, or by email at MacmillanSpecialMarkets@macmillan.com.

First Edition: 2024

10 9 8 7 6 5 4 3 2 1

FOR RENÉE
ALWAYS AND FOREVER

ACKNOWLEDGMENTS

Allow me to acknowledge my debt to Grace Gay, Kayla Janas, Keith Kahla, James McDonald, Susannah Noel, Alison J. Picard, Emily Polachek, Sabrina Soares Roberts, and Renée Valois for their assistance in writing this book.

MAN IN THE WATER

ONE

Nina Truhler screamed when she found the man in the water. Later, she would tell me that she hadn't been afraid, merely startled. I didn't believe her, though, because I heard the scream.

What happened, a mutual friend had invited us to go boating on the St. Croix, the river that formed much of the border between Minnesota and Wisconsin. Dave Deese was pretty excited about it. The weather had improved dramatically by mid-March. Unseasonably bright, warm sunshine had melted the snow and most of the ice and Deese was anxious to get his boat out of dry dock, a forty-two-foot Sea Ray Sundancer that he and his wife often slept on just because. I mean the man had all but given up playing golf so he could spend more time on the river, how nuts was that? He had his "big splash" a few days earlier. Apparently, that's the term luxury boat owners use when they launch their boats; guys with fishing and pontoon boats probably not so much.

Nina and I were excited, too, about the prospect of taking a river cruise and for the same reason—spring. So we accepted the invitation and drove a half hour from Minneapolis to the marina located a few miles north of Stillwater. Only by then the temperature had plummeted to a few degrees below freezing and the sky had turned a dark shade of gray. I half expected to see icebergs floating on the St. Croix and the fact that I didn't, well, that didn't prove they weren't lurking beneath the surface.

The lot was nearly empty; only four vehicles were parked there when we arrived including a black SUV with the name E. J. WOODS TREE CARE SERVICES printed in white letters on all of its doors. We bundled ourselves in heavy coats, boots, and hats, and walked onto the mazelike steel-and-wooden pier that jutted from the shoreline into the river. The marina boasted over two hundred and fifty U-shaped slips but finding Deese wasn't difficult. I counted less than two dozen boats secured to the cleats and plugged in to the electrical outlets. That, plus the sparsely filled parking lot, told me those of us who thought spring had come early to Minnesota were in a true minority.

Before we could reach Deese, though, we were intercepted by a woman; her words came in puffs of condensation.

"Help me," she said. "Please."

I had no idea how old she was. Her eyes were clear and blue; yet her face suggested that she had discovered the fountain of youth in an artful amalgamation of cosmetics and neurotoxins. Her skirt was short, her jacket lightweight, and her head uncovered; shoulder-length blond hair was whipped about in the wind and she used both of her hands to keep it out of her face. The wooden planks beneath her feet were as steady as a concrete sidewalk, yet she bobbed back and forth as if they were being buffeted by heavy waves.

"Please help me," she repeated.

"Help you what?" I asked.

"My husband . . ."

She wrapped her arms around herself as if she suddenly realized that it was cold outside.

"My husband . . ."

"Yes?"

She shook her head.

Nina stretched out a hand and rested it on the woman's shoulder.

"Tell us about your husband," she said.

"I can't find him. I've looked and looked and I can't find him."

"You can't find him?" I asked.

"He was here."

"Here at the marina?"

"But now he's gone."

"Gone where?"

Stop it, my inner voice told me. *You sound like an idiot.*

"I don't know," the woman said. "Can you help me?"

"Of course we can," Nina said.

Her gaze turned from the woman and settled on me.

So, when you say we . . .

I spun in a slow circle, my eyes first scanning the boats moored in their three-sided slips. Next I examined the parking lot. The marina was located on the eastern side of the St. Croix Scenic Byway along with a couple other marinas, a business that rented paddleboats, and the St. Croix Scenic Overlook. On the western side, there was a restaurant, a coffeehouse, a massage parlor, and plenty of houses. Yet, as a man once said, nothing was stirring, not even a mouse. Finally, I turned toward the large red, white, and blue building with the name HEGGSTAD MARINA painted in large white letters above the front door and huge windows. There was a parklike area reserved for picnics and barbecues located between the building and the river, along with a dockside gas pump, only I could see no one moving.

"Did your husband go inside?" I asked.

The woman shook her head.

"Did you look?"

She shook it some more.

"I'll be right back."

I walked across the wooden planks and climbed the concrete steps leading to the building. A sign on the front door told me that cable TV and internet access were available to slip renters as well as free shower rooms and a coin-operated laundry. Bright lights inside Heggstad Marina made the place seem like an automobile showroom, only for boats. There was also a large area devoted to the sale of all the things you might find on a boat, from life jackets to bumpers and fenders to ropes and harnesses to bags of Fritos and precut fruit, plus a section where a fellow might buy dry clothes, deck shoes, and rain gear. I started walking through the building, my head on a swivel, searching the empty spaces between the boats.

A man called to me.

"May I help you?"

He had a name tag above his left pocket that read BRAD HEGGSTAD.

"Hey," I said. "I met a woman outside who's looking for her husband. I thought he might have wandered in here."

"I haven't seen anyone."

"Restrooms?"

"Good idea."

He gestured at a corridor between the showroom and the boat supplies. I found the men's room. It was large with several shower stalls and empty. I tried the women's restroom on the off chance. It was vacant as well.

Heggstad was waiting for me when I returned.

"Nothing, huh?" he asked.

"No."

"When did he get here?"

"I don't know."

"What's his name? Does he have a boat?"

"I don't know."

"Could he be visiting one of my early rentals?"

"His wife didn't say."

I expected him to be annoyed by my answers. God knows I was. Yet there was genuine concern in his voice when he said, "Maybe he's not here at all. Maybe he wandered across the street to get a cup of coffee."

"I'll look," I said.

I went to the door, opened it, and stepped outside. The cold wind slapped me in the face, yet the scream hit me harder.

Nina's scream.

I didn't see her as much as her long blue winter coat. The coat was at the far end of the marina where two boats were parked. It was standing at the very edge of the dock and looking down. A sleeve came up to cover Nina's mouth and the coat backed away from the edge. Another sleeve seemed to search behind her for a bench. Finding none, the coat sat down in the middle of the dock.

By then I was running. I sprinted down the stone steps to the pier and past the woman who was standing exactly where we had left her, staring at nothing in particular. The dock was wide and stable and I had no trouble jogging the length that stretched along the shoreline and then over one of the arms that jutted out into the water. My heavy Columbia hiking boots pounded on the wooden planks and seemed to echo across the water beneath them. I was chanting Nina's name by the time I reached her.

"Nina, Nina."

"I'm okay, I'm okay," she chanted back.

I knelt next to her; my arm circled her shoulder.

"I'm okay. The woman, she told me—after you left she told me that she thought she saw her husband on the dock next to these boats." Nina shrugged a shoulder toward the cabin cruisers moored behind her on opposite sides of the dock from each other, one very near where we were sitting and one closer to the shore. "No one is on the boats, but McKenzie"—she raised a hand and pointed—"I went to the edge of the dock and looked down. I don't know why."

I followed Nina's pointing finger to the edge. There was a wooden ladder attached to the dock. I looked down, went to my knees, and looked some more. I wasn't sure what I was looking at; the water was clear, only the overcast sky wasn't giving me much help. As my eyes adjusted, I realized I was staring at the top of a man's head about a foot and a half beneath the water. He was fully clothed for winter, his gloved hands were tightly gripping each side of the ladder, and he was looking straight ahead as if there was something under the dock that demanded his complete and undivided attention. I removed my own glove and immediately felt the cold. I was about to dip my hand into the icy water, yet thought better of it.

What are you going to do, check for a pulse?

I spun on my knees toward Nina.

"I'm sorry," I said.

Her expression suggested that she had no idea what I was talking about. Probably because I had never told her that the thing I hated most when I was a cop was delivering bad news.

"I'm sorry, there was an accident . . . I'm sorry, there was a shooting . . . I'm sorry, we conducted a welfare check . . ."

Now I was going to have to deliver some more bad news, even though I hadn't been a cop for a long time, and I was not looking forward to it. I stood and gazed across the marina.

The woman was still standing where we had left her, her weight shifting from one foot to the other. What I found re-markable, though, was that despite enlisting our aid to find her husband, Nina's scream, and my mad sprint to Nina's side, the woman wasn't looking anywhere near us but instead gazing across the river toward Wisconsin.

Don't you think that's a little off?

If I was still a cop, I would have questions to ask her, I told myself.

I looked down at Nina.

"He's dead, isn't he?" she said. "I mean, of course he is, but how? Did he drown?"

"I don't know."

Aren't you getting tired of saying that?

"Geez, McKenzie, I knew these things always happened to you but I didn't know when we got married that they would happen to me, too."

"I'm sorry."

The operator said, "911, what's your emergency?"

I told her where we were; I told her about finding the man in the water. I told her to contact the Stillwater Police Department, water rescue, and the medical examiner, in that order. She didn't seem interested in my advice and instead asked for my name. I gave it to her and she told me to remain where I was.

"Help is on the way," she told me.

She also told me to remain on the line until help arrived. I apologized, said I had things to do, and hung up.

By then Nina and I had reached the woman. She waited for us to speak.

"I'm sorry," I said.

She waited some more.

"I'm sorry, but we found a man in the water."

"He must have fallen in the river by accident and drowned," the woman said.

Nina opened her arms and stepped toward the woman. The woman stepped backward, avoiding the hug.

"I was afraid that might have happened when I couldn't find him." She sounded like she was explaining why she had missed a sale at Cub Foods. "E. J. wanted to look at the boats and at the river. He liked boats and the river. I was waiting in the car for him."

The woman gestured at the SUV in the parking lot with the words E. J. WOODS TREE CARE SERVICES painted on the door.

"I waited in the car because it was cold," the woman added. "When he didn't return—I waited at least a half hour." She glanced at her watch as if to confirm the time. "When he didn't return, I went looking for him. I didn't find him. I feared the worst. I met you two. You were very kind. I'm grateful for what you've done."

Geez, lady, my inner voice said. *Your husband just drowned in the St. Croix River. When are we going to see some tears?*

"Did you call 911?" the woman asked.

"Yes."

"I'm grateful for that as well. It saves me the trouble. I guess there's nothing to do now except wait."

We didn't wait long. The woman spun toward the parking lot at the same moment that another black SUV pulled into the lot, this one with the name STILLWATER POLICE printed in white on the side. When she saw the vehicle, the woman moved away from us and sat down on the dock. She brought her knees up, holding her skirt around her thighs, and leaned forward, resting her face against her knees. After a moment, she uncurled enough to glance behind her. She watched a female police officer slide out of the SUV. The officer was dressed in full battle regalia, her long hair piled on top of her head. As the officer approached, the woman resumed her near-fetal position and began rocking side to side.

Okay, now this is really off.

The officer landed on the dock and started moving toward

us. She stopped when she reached the woman, who was now humming unintelligible sounds filled with grief and sorrow.

The officer knelt and rested her hand on the woman's back.

"Ma'am," she said.

"My husband, my husband . . . He's gone. It's the marina's fault."

"Ma'am, what's your name?"

"Bizzy."

"Ma'am?"

"It's the marina's fault."

The officer looked up at me. The name tag above her left pocket read STOLL.

"Are you McKenzie?" she asked.

I nodded in reply.

"You found the body?"

I gestured at Nina.

"Both of us. This woman"—I pointed at her—"apparently, she's the vic's wife."

I purposely used the word "vic." It's a cop word, slang for victim. I wanted the officer to know that we were both on the same side.

"Show me."

Officer Stoll rose and I led her across the dock to the far end of the pier. She asked me how I had come to the marina.

"It's still off-season," she said.

I explained.

"Did you see anything?" she asked.

"Only the body," I replied.

I led Officer Stoll to the edge of the dock. She looked down, went to her knees as I had done, and looked some more.

"Wow," she said.

Wow, indeed.

"McKenzie, were you on the job?"

"Almost twelve years in St. Paul."

"Have you seen anything like this?"

"I didn't catch many drownings."

"I have. A couple, anyway. This is . . . the way he's hanging on to the ladder like that. Wow."

Stoll did something then that convinced me she was a good cop. She crawled away from the edge and, while still on her knees, began running her bare hands back and forth over the wooden planks. She did this until she covered at least a couple of square yards.

"I don't feel any moisture," she said. "I don't feel any ice."

"He could have tripped over his own feet," I said. "I've done that."

She hummed a reply and we made our way back to where Nina and the woman were standing.

By then more officers had arrived, all men. Unlike the female cop, they had come with sirens blaring. The sirens drew a crowd. Brad Heggstad climbed down the hill from the marina building to the pier. I didn't know if he was interviewing the cops or they were interviewing him. My pal Dave Deese and his wife, Barbara, sat on the deck of their Sundancer and watched from a distance. Neighbors lined the fence above the marina and looked down on us.

Nearly all the cops went one by one to the edge of the dock to see the man in the water for themselves. It was like he had become a tourist attraction. Meanwhile, Nina and I were separated and interviewed. The wife of the man in the water was interviewed as well. By then she had dried her tears and was telling the cops almost exactly what she had told us. From what little I overheard, I discovered that her name was Elizabeth Woods and her husband was Earl Woods. She told the cops that she felt indebted to Nina and me. I couldn't imagine why.

Not long after, deputies belonging to the Washington County

Sheriff's Office arrived. I failed to recognize them at first; their uniforms closely resembled the Minnesota Highway Patrol's. I didn't know which incidents fell within the Stillwater PD's jurisdiction and which belonged to the county, but the deputies immediately took charge of the crime scene, if you want to call it that. One by one, like the police officers, they also went to the edge of the dock and looked down. Afterward, they interviewed Elizabeth Woods, Brad Heggstad, and Nina and me all over again. One deputy made his way up the dock to where Deese's boat was moored and chatted with him and his wife. Afterward, he visited one by one the other boats in the marina; they all seemed to be empty.

Shortly after, the county's Water, Parks, and Trails Unit appeared—two deputies in a car and a few more in boats that had come up the St. Croix.

"They're the ones who investigate deaths and accidents on the river," Officer Stoll told me.

They converged on the man in the water. Photographs were taken; measurements were made. At the same time, a deputy started shooing people off the pier.

"There's nothing to see," he said. Swear to God.

Nina and I made our way to my friend's boat. The name printed across the stern read DEESE AND DOSE.

"Permission to come aboard?" I was told you're supposed to ask that before stepping on someone's boat; a form of knocking, I was told.

"What have you done now?" Deese said. "Is this one of your"—he quoted the air—"'cases'?"

Like you should talk, my inner voice said.

Not too long ago, I had used DNA to connect him to a couple of half brothers and a sister that he didn't know he had. They grew close. Eventually, Deese traded a chunk of his liver to one of them for the boat, which wasn't nearly as mercenary as it sounds. His newfound family had more money than everyone you had ever known combined and was exceedingly grateful and generous. Complicated story.

While we were chatting, the medical examiner arrived and the body was retrieved from the river; three men pulled the dead man up as gently as possible. Given his dark winter clothes, from a distance Mr. Woods looked like a small whale. I couldn't see his face as they laid the body across the dock.

"Is this your idea of a boat-warming gift?" Barbara said.

"That's not funny," Nina said.

Her tone of voice changed the mood. We were brought aboard and taken down the narrow companionway into the salon. The four of us fit comfortably around a folding table. Surrounding us was the stuff of the boat's galley—refrigerator, stove, micro-wave, coffeemaker, stainless-steel sink with a single lever faucet, and storage cabinets. Forward was a stateroom. The partition was open and we could see the queen-size bed, cabinets, a flat-screen TV, and a head, what they call a bathroom on a boat. Drinks were dispensed.

"What did the deputy ask you?" I said.

"He wanted to know if I saw anything, if I heard anything," Deese said.

"Did you?"

"No. Well, not today; not this morning when we arrived. Thursday I saw a couple of people wandering around, though. Brad Heggstad, who runs the marina, plus a few others. I didn't pay any attention to them. I figured they were from the other boats. You see people on the pier all the time during the summer, but . . ." Deese gestured at the ceiling of the boat's cabin, although, I'm sure he meant the sky. "People say I splashed too early, only there were already a dozen or more boats here before I arrived."

"Can you describe the people?"

"Nah."

"Men? Women?"

"No, what I told the deputy during the interrogation."

"Interview," I said.

"What's the difference?"

"Out here in the open it's an interview. It becomes an interrogation when it's conducted in the house where there's no one to see."

"I'll keep that in mind."

"How 'bout you, Barb?" I asked. "Did you see anything?"

"Yes, I did, thanks for asking."

"Wait," Deese said. "You did? Why didn't you speak up?"

"The deputy didn't ask me," Barbara said. "He only spoke to you like I wasn't even there. Remember? Asked for your name, which he wrote down, but didn't ask for mine."

Ah, geez. C'mon.

"What did you see?" I asked.

"I didn't see anything this morning, either," Barbara said. "As far as I could tell we were the only ones here, which I thought was kinda creepy. Thursday, I saw the same people that Dave saw. Yesterday, though, I saw a couple, a man and a woman, walking together. They were holding hands."

"When was this?"

"Friday. Right before we left. When was that, Dave? Seven? Seven thirty? I remember thinking—Friday was a lot warmer than today, but I thought 'a skirt?' The woman was wearing a skirt in winter in Minnesota and I couldn't remember the last time I wore a skirt in winter in Minnesota."

"You wear skirts in the winter," Dave insisted.

"Only when my husband takes me to someplace nice which, let's face it, he hasn't done lately." Barbara blinked several times at Dave. "Hint, hint."

"Where would you like to go?" Deese asked.

Barbara pointed at Nina.

"How about Rickie's?" she said. "I bet we could get a good table. We know people."

Usually that would generate a response. Nina would say something like, "Maybe if you tip the hostess a twenty," something like that, only she didn't speak. Instead, she just stared into her drink.

"Tell me about the couple," I said.

"Honestly, McKenzie, I wasn't paying that much attention. All I can tell you is that he was taller than she was and they were walking that way."

Barbara pointed at the hull of the *Deese and Dose,* yet I knew that beyond the hull was the far side of the marina where the body was discovered.

"And you didn't tell the deputy," I said.

"Like I said, he didn't ask."

"If they talk to you again, tell them."

"Do you think it's important?" Barbara asked.

"The woman, the vic's wife, she was wearing a skirt."

I glanced at my own watch and did the math. Nina and I had arrived at Heggstad Marina at about eleven. When the woman approached us, she said she had been waiting for her husband for over a half hour. Make it ten fifteen to be on the safe side. Only Barbara said she and Dave were the only ones at the marina since . . .

"When did you arrive this morning?" I asked.

"Nine, nine thirty," Dave said.

"Did you spend much time on deck?"

"No, mostly we were below. It's cold outside."

"What are you thinking?" Barbara asked.

"I'm not thinking," I said.

"Yes, you are. I can tell by the way you stare off into the

distance like you're reading a billboard except there's no billboard."

"I don't do that."

"Yes, you do," Nina said. "Only I hadn't thought of it in quite
that way."

She raised her glass toward Barbara as if she had just been
given a gift. I was pleased to see the slight grin on her face.

"What I'm thinking is that this is none of my business," I
said. "What I'm thinking is that we should get this boat on the
river. There's a bar in Prescott serving Bloody Marys with my
name on them."

"Yeah, about that," Dave said.

"What?"

"I took the temperature of the water in the marina. It's probably warmer in the middle of the St. Croix, only here it's thirty-
two degrees. There's a chance the icy water could damage my
engines, so I figured we might hang around here."

*Thirty-two degrees. If a man jumps, falls, or is pushed into
water that cold, he'll experience shock, nearly always accompanied by an involuntary gasp, what they call a torso reflex,
in which he'll swallow water—it takes less than a half cup of
water in your lungs to drown. He could drown in a minute. If
that doesn't do it, he'd lose muscle control in what? Just a few
minutes more, anyway.*

So the vic somehow ends up in the river, I told myself, swal-
lows enough water to kill him, yet somehow manages to make it
to the ladder. Only time and the weight of his now waterlogged
clothes work against him and he drowns before he can climb up,
gripping the side rails of the ladder that might have saved him.

"Look," Barbara said. "He's doing it again."

"Now what are you thinking, McKenzie?" Nina asked.

"I'm thinking how glad I am that we didn't bring a boat-
warming gift," I said.

TWO

Maryanne Altavilla was the smartest person in the room no matter what room she happened to be in. It was a big reason why she was the chief investigator in the Midwest Farmers Insurance Group's Special Investigative Unit at the tender age of thirty-one, which you might have found impressive if you didn't already know that she was promoted to the position when she was twenty-seven.

I opened the door to our high-rise condominium in downtown Minneapolis before she knocked; the security people had called before sending her up. She was wearing a heavy winter coat and boots because it was snowing. The temperature had gone from a high of eighty-eight degrees to a low of thirty-one in less than forty-eight hours and now it was snowing. On April 16. It made even the heartiest Minnesotans ask, "Why do we live here again?"

When Altavilla saw me, she said, "Mr. McKenzie."

"Really? Mr. McKenzie?"

I opened my arms and she stepped into them.

"I'm trying to be professional," she said as we hugged.

"You mean this isn't a social call?"

"How's Nina?"

"Spectacular."

"Is she here?"

"Yes."

Altavilla stepped out of my grasp.

"I need to speak to both of you," she said.

Nina moved toward the door as Altavilla removed her coat to reveal a severe black jacket and skirt and a white dress shirt. Her hair was the same color as the jacket and skirt; it was pulled back into a ponytail.

"Oh my God, Maryanne," Nina said.

She and Altavilla hugged, too, although theirs seemed to carry greater affection.

"How long has it been?" Nina asked. "At least two years."

"At least. Can I talk to you guys?"

"Of course."

Our condo had a master bedroom and guest room with en suites, plus a bathroom for visitors. Beyond that, we didn't have rooms so much as areas—dining area, music area where Nina's Steinway stood, office area with a desk and computer, and a kitchen area that was elevated three steps above the rest. The south wall was lined almost to the ceiling with books. The entire north wall consisted of tinted floor-to-ceiling glass with a dramatic view of the Mississippi River where it tumbled down St. Anthony Falls. Across from it was our living area where a sofa and chairs were arranged around a fireplace. Nina led Altavilla to a chair and sat across from her. I sat next to Nina.

Altavilla carried a large black bag that hung from a thick strap resting on her shoulder. She opened the bag and removed a notepad and pen.

"What's going on, Maryanne?" I asked.

"I have copies of reports filed by officers of the Stillwater Police Department and deputies with the Washington County Sheriff's Office. They state that you and Nina discovered the body of Earl John Woods, an African-American male, age sixty-two, at approximately eleven thirty A.M. on Saturday,

March twenty-fifth at the Heggstad Marina just outside Still-water."

"Earl John Woods," Nina said. "A name to go with the face."

That caused Altavilla to pause.

"But Nina, according to the reports, you couldn't see his face," she said.

"I do in my dreams."

I rested my hand on her shoulder.

"You never said . . ."

"You have enough dreams of your own to worry about."

"Nina . . ."

She rested her hand on top of mine.

"It's all right."

"I could come back another time," Altavilla said.

"Tomorrow won't be any different than today, Maryanne," Nina said. "Earl John Woods, you say. We knew the name from when the police interviewed us, only I never really connected it to the man in the water. That's kind of odd, don't you think? Something else—you say he was a Black man?"

"Yes."

"I didn't actually know that until this minute, yet in my dreams, he was Black. How is that possible?"

Neither Maryanne nor I had an answer for her.

Spooky, my inner voice said.

"Maryanne, why are you here?" I asked.

"I wanted to confirm that the statements you gave are accurate before the lawyers make their determination."

"Before the *lawyers* make their determination?" I said.

"Yes, although I'm pretty sure, based on the intelligence I've gathered so far, I know what they're going to decide."

"I don't understand," Nina said.

"Maryanne," I said. "What did the ME rule?"

"Oh, he didn't."

"Now I don't understand."

Altavilla rummaged through her bag and found another sheet of paper—why all this information wasn't stored on her phone, I couldn't say. She found the sheet of paper, yet quoted it from memory instead of reading it verbatim.

"The Ramsey County medical examiner serves as the medical examiner for Washington County as well as Aitkin, Blue Earth, Cass, Clay, Crow Wing, Freeborn, Hubbard, Kanabec, Le Sueur, Martin, Murray, Nicollet, Nobles, Redwood, Waseca, and Wilkin Counties."

"Maryanne—"

"The ME ruled that Earl John Woods, aka E. J. Woods, died by drowning, with hypothermia listed as an associated significant condition. However, the manner of death was classified as undetermined. There was no alcohol in his system; no drugs. There was no sign of trauma. He didn't hit his head on the dock and roll into the water; there were no contusions or lacerations."

"I get it now."

"I don't," Nina said.

Maryanne said, "When existing evidence supporting a specific manner of death—natural, accident, suicide, or homicide—is unavailable, the ME will rule that the manner of death is undetermined, which is the same thing as saying that they don't know why the man died, only what killed him."

"Which means your lawyers will decide based on what's best for the Midwest Farmers Insurance Group," I said.

"That's what they're paid for."

"I know you're both getting tired of hearing this, but I still don't understand," Nina said.

"The lawyers will rule that Earl Woods died by suicide," Altavilla said.

"Which means they won't pay off on his life insurance policy," I said.

"Oh, they'll pay," Altavilla said. "Only not as much."

"He didn't have a suicide exclusion?"

"That expired long ago. He set up the original policy with Midwest Farmers in the 1990s. However, he added a double indemnity rider just over a year ago."

"Really?"

"Makes an insurance investigator go 'hmm.'"

"Did he have any health issues?"

"None that I'm aware of, although I'll keep searching, especially since Midwest Farmers will probably be sued the moment the lawyers make their determination. You know how it works."

"I don't," Nina said.

I turned toward her.

"The way it works . . ." I said.

"No." Nina pointed at Altavilla. "You tell me."

"Nina, how often do I get a chance to prove how smart I am?"

She patted my hand and said, "Maryanne, be a friend."

"I love you guys," Altavilla said. "Double indemnity is an accidental death benefit rider. It provides an additional payment if death occurs as the result of an accident, often double the face value of the life insurance policy."

"How much is Mr. Woods's policy worth?"

"The original policy was for $500,000."

"That's a lot."

"No, not really. The average life insurance payout was $618,000 the last time I checked. What's unusual is the rider itself. Most people who have double indemnity riders work in dangerous occupations like construction or mining or they have really persuasive insurance agents. That's because only about five percent of all deaths in the United States are ruled accidental. In Mr. Woods's case, the DI rider boosts his payout an additional $500,000."

"A cool million," I said.

"However, double indemnity is usually not paid if the death occurs as a result of illegal activities or self-inflicted injuries," Altavilla said.

"That's why you expect to be sued," Nina said.

"Wouldn't you file a lawsuit? Half a million dollars is a lot of money and nobody wants to be told their loved one committed suicide."

"Now I understand."

"Unfortunately, it's going to get worse for you. I'm sorry, but Mr. Woods's beneficiaries will absolutely be sending lawyers to interview you, not to mention the other insurance companies."

"What other insurance companies?" I asked.

"Turns out Mr. Woods was stacking."

Nina shook her head.

"That means he had multiple life insurance policies, at least three besides the one he opened with Midwest Farmers," Altavilla said. "All activated within the past two years."

"The past two years," I repeated.

"Yes."

"For how much?"

"I don't know yet. Could be millions."

"Is that legal?" Nina asked.

"Yes, only you're not supposed to have policies totaling more than your net worth. The industry believes the purpose of life insurance is to replace income, not generate wealth. If a policyholder qualifies for, say, $500,000 and has a policy from Company A for $100,000, Company B will usually only go as high as $400,000."

"Why didn't that happen in Mr. Woods's case?" Nina asked.

"Insurance agents are paid by commission and they mostly only care if you can pay your premiums, so . . ."

"Let me guess," I said.

"Yes, McKenzie, the policies all have two-year suicide exclusions."

"What does that mean?" Nina asked.

"An insurance company usually will not pay a death benefit if it can prove the insured died by his own hand within the first two years of coverage, although most will return the premiums that were paid. After two years, they usually decide that the insured had not intended to take their own life when the policy was activated and will pay."

"Are you saying that Mr. Woods planned to kill himself and took out the policies to enrich his family?"

"That's the position I expect the lawyers will take, yes. Why else did he take out all those policies in such a short period of time? They'll argue that it's their responsibility to protect the insurance pool by blocking undeserved payouts, although, probably they'll need more than that in court or risk a summary judgment in the plaintiff's favor for lack of evidence."

"Which you will provide," I said.

"Which I will provide if it exists," Maryanne said. "What I do isn't vastly different from what you did when you were a police officer, McKenzie. You work the case as best you can, as diligently as you can; gather the evidence, present it to the attorneys. After that, it's on them."

"Long story short—the insurance industry will attempt to prove that Earl Woods committed suicide while his estate, his beneficiaries, will try to prove that he died by accident," I said.

"With you two in the middle," Altavilla said.

"Why us?" Nina wanted to know.

"Because you're not law enforcement officers or medical examiners or evidence technicians explaining, usually in a monotone while consulting their notes, the specific details of the case. You're actual eyewitnesses. Studies prove that juries *love* eyewitness testimony."

"Except we didn't see anything. Not really."

Altavilla shrugged her reply.

"If we just keep repeating the truth about what we saw . . ." Nina said.

"It might become a bit acrimonious anyway," Maryanne told her.

"Why?"

"Because of McKenzie's history with Midwest Farmers."

"I don't see—oh."

"McKenzie has a track record with us. The millions we paid him after he caught the embezzler; the money that allowed him to retire from the St. Paul Police Department and do what he's doing now. Recovering the Jade Lily for us, the Countess Borromeo— he'll be accused of favoring Midwest Farmers if not actually lying on our behalf. You're his wife, so . . ."

"Maryanne, up until this moment I was actually happy to see you," Nina said.

Nina and I answered Altavilla's questions as best we could, confirming that we actually did say and do what the Stillwater PD and Washington County sheriff's deputies claimed that we said and did in their reports. Afterward, it was all small talk until Altavilla chose to return to her office.

As soon as she was out the door, Nina turned toward me.

"I noticed that you didn't mention anything about the woman, Mrs. Woods," she said. "I noticed you didn't say any-thing about her odd behavior."

"I noticed that you didn't, either."

"I love Maryanne . . ."

"Yeah."

"But I guess I'm kinda on Mr. Woods's side."

"Yeah."

"I can't even imagine—I mean is there anything more tragic than taking your own life? The pain and hopelessness that would drive you—and he was thinking about his family when he did it. Holding on to that ladder, waiting for death to come, my God . . ."

"The strength and discipline that would have required . . ."

"My God," Nina repeated. "Do you think his wife was in on it?"

"She didn't seem surprised when we found him, did she? Nina, listen. All the insurance policies he took out are pushing us to that conclusion, yet it's entirely possible that Woods didn't commit suicide; that it really was an accident. We know nothing about this guy. His history. His state of health. Maybe he took out the policies just because he was getting old and wanted to die rich. Whatever. Something Maryanne only touched on: the burden of proof lies with the insurance companies. Midwest Farmers is probably going to have to come up with a specific reason why Mr. Woods took his own life if it wants to win its case.

"But you know what?" I added. "Nina, this is none of our business. We're kinda, sorta involved, only it isn't about us. This is someone else's problem."

"You're right, you're right."

Nina thought about it for a few moments before shaking her head vigorously.

"Enough," she said. "I'm going into Rickie's to intimidate my staff."

"I thought you were taking the day off."

"Suddenly I feel like I could use a distraction."

"In that case . . ."

"I mean for more than an hour."

"Who's in the big room tonight?"

"Lori Dokken and Friends."

"Which friends?"

"Judi Vinar, Patty Peterson, Ginger Commodore, Rachel Holder, Jennifer Grimm, Erin Schwab . . ."

"How 'bout I meet you there, later? I'll buy you a drink."

"Oh, you will, will you?"

"If we can get a table."

"I might be able to manage that."

"I wish you would have told me about your dreams."

"It's not as bad as it sounds. I only had them a couple of times."

"Nina."

"It'll pass," she said. "Or I'll just learn to live with it like you do; you and Bobby Dunston, all the pain you've seen, the suffering, as police officers and what you do now; the people you've seen killed, the people you were forced to kill. It's my problem."

"No. It's our problem."

"If my dreams get worse, I can always reach out to your ex-girlfriend. What's her name? Dr. Jillian DeMarais?"

"Okay, now you're just messing with my head."

Nina's response was to wrap her arms around me. Her hug was followed by a kiss. And then another.

It was well over an hour before she left for Rickie's.

Events unfolded exactly as Maryanne Altavilla suggested they would. Midwest Farmers refused to pay Earl Woods's family the full value of his life insurance policy while the other insurance companies refused to pay anything at all. Woods's family immediately filed a lawsuit in federal court alleging breach of contract. Other lawsuits quickly followed.

I learned this in a roundabout way, though. Dave Deese called me.

"I need a favor," he said.

"I already did you a favor."

"Another one."

Heggstad Marina in mid-May was a picture postcard, hundreds of expensive boats at rest, nesting next to the sparkling blue St. Croix River, a brilliant sun and cloudless sky above. All it needed was a banner—"Greetings from Stillwater."

It took me a few minutes to find the *Deese and Dose,* this time because nearly all the slips at the marina were filled and the docks were loaded with pedestrians. I might have missed it if Dave hadn't waved at me from the cockpit.

"McKenzie," he said.

"Permission to come aboard?"

"What are you drinking?"

There was a four-step ladder that allowed me to climb to the gunwale of his Sundancer and a two-step ladder that let me descend to the deck in the stern.

"What are *you* drinking?" I asked.

Deese was holding a tall, thin glass filled with an orange liquid and topped with a wedge of pineapple, a slice of lime, three cherries skewered by a plastic sword, and an umbrella with all the colors of the rainbow if the rainbow was pastel.

"A Hawaiian margarita," he said.

"You have sunk so low since you became a boat owner."

"Jealous."

"Swear to God, the guys we play hockey with would stop drinking in the same bars as you do if they saw this."

"They don't know what they're missing."

"I'll have a Summit Ale, if you have it."

"I don't have. How 'bout a Summer Shandy?"

"Only if you promise not to tell anyone."

Deese fetched a cold bottle from the refrigerator inside the salon of his boat. It was a pilsner mixed with lemonade brewed by Leinenkugel and was pretty refreshing on a hot summer's day except it wasn't summer, it wasn't hot, and I wasn't going to tell Deese that anyway.

"The marina seems to have become pretty busy since the last time I was here," I said.

"It always reminds me of a sprawling apartment complex. People come and go during the day when it's open to the public. After hours, though, when it's locked down and you can only gain entry through the main building, it's just neighbors calling from one boat to another, gathering on the dock, playing their music too loud. It can be very cool and very annoying at the same time. You have money. You should buy a boat. We could be marina buddies."

"I don't like you now. Why would I want to be your marina buddy? This favor you need . . ."

"We're waiting for someone."

Dave planted himself on the captain's chair in the cockpit of the boat and swiveled it toward me. I stretched out on one of the boat's bench seats, my feet on the gunwale, my beer balanced on my chest, and watched the St. Croix River slide by.

"You know, I could get used to this," I said.

"Right?"

After that it was all chitchat—How's Nina? How's Barb? Are you playing summer hockey? No, you? What's this about Bobby Dunston starting a curling team? Do you believe that? Not once did we mention the man in the water.

A few minutes later, I heard the words, "Permission to come aboard?"

So, people actually do say that, my inner voice said. *It's not just you.*

It was a man, mid-forties, dressed casually. I recognized him as he climbed aboard. He was the gentleman I had met working the marina building that Saturday in March. He wore the same name tag. Brad Heggstad.

Desse introduced us anyway.

After he shook my hand, Heggstad said, "I appreciate this, that you're willing to help me."

"I honestly don't know what you need much less whether or not I can help you."

"Dave didn't say?"

"No."

"I thought it would be better if it came from you," Deese said.

"I appreciate that you came down to listen, then," Heggstad said.

"Drink?" Deese asked.

"No." Heggstad waved more or less in the direction of the marina headquarters. "I need to get back soon."

We were all settling onto the boat cushions when Heggstad came out with it.

"We're being sued," he said. "The marina, I mean. The family of the man you found in the water . . ."

"Earl Woods," I said.

"You know who he is?"

"I only know his name."

"Well, his wife, she's suing us for—they filed a wrongful death lawsuit against the marina. They said we were, I'm trying to remember the exact words—we were complicit in Woods's death because we neglected to sufficiently warn visitors of the river's dangers . . ."

The river's dangers?

"And the danger of walking on our docks and that we didn't have sufficient safety equipment and that we were guilty of inflicting emotional distress on the Woods family."

"I don't know what to tell you, Brad," I said. "I hope you have insurance."

"Of course we have insurance, McKenzie. It's not like we started this business yesterday. It's been in the family for nearly fifty years and from the first day to this we've been insured up the wazoo if for no other reason than we know that the first thing lawyers learn in law school, maybe the only thing they learn, is how to get rich by accident. I knew we were going to take a hit when you walked into the building that day and asked if I had seen that old man."

Sixty-two isn't old, is it?

"It doesn't matter that we did nothing wrong," Brad said. "He drowned while he was at our marina so it must be the marina's fault, that's how juries think. That's why there are so many ridiculous lawsuits, because of how juries think. Only this is different."

"How is it different?"

"My lawyer, well not my lawyer, the insurance company's lawyer—he said the family, Woods's family, isn't interested in a settlement. They won't take our money and go away. They're desperate to take us to court. They want a jury to say that we were negligent, that the marina was negligent, that Woods's death was an accident and it was our fault. I'm like, settling a lawsuit out of court says that, doesn't it? A company, in the language of the settlement, it might refuse to admit wrongdoing, but we all assume that it screwed up. That's why it's paying the money. Only that's not enough for these guys. You know why?"

Yes, I think I do.

"They're using me, us, the marina—they're using us to get at Woods's life insurance companies," Heggstad said. "What I was told, according to my insurance company's lawyer, Woods had policies with four other insurance companies. Only they've all refused to pay out any benefits. They claim that Woods committed suicide and I guess there are rules about that. So, Woods's wife wants to take us to court to get a verdict saying that Woods died by accident that she'll then use in the breach-of-contract lawsuits she filed against the life insurance companies."

"Okay," I said.

"You see my problem."

"I see your problem, only I don't think I can help you."

"Dave here told me that you help people. He told me about what you did for him and some others."

"It's not that I don't want to help you, Brad. I just don't know if I can. Has your lawyer—first of all, do you have a lawyer?"

"No, I've been relying on the insurance company's lawyer."

"Well, stop it. Get your own lawyer. The lawyer from the insurance company is working for the insurance company, not you. Get a lawyer that represents Heggstad Marina. You want someone who's on your side. That I can help with."

I reached into my pocket, pulled out a wallet, and removed a business card. The card read ASSOCIATES AND BONALAY.

"Ask for G. K.," I said. "Tell her I sent you. She's the best lawyer I know. She's kept me out of trouble more times than I can count."

"Thank you," Heggstad said. "I appreciate it, only what I was thinking . . ."

"What?"

"What I was thinking—I want to fight back. I was all set to take the insurance company's advice. They were like it was our turn, okay. Our turn to be sued. Just pay the money, keep the bad publicity to a minimum, and move on even though we didn't do anything wrong. Except Woods's family won't let us. Okay, fine. They want to go to court, let's go to court."

I pointed at the white card Heggstad still held in his hand.

"She's the woman for you," I said.

"What I was thinking—if the other insurance companies can claim that Woods killed himself, why can't I?"

"Sounds logical," Deese said.

"It is logical," I said. "Why don't you have your insurance company contact the other insurance companies and ask them what they have that led them to that conclusion?"

"We're not allowed," Heggstad said. "What I was told— maybe I should have that drink."

Deese rose, only Heggstad waved him back to his seat.

"No, no, no," he said. "What I was told, the four insurance companies formed what they call a joint defense agreement."

NATO, my inner voice said.

"Because they have a common interest, not paying the insurance benefits, and a common defense, the guy committed suicide, they're able to act together, which I guess makes it easier. Instead of four court cases, there'll be just the one . . ."

Which is why you haven't been interviewed by investigators from the other insurance companies. They're all relying on Maryanne Altavilla's work.

"Only our interests, our case, defending against a wrongful death lawsuit, isn't the same as theirs so they're not allowed to share information with us," Heggstad added. "At least that was what I was told."

"Doesn't matter," I said. "Whatever their investigators found out your investigators can find out."

"Well, yeah. That's why you're here."

"No."

"No?" Deese sounded like he was surprised to hear that word come out of my mouth.

"Here's the thing," I said. "Both Dave and I will be made to testify and so will our wives in all of these cases . . ."

"We will?" Deese asked.

"Brad, anything I do for you I will have to disclose to the other side whether it's to your advantage or not. Let's say I find a loose plank on your dock. I'd have to tell them."

"Ah, geez," Deese said.

"Besides, you don't need me." I pointed at the business card again. "My lawyer, G. K. Bonalay—she'll take care of you, I promise."

Brad Heggstad wasn't thrilled by my declaration, yet he wasn't particularly upset, either. I guess his expectations were low. Dave Deese, on the other hand, became somewhat emotional over the prospect of testifying in court.

"What should I say?" he asked me.

"The truth and nothing but the truth."

"What if I get it wrong?"

"They'll lock you up and throw away the key."

"You're kidding."

I didn't say if I was or wasn't, yet by the time I left the *Deese and Dose,* he had switched from Hawaiian margaritas to Scotch.

I explained all of this to Nina at Rickie's, the jazz club on Cathedral Hill in St. Paul that she had named after her daughter, Erica. Rickie's was divided into two sections, a casual bar on the ground floor with a small stage for happy hour entertainment and a full restaurant and performance hall upstairs. We were downstairs, me sitting on a stool on one side of the bar and Nina on the other.

"Why would you tease him like that?" she asked.

"Deese had it coming. He should have told me about Brad Heggstad before I arrived at the marina."

"What would you have told him if he had?"

"I would have said no, I won't get involved in this. I don't know who the good guys are. I don't know who the bad guys are. I don't know if there are any good guys or bad guys. Who would I be helping, anyway? The marina? The insurance companies? Against who? The family of a guy who may or may not have committed suicide? Of all the things I've done that were none of my business, this is the most none of my business of all."

Nina made a production out of waving her hand back and forth while she silently reviewed what I just told her.

"Wait, wait, wait," she said.

"You know what I mean."

"When will the games begin?"

"The trial date? Who knows? These cases take forever to wind their way through the courts. It could be six months. Could be a year or more. It's already been over fifty days since we found the man in the water."

"I meant our part."

"I suppose they could start taking depositions any day now."

THREE

Any day now turned out to be Wednesday, June 7, at the offices of O'Hara, O'Hara, and Thomas. I was invited to appear at exactly one P.M. to be deposed in the case of *Woods v. Heggstad Marina,* if you call a subpoena an invitation. What surprised me was that Nina had not also received a subpoena.

What the hell? my inner voice wanted to know. *Why are they picking just on you?*

I actually arrived on time for the deposition; the law offices were a seventeen-minute walk from our place in downtown Minneapolis. I was dressed in a white dress shirt, black dress slacks and shoes, a black suit jacket, and a dark blue tie, because that's how I was trained to dress for a deposition by my attorney many years before.

"How you present yourself matters," G. K. Bonalay told me at the time. "Maintain a professional attitude from the moment you enter your deposition until after you leave. Clothes, body language, your overall demeanor speak just as loudly as your words especially in the event of a video-recorded deposition. And for God's sake, McKenzie, I'm begging you—no jokes."

Just because I was on time, though, didn't mean everyone else was. I was forced to wait a good fifteen minutes before I was ushered into a conference room by an admin who clearly had other things on her mind. At the door to the conference room, I was met by a tall man with silver hair impeccably dressed in a suit that looked as though it was selected for him by a costume designer. He, in contrast to the admin, was all business. He took my hand, introduced himself as Garrett Toomey, and, while still holding my hand, led me the length of the room to the head of a long table where I was asked to sit. I came *this*close to telling him the last time someone held my hand for that long I married her.

Don't even think about it.

There were seven people in the room in addition to Toomey. I knew two of them yet pretended not to. The first was Brad Heggstad. The second was the woman seated next to him at the conference room table. Her name was Genevieve Katherine Bonalay, aka G. K. Bonalay, the woman who had been acting as my attorney ever since she helped me dodge an obstruction charge and I helped her client escape a murder conviction eight years ago. While everyone else in the room including me was dressed for a wake, she wore a red equestrian-style jacket over a white pleated skirt, black tights and pumps; her long hair was pulled back and green eyes peeked out from under schoolgirl bangs. It was a ploy, of course. Although in her late thirties, G. K. looked as if she had graduated from law school last month. You'd think that would be a good thing, yet in her profession, at least, not so much. Other attorneys, mostly men, refused to take her seriously, one of the reasons she started her own law firm. Now she often used her appearance to her advantage.

"I love it when men underestimate me," I was once told.

Toomey took the time to remind me why I was there—to get at the truth, he said—although it was a little more complicated than that. What G. K. taught me, a deposition is often the first time that a lawyer can evaluate how a particular witness may appear in front of a judge or jury; it's used to assess the witness's credibility and to present an overall impression of them.

"So, please, McKenzie, try to behave yourself," she said. "And no swearing, dammit."

After explaining himself, Toomey went around the room. He started first with the court reporter that was charged with keeping a written record of the deposition followed by the videographer whose job apparently was to turn on and off the camera that was pointed at me from the other side of the conference room table.

Next came Mrs. Elizabeth Woods, "wife of the deceased," Toomey said. I nodded at her. She nodded back. The last time I saw her, Mrs. Woods's long blond hair was being whipped about in the wind. This time it fell neatly to the collar of a tailored black blazer that was tied at the waist with a cloth belt. Her expression gave me nothing. There was something about her, though, that I couldn't place until I did. I had never watched a single episode, yet I had seen plenty of promos for the show. Elizabeth Woods reminded me of a character on *The Real Housewives of Beverly Hills*.

The woman sitting next to her was about ten years younger. She was introduced as Nevaeh Woods, "daughter of the deceased," and was dressed like an elementary school principal. Yet the biggest difference between the two—Nevaeh was clearly Black while Elizabeth clearly was not.

"Hey," Nevaeh said.

Brad Heggstad sat across the table from Elizabeth and Nevaeh. He was introduced to me as "the defendant." Toomey said the word like it was an accusation. Heggstad stared straight ahead and I could almost hear G. K.'s voice telling him what she had told me years before—"You're not here to make friends."

Next I was introduced to an attorney named something Fisher who represented the Heggstad Marina's insurance company and who pointed at me like he was already pissed off.

Finally, "G. K. Bonalay, attorney for the defendant," Toomey said.

G. K.'s response to that was to lean forward and jot something on the yellow legal pad in front of her.

Well, this is going to be fun.

"Let's begin," Toomey said.

The videographer turned on his camera. The court recorder began typing on her stenotype machine. I swore on a Bible to tell the truth, the whole truth, and nothing but the truth so help me God.

(In Minnesota, maybe everywhere, a copy of the transcript of a deposition will be sent to you. You'll then have thirty days to review the document and, if there are changes you want to make, sign a statement indicating the changes and the reason for making them. This is only a partial transcript of my deposition. Trust me when I tell you it was much, much longer.)

Q: Mr. McKenzie, good afternoon.

A: Good afternoon.

Q: My name is Garrett Toomey. I'm an attorney and I represent the Woods family, which has brought suit against Heggstad Marina in Stillwater, Minnesota, arising out of an accident that occurred on March 25th. Do you know what accident I'm talking about?

Ms. Bonalay: Objection. Did an accident occur on March 25th?

Q: Mr. McKenzie, are you aware of the incident I am referring to?

A: Yes, sir.

Q: I'm going to ask you some questions about yourself and about that incident. If at any time I ask you a question and you don't hear it or you don't understand it, please tell me that, and I'll repeat the question for you or I'll ask it in a different way. You're sworn today with the same oath that you will take at the trial of this case. So, if you answer any question for us today, we all shall take it that you heard the question and that you understood the question and that you then gave us your sworn answer. Is all that clear?

A: Yes, sir.

Q: What is your name?

A: Rushmore McKenzie.

Q: Where do you live?

I recited my street address in downtown Minneapolis.

Q: What do you do for a living?

A: I'm retired.

Q: What did you do before you retired?

A: I was a police officer.

Q: Where?

A: St. Paul Police Department.

Q: How long were you a police officer?

A: Approximately twelve years.

Q: Why did you retire?

A: I came into some money and thought I'd try something different.

Q: In fact, you quit in order to collect a reward on an embezzler that you captured. You quit because serving police officers are not allowed to collect rewards. Is that correct?

A: Yes.

Q: How much money did you collect?

A: Three million dollars and change.

Q: $3,128,584 to be exact, is that correct?

A: $3,128,584 and fifty cents—to be exact.

G. K.'s head came up and she looked at me for the first time. I knew what she was thinking, too—"I taught you better than that." Stay calm, she had insisted. When you become emotion-

ally involved or angry, you are more likely to lose control of the answers you are providing.

Q: What did you do with that money?

A: I invested it, or rather I had my financial advisor invest it.

Q: Would you consider yourself independently wealthy?

A: Independent, anyway.

Q: And now you're a vigilante.

Again I could hear G. K.'s voice in the back of my head. "Stand up for yourself during questioning. Likely the lawyer will make a statement that you disagree with. When that happens, say so. Can you do that, McKenzie, while remaining cool and calm?"

A: I disagree with your characterization of me. A vigilante acts outside of the law; puts himself above the law. A vigilante will break the law to punish or avenge a crime real or imagined. If you have even a scintilla of evidence proving I have ever done such a thing you should bring it to the police and have me arrested, otherwise you're just committing slander.

Surprisingly, at least I was surprised, the only one who reacted to my statement was Woods's daughter, Nevaeh, and the way she snorted I didn't know if she was on my side or not.

Q: Your activities often involved helping insurance companies.

Ms. Bonalay: Objection. Is that a question?

Q: Mr. McKenzie, have you often helped insurance companies?

A: On occasion I have helped them recover art that was stolen.

Q: Were you paid for recovering this stolen art?

A: No.

Q: What?

A: I was not paid.

Q: I thought . . . Why would you . . .

A: I did it as a favor for friends. Not the insurance companies. That they benefited from what I did made no difference to me.

*Everyone was watching me, of course, yet Wood's daughter
seemed to stare more intently when I said that and I wondered
what she was thinking.*

Q: Yes, of course. Tell me, is Mr. Bradley Heggstad your
friend?

A: No.

Q: But you know him?

A: I met him. That's not the same thing.

Q: When did you meet Mr. Heggstad?

A: On the morning of March 25th.

Q: Where did you meet him?

A: At the Heggstad Marina.

Q: Why did you go to Heggstad Marina on the morning of
March 25th?

A: I have a friend who has a boat there. He asked if we
wanted to go on a cruise. I thought it would be fun.

Ms. Woods: Yeah, what fun.

Mr. Toomey: Ms. Woods, please. We discussed this.

Ms. Woods: Sorry.

*Elizabeth set her hand on Nevaeh's hand, only the younger
woman pulled it away.*

Q: Mr. McKenzie, you said "we." Who was with you?

A: My wife.

Q: What is your wife's name?

A: Nina Truhler.

Q: Ms. Truhler does not share your surname?

A: No.

Q: Do you live together?

A: Why yes. Yes, we do.

Nevaeh snorted again.

Q: Ms. Truhler was with you when you went to the marina to visit your friend?

A: Yes.

Q: What is your friend's name?

A: Dave Deese.

Q: Was he alone?

A: No.

Q: Who was with him?

A: His wife.

Q: What is her name?

A: Barbara Deese.

Q: They have a boat at Heggstad Marina?

A: Yes.

Q: What is the name of the boat?

A: Deese and Dose.

Q: That's . . . Okay. Tell us what happened when you arrived at Heggstad Marina.

A: Nina and I walked out onto the dock to go to Dave Deese's boat. We met Mrs. Woods.

Q: Did you know Mrs. Woods?

A: No.

Q: You never saw her before?

A: No.

Q: What did she want?

A: She said that she couldn't find her husband. She asked Nina and I to help look for him.

Q: Did you help?

A: Yes.

Q: Why?

A: Because she said she needed help.

Q: Is that the only reason?

A: Do I need another reason?

Again, Nevaeh seemed to stare at me more intensely than everyone else.

Q: What did you do?

A: I went into the marina's building to see if he had gone inside.

Q: Did he?

A: I did not find him there and Mr. Heggstad said he hadn't seen anyone.

Q: Is that the first time you met him, met Mr. Heggstad?

A: Yes.

Q: What did you do next?

A: I went outside.

Q: What happened when you went outside?

A: I heard my wife scream.

Q: What did you do?

A: I ran to her side.

Q: Why did she scream?

A: She said she had been startled.

Q: What startled her?

A: She found Mr. Woods in the water.

Q: Under the water.

A: Yes.

Q: Clutching the ladder leading to the dock.

A: Yes.

Q: He had drowned.

A: Yes.

Q: What did you think when you saw that?

Ms. Bonalay: Objection. Immaterial.

Q: Mr. McKenzie, what did you think when you found the man in the water?

A: I wondered how he got there.

Q: Did you think he fell?

Ms. Bonalay: Objection. Mr. McKenzie's opinion is immaterial.

Mr. Toomey: Why don't we let a judge decide what is material and what isn't?

Q: Mr. McKenzie, answer the question.

A: I couldn't think of any reason why he fell.

Q: Ice, wind . . .

A: The wind wasn't strong and there wasn't any ice.

Q: How do you know? Did you look?

A: No, but Officer Stoll did. I was with her when she got on her knees and used her hands to search for ice and moisture in the area at the end of the dock where Mr. Woods was. She didn't find any.

Mr. Fisher: You're referring to Officer Eden Stoll of the Stillwater Police Department?

A: I didn't know her first name.

Ms. Woods: This is a load of crap. We all know what happened.

Mr. Toomey: Ms. Woods, if you cannot remain quiet I will ask you to leave.

Mrs. Woods: Nevaeh, please.

Q: Mr. McKenzie, are you saying this to help Mr. Heggstad

defend the wrongful death lawsuit that has been filed against him?

A: No.

Q: You met Mr. Heggstad some weeks after the events of March 25th, is that not true?

A: I'm not sure I understand the question.

Q: Did you meet with Mr. Heggstad weeks following the events of March 25th, yes or no?

A: Yes.

Q: You met him on the boat owned by your friend, Dave Deese, on May 18th, yes or no?

A: Yes.

Q: What did you talk about?

A: He spoke about the lawsuit.

Q: What else?

A: He asked me if I would try to find evidence to prove that Mr. Woods committed suicide.

Q: What did you say?

A: I said no, I would not.

Q: A friend asked you for a favor and you said no?

A: He's not my friend. I barely know the man.

Q: What did you do?

A: I gave him the name of a good lawyer.

Things happened after that. Toomey turned to glare at G. K. and G. K. smirked in return. At the same time, Nevaeh stood up and shouted.

Ms. Woods: This is so much bullshit. We all know what happened to my father. He didn't fall into the river by accident and he sure as hell didn't kill himself. He was murdered.

Mr. Toomey: I move for an immediate recess.

"Recess" seemed to be a magic word. Immediately after Toomey uttered it, the stenographer's fingers came off her stenotype machine and the videographer reached quickly to the camera and turned it off.

Toomey moved to Nevaeh's side, grabbed her arm, and pulled her out of her chair. He directed her toward the conference room door. She seemed to go willingly.

"I told you," Toomey said. "I told you."

"Where are you going?" Fisher wanted to know.

Elizabeth followed closely behind her daughter and the lawyer.

Fisher said, "Wait. What? No." He circled the conference room table and followed the trio.

Once they were out of the room, Brad Heggstad turned toward his attorney.

"What just happened?" he asked.

"Something good," G. K. said. "Let's get out of here and I'll explain."

A moment later, both G. K. and Heggstad also exited the conference room.

I watched the stenographer and videographer; both were sitting quietly next to their equipment.

"I guess we're done here?" I asked.

The answer came in the form of the admin I had met when I first arrived at the law offices.

"The deposition has been postponed to a later date," she said. "The date to be determined."

The stenographer and videographer started packing up their equipment. I rose from my perch at the end of the conference room table and followed the admin out of the room, down a corridor, and out of the office. No one spoke to me except my inner voice once I reached the elevators.

He was murdered? it asked.

* * *

I had questions and plenty of them, only I didn't know who to ask or even if I was legally allowed to ask. Normally, I would have called my lawyer for advice. Instead, I walked back to the condo. I had just finished changing clothes when I received a call from the security desk.

The guards working the two P.M. to midnight shift four days a week were friends of mine. Smith and Jones had explained when Nina and I first moved into the building that they had checked me out—acting under building management's orders, of course; it was SOP for all new tenants—and they knew who I was and what I did. They had also made it clear that they were ready, willing, and able to assist me should ever the need arise. "The job can get so boring," they told me. Sometimes they did help in exchange for Wild tickets or a case of very good bourbon or some other form of contraband that I would "find" in the hallway or on an elevator and dutifully turned in to the lost and found because the security firm that employed Smith and Jones had a strict policy against employees accepting gratuities of any kind from tenants.

For the longest time, I couldn't tell Smith and Jones apart without reading their name tags; they were always dressed in the identical dark blue suits, crisp white shirts, and dark blue ties of their profession. Now I could but sometimes pretended not to. It was a running gag between us.

"This is Jones from downstairs," the voice told me.

"Are you sure?" I asked.

"Pretty sure. Listen, McKenzie, there's a young woman in the lobby who claims she needs to talk with you."

"What's her name?"

"Nevaeh Woods."

* * *

It took me about five minutes to reach the lobby. Nevaeh didn't seem to mind waiting, though. She was sitting in one of the four stuffed red chairs gathered around a low, round table in front of the security desk, her hands resting on the arms of the chair, her eyes staring out the large windows at the apartment complex across the street. Jones had pointed her out to me after I emerged from the elevator, although it wasn't necessary. It was the lobby of a condominium, not a hotel. Counting Smith, who was seated behind the security desk next to Jones, there were only the four of us.

I approached soundlessly across the carpet. Movement was enough to startle the woman, though. She leapt to her feet.

"McKenzie," she said. "Your name is Rushmore McKenzie."

"Yes."

She offered her hand and I took it.

"I'm Nevaeh Woods."

"Yes."

We stared at each other for a few beats. I had no idea what she was thinking so I told her what I was thinking.

"I bet your lawyer would not like it if he knew you were here."

"Toomey isn't my lawyer," Nevaeh said. "He's my stepmother's lawyer."

"Stepmother?"

"I know what you're thinking. I say stepmother and people nearly always add the word 'evil.' Evil stepmother. Bizzy is all right, though. Besides, do I look like Cinderella to you?"

"Sure, why not? I mean if the shoe fits."

"It doesn't."

"Okay."

Nevaeh gestured at the red chairs.

"Will you sit with me?" she asked.

We sat and stared at each other some more.

"You're probably wondering why I'm here," Nevaeh said.

"I'm also wondering if you should be here. Talking to me, won't that compromise your lawsuit?"

"Toomey said I already did that. Mr. McKenzie, we checked you out; the lawyers I mean. Wanting to know if your testimony can help the case; if it should be endorsed. Wanting to know if it'll hurt, if you should be discredited. What Toomey said about you working with insurance companies to recover that stolen art, that's only part of what they discovered."

"That doesn't explain why you're here?"

"I need your help."

"My help?"

"That's what you do, isn't it? You help people? You helped Bizzy, tried to help Bizzy, anyway, and all she did was ask."

"Bizzy?"

"My stepmother's nickname, what she likes to be called. Her real name is Elizabeth."

"Yes, well, helping your stepmother is a little different than helping you," I said.

"How is it different?"

"I wasn't being deposed at the time."

"My father didn't commit suicide," Nevaeh said. "He would never, never, never have done that."

"Okay."

"He sure as hell didn't fall off a dock, either. He wasn't a feeble old man."

"Ms. Woods—"

"Nevaeh. Call me Nevaeh."

"Nevaeh—"

"I'll call you Rushmore."

"McKenzie will do. Nevaeh, why do you believe your father was murdered?"

"Because he didn't jump and he didn't fall into that river."

"We don't actually know that."

"Something else. Bizzy—she said that Dad liked boats, that he liked the river. That's bullshit. Excuse my language."

"It's okay."

"He didn't fish, he didn't water-ski, he didn't hang around rivers or creeks or lakes or ponds or swimming pools. I mean c'mon now."

"If that's true . . ."

She leaned toward me and spoke almost in a whisper.

"If Dad wanted to drown himself, he lived ten minutes from the Mississippi River," she said.

"Then why was he in Stillwater?" I asked. "Why the Heggstad Marina?"

"Exactly."

"Nevaeh . . ."

"He was lured there."

"By whom?"

"I don't know. You tell me."

"Do you believe your stepmother was involved?"

"I don't know." Nevaeh dropped her head into her hands, rubbed her face, and lifted her head again. She looked directly into my eyes. "I don't know. That's why I'm here. McKenzie. Help me. Please."

Which is exactly what her stepmother said.

"Nevaeh, I assume your lawyer—"

"Bizzy's lawyer."

"Has a copy of the autopsy report," I said.

"I guess."

"I haven't read it, but I was told that the medical examiner could find no sign of trauma, no contusions or lacerations or any other evidence that might indicate foul play—I'm sorry to use those words; I know it sounds frivolous."

"That doesn't mean there wasn't any, though."

"Yes, that's exactly what it means."

"How do you know? Have you looked? Has anyone looked?"

"Nevaeh . . ."

"No one has done anything. The insurance companies don't want to pay so they say Dad was a veteran, which means he must have had PTSD, which means he must have jumped. Bizzy and her lawyers want them to pay so they say the marina didn't protect him during poor weather conditions so he must have fallen. Yet nobody—nobody—has said you know what, maybe he was pushed."

Maybe he was, my inner voice said. *Yet would anyone have thought that would have been enough to kill him even in freezing water?*

I shook the thought from my head.

"Nevaeh, I'll tell you the same thing I told Brad Heggstad—both me and my wife will be forced to testify in this case and probably others as well. You saw a little of what that means for us this afternoon. Also, if I did try to help you, anything and everything I found out I'd have to disclose to the other side. Let's say I did learn that your father had symptoms of post-traumatic stress disorder—"

"He didn't."

"Let's say he did and he was hiding it from you and I found out about it, I'd have to inform the insurance companies."

"Why would you?"

"Toomey made a big deal about my meeting with Brad Heggstad and what I promised or didn't promise to do for him. Another lawyer could make a big deal about my meeting with you. I told the truth about Heggstad and I would be forced to tell the truth about you or risk going to prison for perjury."

Nevaeh stared at me for a few moments, rose from her red

chair, and paced the lobby for a good half minute before coming to a halt directly in front of me.

"I need to know the truth," she said.

Still, as much as it pained me, I told her that this was something I just couldn't get involved in. I apologized and told her that I hoped she'd find the answers she needed. She responded by insisting I take her contact information and then begged me to reconsider. That's how she phrased it—"I beg you to reconsider."

I explained it all to Nina while sitting on a stool in front of a Maker's Mark on the rocks at Rickie's downstairs bar. The bourbon was mine; Nina seldom drank in her own place.

"The poor thing," she said.

"What Nevaeh might not realize is that claiming her father didn't like boats and rivers actually supports the insurance companies' theory more than hers. If he didn't like them, why was he at the marina except to, well . . ."

"She said he was lured there."

"By whom? His wife?"

"She was the only other person we saw."

"Are you suggesting she pushed him?" I asked.

"She didn't cry until the police arrived."

"Maybe her husband's death didn't become real to her until the police arrived."

"I suppose that's possible."

"Around and around we go. You see the problem? We can come up with plenty of theories yet not a shred of evidence to support any of them."

According to the internet, the term "object permanence" referred to a child's ability to recognize that objects continue to exist even though they can no longer be seen or heard. It's a skill I hadn't quite mastered. For example, often when I woke in the middle of the night, I'd reach out a hand or a foot to make sure my wife was still sleeping next to me. Afterward, reassured by the touch of her, I'd go back to sleep. Except, when I reached out at 4:13 A.M. according to the clock radio, I discovered that Nina wasn't there.

I called her name. She didn't reply. I turned on lights. The bedroom was empty. I checked our ridiculously large bathroom, the one with double sinks and a glass-enclosed walk-in shower big enough for two people to play tag in. Also empty. I ventured into the condominium, turning on lights as I went.

"Nina?" I called.

"Did I wake you?" she asked.

Nina was standing in the kitchen area, her back against the refrigerator, eating a bowl of French vanilla ice cream in the dark.

"You weren't in bed," I said. "I think that's what woke me."

"Sorry about that."

"Are you okay?"

"Why wouldn't I be?"

"You're eating ice cream in the dark at four thirty in the morning."

"When do you eat your ice cream?"

"Nina."

"The dream came back. I hadn't dreamt it for a couple of weeks now but it came back tonight. In the dream I was standing on the dock in the marina and looking down at Mr. Woods like I always did only this time—I didn't just see his face, McKenzie. This time he was looking up at me; staring at me. He seemed so confused, his expression so haunted. That's the word. Haunted. It was as if he had no memory of what had happened to him and he was desperate to learn the truth; that he wouldn't have any peace in this world or the next until he did."

I do not like where this is heading, my inner voice told me.

"I was told that when we die, all of our questions will be answered," I said. "Isn't that how it's supposed to work?"

"How should I know?"

Nina ate another spoonful of ice cream and set the now empty bowl in the sink.

"Let's go back to bed," she said.

"Okay."

Only she didn't head toward the bedroom. Instead she looked down at me standing in the light in the dining area while she stood in the dark three steps above me and behind the island in the kitchen area.

"McKenzie, will you do me a favor?"

I didn't need to ask her what she had in mind.

"I don't know if I can," I said.

"It isn't just Nevaeh who wants to know what happened to her father. I want to know. If we can determine why he died, I'm convinced the dream will go away."

"I'm not sure it works that way."

"McKenzie . . ."

"Nina, the truth is we might never find out what actually happened on that dock. Whatever I do, I can't promise that we'll ever learn anything more than what we already know, which, I admit, isn't very much. That's just the way life works sometimes."

"But you can try, can't you?"

"Yes, Nina, I can try."

FOUR

I was standing at the edge of the dock and looking down. The sun was shining and the water was clear and I could easily see that there was nobody under the water gripping the ladder with both hands and looking up at me with a haunted expression on his face. Although, I knew if I stared long enough . . .

I heard a male's voice behind me.

"Boy, oh boy," he said. "I bet I could sell tickets."

I spun toward the voice. The man was standing on the bow of his luxury boat and looking down at me. It was one of the two boats that had been moored at Heggstad Marina when Nina and I had discovered the man in the water. I raised my hand to shield my eyes from the sun as I spoke to him. He was wearing a red short-sleeve polo shirt, gray cargo shorts, and Top-Siders.

"Getting plenty of tourists, are you?" I asked.

"Seems everyone and their brother wants to see where Earl Woods drowned."

"Did you know Mr. Woods?"

"What? Me? No. Never met the man."

"But you know his name."

"He's become kind of a celebrity in these parts."

"Is this your boat?" I asked.

"Yacht."

"Excuse me. Is this your yacht?"

"Yeah. I call it the *Miss Behavin'*."

"It was one of the few boats anchored at the marina when Mr. Woods drowned."

"You're one of them investigators, aren't you? Yeah, I met a couple of them. Mostly they work for one insurance company or another. Is that you?"

"In a manner of speaking."

"Yeah, yeah," he said. "I can tell by the way you're dressed."

I was also wearing a short-sleeve polo shirt, only mine was green, my jeans were black, and my Nikes were white.

And that makes you look like an insurance investigator? my inner voice asked. *Huh*.

"What I told the others, I wasn't here when it happened," the man said. "When Woods drowned. I didn't get here until the following Monday. Hey, you want a beer?"

"Why, yes. Yes, I would."

"Well, come aboard."

I moved along the main dock and then veered off onto the narrow wooden walkway that served him and his neighbor. He came up the passageway that led to his salon as I stepped aboard his large boat. Up close he looked to be in his late fifties with hair that was black on top and gray at the temples, making me wonder if it was Father Time's doing or the product of a very competent stylist. He had an easy smile that never entirely left his face and I wondered if that was also an affectation.

Not that you're as cynical as some people say.

"I'm Nelson LeMay, by the way," he said. "Call me Nels."

"McKenzie."

We shook hands and he handed me an aluminum beer can with the name AURORA HAZE printed on it.

"You like your IPAs?" LeMay asked.

"I do."

"You'll like this one, then. Brewed by Castle Danger up there in Two Harbors on Lake Superior. Ever been?"

"Two Harbors, yes, but not the brewery."

While we chatted, I glanced around his boat. It was much larger than Dave Deese's.

"Nels." I used his first name because we were such good friends now. "Nels, what's the difference between a luxury boat and a yacht?"

"Depends on who you talk to. Most of the people in the marina, I mean they can call their boats yachts, only they're really just cabin cruisers. To be a yacht, you gotta sleep more than two. You need a well-ventilated galley with a stove, a refrigerator, and a sink. A head with a shower. Air-conditioning. Plus, cruisers generally range from twenty to forty feet. The *Miss Behavin'* is fifty-five feet."

"So, size matters," I said.

LeMay thought that was funny.

"In my experience," he said, "it matters a lot. On the other hand—you see all the electrical outlets the boats are plugged in to? Mine costs me over six thou and that's just for the summer."

"Is that the standard price?" I asked.

"No. The bigger the boat, the bigger the charge."

LeMay laughed at his own pun.

"Yours was one of the first boats in the marina," I reminded him.

"This spring, yeah, I splashed early. Too early, actually. It's kind of an ego thing, I admit. Gotta be the first one on the river. I wasn't though."

LeMay gestured at an empty slip across the dock and down four boats from his.

"*Maverick* was first," he said. "At least it was here before I was."

"Is that the name of the boat?" I asked.

"No, the name of the owner. Bret Maverick. Nah, I'm messing with you. *Maverick* is the boat's name, owned by Richard Bennett. Most call him Rick, but I've also heard people call him Dick." LeMay smirked at the nickname. "I only know him because we're neighbors. He doesn't associate with the riffraff in the marina; thinks he's special, although, c'mon. His boat—it's only a thirty-six-foot Carver. One time—I guess he wanted to be friends because he offered me a can of caviar."

"Caviar?"

"Said it was left over from something, but you know what? It was Iranian. Tasted like shit."

I tossed LeMay a changeup just to see what he would do with it.

"Was he on his boat when Mr. Woods drowned?" I asked.

LeMay spread his arms wide as he let the pitch go by, the gesture suggesting that he couldn't possibly know the answer to my question.

"That's right," I said. "You told me you weren't here."

"It was too cold. Temperature dropped below freezing. I could have stayed on board; fired up the space heaters. What happens, though, when the difference in temperature between the inside of the boat and the outside becomes too great, you get a lot of condensation. Everything inside gets wet. The *Miss Behavin'* has pretty good insulation, but ah, I decided it was best to stay in town."

"Do you live in Stillwater?" I asked.

"No, I have a condo in New Hope."

"New Hope, that's what? About an hour from here?"

"Not the way I drive."

"You're saying that you were in New Hope when Mr. Woods drowned."

"I don't actually know when he drowned, so I'm going to say yes. I didn't even know what happened until a couple days later when I drove back down here. It was a Monday. Most people, what they do, they live and work in the Cities, the suburbs, and come out to the marina on the weekends. Me, I'm here most of the time when the weather is good, and go to New Hope on the weekends to check my mail."

"What do you do for a living, Nels?"

"I'm a certified financial planner. I help individuals and small business owners manage their investments, life, health, disability, and long-term-care insurance needs, estate and tax planning; that sort of thing."

"You work from your boat?"

"Man, I gotta tell you, the best thing that ever happened to me was COVID. Before that every meeting was held in the office in Golden Valley or at a client's business or home. Now everything's done on Zoom. Clients got used to it and now most of them prefer it. It's easier, you know? More convenient for both sides. What I do, I put on a jacket and tie and conduct business from my salon. Clients don't even know. Probably wouldn't care if they did. Anyway, it's perfect for me. Not just for me, either. I think half of the New Money staff works remotely."

"New Money?"

"New Money Management Group. The guys who started the firm in the early nineties were all about the tech industry; about hooking up with people who were acquiring their own wealth instead of inheriting it. The nouveau riche, they called them, although it's the riche that matters, am I right? Do you have a financial planner, McKenzie?"

"I do. She works out of a houseboat."

LeMay thought that was funny, too.

"A houseboat?" he asked. "We should start a club."

"You said you didn't get here until the Monday after Mr. Woods drowned."

"Yeah, yeah, yeah. I splashed on Wednesday yet didn't stay

the night. I was here Thursday night and Friday, though. The weather was great on Thursday and Friday. The forecast for Friday night and Saturday, though . . . I left Friday, I don't know, seven? Just before sunset, anyway. It was still pretty warm, but like I said, the weather was going from warm to below freezing."

"Did you see anyone hanging around the docks on Thursday and Friday?"

"No, it was pretty dead. I didn't mean—you know what I meant."

"Sure."

"When the weather is great like it is now, you'll get a lot of people in the marina, boat owners, friends visiting friends, the occasional tourist; the place can get pretty crowded sometimes before they close the gates."

"The gates?"

You didn't see any gates when you were last here.

"Between eight and eight—eight in the morning and eight at night—people have easy access to the marina," LeMay said. "It's just more convenient for the people who have boats here. From eight at night to eight in the morning, though, it's shut down. Only people who own boats and their guests can get in. Only you're asking about late in March and I gotta say, I didn't see anyone."

"Are you sure?" I asked. "It's starting to be a long time ago."

"I know it is. I remember, though, because people were asking me the same questions as you back then, too. This female cop from Stillwater; what was her name?"

"Officer Eden Stoll?" I asked in reply.

LeMay pointed at me like I had won a prize.

"Yeah, yeah, yeah," he said. "You know her?"

"We've met."

You didn't know she was an investigator, though. You thought she was a street cop.

"I offered her a beer, too. She turned me down; said she was on duty. I told her that she was welcome to drop by anytime when she was off duty only she never did." LeMay spread his arms wide. "What can I say? You can't win them all. Anyway, I told her the same thing I just told you and then there were the insurance guys. Well, not just guys. This one woman, black hair, a babe but didn't smile once—she managed to ask the same questions six different ways. I didn't even think of offering her a drink. Way, way too serious for me."

Good for you, Maryanne.

"What I'm trying to say, McKenzie, is that this was way back in March and now it's what? June eighth? I probably don't remember much of what I saw or heard, only what I told the investigators that I saw and heard."

"You said you splashed on a Wednesday," I said.

"Yeah."

"Tell me about that."

LeMay did, explaining where he stored his boat during the harsh winter months and what he went through to get it back on the river and into Heggstad Marina. I kept asking specific questions, compelling him to provide details. He supplied them, telling me about the difficulty he had moving supplies and equipment from the parking lot to his boat.

"Every year I tell myself to get a dolly and every year I forget," he said.

"You carry everything from your SUV to the boat?"

"No. I carry everything from the SUV to the dock and then I lock up the SUV and carry everything from the dock to the boat."

"Who else was on the dock when you were doing this?" I asked.

"Brad Heggstad for a minute or two and this guy—hey, I do remember. There's a guy has a cabin cruiser on the far side of the marina." LeMay waved more or less in the direction of the main building. "Guy has a honey for a wife, but I don't know his name. He splashed on Thursday. How did you do that?"

I admit my smile was a little self-satisfied.

"Something I picked up over the years," I said. "Cuing one memory can often lead to another."

LeMay's smile disappeared and he stared at me for a few beats as if I had just shown him a weapon that he found dangerous.

"I'll remember that," he said. The smile quickly returned. "The guy with the good-looking wife, I watched him tying up and plugging in. His boat has the goofiest name."

"*Deese and Dose*?" I asked.

"There you go. Do you know them?"

"We've spoken."

"If you get a chance, introduce me to the wife."

I said I would, only I didn't mean it. I gave LeMay a card, though. It was white and printed with my name and cell number and nothing else. I told him if he remembered anything else to give me a shout. He waved the card at me like it was a gift.

"Will do," he said.

Brad Heggstad wasn't surprised to see me.

"G. K. Bonalay said you might come poking around," he said.

"Poking around?"

"Words she used. She also said I was supposed to call her if I found you poking around."

"Did she tell you why I would be poking around?"

"She said you thrive on chaos. She also said I was supposed to tell you that if you learn anything she expects you to share."

"If I do learn anything, I'll share it with everyone including the Stillwater PD and the Washington County Sheriff's Office. Speaking of which . . ."

"Yeah?"

"Security cameras."

Heggstad sighed deeply.

"The authorities, the cops, even the insurance companies, they all asked about the same thing," he said.

"I thought they might."

"We have them watching all the boats on the marina as well as the gas pump and the parking lot. Sometimes people leave their cars in the lot for more than a week at a time."

Cars in the parking lot, my inner voice said.

"That's right," I said aloud. "I forgot."

"What?" Heggstad asked.

"Can I see the video footage?"

"No. Unfortunately, the cameras weren't on in the winter."

"Really?"

"What would we be watching? That's what I asked the cops when they gave me the look you're giving me now. I told them in the past we usually only turned on the cameras when the marina started getting busy again in the spring."

"Meaning they weren't on when Mr. Woods drowned."

"Uh-uh, and you just know they're going to use that against us in the lawsuit; an example of our negligence I was told. We'll leave 'em on next winter, I promise."

"When Nina and I arrived that Saturday, there were four cars in the parking lot. One of them belonged to Mr. Woods; his name was painted all over it. One belonged to Dave Deese. Am I right in assuming that the third belonged to you?"

"Well, yeah, I drove here, so . . . ."

"Was anyone else working here that day?"

"No. It's pretty slow in the winter and a Saturday . . ."

"Then who drove the fourth car?"

Heggstad stared at me for a few beats before shaking his head.

"I couldn't say," he told me. "Someone who parked here and went for a walk, maybe? I don't know."

"Could it have belonged to one of your—what do you call them? Tenants?"

"None of the other boat owners were here that day. The cops checked."

"I'm sure they did. Tell me about Nelson LeMay."

"Been a customer for what? Five, six years? Nice enough guy except Nels likes to party and sometimes the parties get out of hand. He's supposed to be some sort of financial guy. Personally, I wouldn't let him manage my finances at gunpoint."

"Why not?" I asked.

"He acts like a big kid, you know? And like I said—he loves to party; always tries to be the life of the party. You see him with lots of different women, too. He uses his boat to get women."

"Maybe he can't keep a girlfriend."

"What makes you think they're girlfriends?"

"Professionals?"

Heggstad shrugged.

"I wouldn't say that," he told me. "The women I've seen him with, though—they always look to me like they know they shouldn't be on the *Miss Behavin'* but are hanging around, anyway."

"What about Richard Bennett?"

"Owns *Maverick Two*. I call it *Maverick Two* because there must be half a dozen boats in the marina called *Maverick*. Bennett's been here for, well, the same number of years as Nels, only I don't know him very well. When we talk it's mostly about marina stuff. He likes to keep to himself except from time to time when he complains about Nels and his loud parties."

"His boat isn't here today," I said.

"Not surprised. He's one of those guys who'll disappear for a week, two weeks at a time. Sometimes longer."

"Do you know where he goes?"

"Nah. It's not like people file flight plans or anything like that."

"Can you do me a favor?"

"G. K. said I should do whatever you ask," Heggstad said. "Within reason, she said, whatever that means."

"Give me a call when Bennett comes back."

"You think he knows something?"

"His was the only other boat docked on that side of the marina when Mr. Woods drowned, so who knows?"

Barbara Deese *was* surprised to see me. Truthfully, I was surprised to see her. At least I was surprised to see her alone on the *Deese and Dose* when I came knocking. We ended up sitting across from each other in the salon. I asked where Dave was.

"Dave does have a business to run, you know, although these days he's been giving more and more responsibility to his people," Barbara told me. "I think they like it that way."

"I'm surprised to see you here alone. I thought the boat was all Dave's idea."

"It is. He loves it."

"What about you?"

"It gets old sometimes. Don't tell him I said that."

"Why are you here?"

"Cleaning. I'm not only Dave's housekeeper; I'm his boat keeper, too."

"I think a little more than that."

Barbara reached over and tapped my knee.

"What are you doing here?" she asked.

I explained.

"Murder," she said. "Really?"

"It does seem unlikely," I admitted. "You didn't see anyone that Saturday morning?"

"No, like I told you back in March. No one."

"You didn't see a Black man with a white woman?"

"Not on Saturday."

"You said you arrived at eight A.M."

"No, closer to nine."

I knew that, only I was trying to use the same memory tricks on Barbara that I did on LeMay. Unfortunately, I learned nothing more than what she had already told me except that the couple she remembered seeing early Friday evening before she and Dave left the marina "were walking fast. They were walking as if they knew exactly where they were going and were anxious to get there."

"Was one of them Black?"

"No," Barbara said. "Why do you keep asking that?"

"Earl Woods, the man who drowned, was Black."

"I didn't know that. And his wife was white. Okay."

I kept plugging away, although, if there was anyone else on the dock Thursday, Friday, or Saturday, Barbara hadn't noticed.

"Sorry," she said.

"For what it's worth, Nelson LeMay thinks—and I'm quoting now—LeMay thinks you're a honey."

"Is that a compliment or a warning?"

"Why would it be a warning?"

"Some men believe you should be thrilled when they compliment you and then become angry when you're not."

"I hadn't thought of it that way."

"Ask Nina. She knows."

I spied the note pinned beneath the windshield wiper of my Mustang long before I reached it. My first thought was that a local retail outlet was handing out flyers for ten percent off on whatever it was they were selling. Only a quick glance told me that no other vehicle owners in the parking lot of Heggstad Marina had been invited to the sale. I pulled the note out once I reached my car and glanced around to see if anyone was watching. There was no one that I could see. I unfolded the note and read the message. It was handwritten in block letters on an otherwise blank sheet of white paper.

MIND YOUR OWN BUSINESS OR ELSE!

"C'mon," I said aloud. "Really?"

I thought of jogging to the marina building and asking Heggstad to let me take a look at the security footage of the parking lot, assuming that he had actually turned the cameras on, yet thought better of it.

Why bother? my inner voice asked.

Instead, I fired up the Mustang and drove out of the parking lot. It was while I was threading my way through the city of Stillwater that I made a hands-free phone call using the car's onboard computer.

"Associates and Bonalay, attorneys at law," a woman's voice said.

"Caroline, it's McKenzie. Put the boss on the line."

"Someone sounds cranky."

"Caroline . . ."

"She told me to expect your call . . ." *So, you were right.* "Just a sec."

A couple of moments later a different woman's voice said, "G. K. Bonalay."

"What the hell, Gen?" I asked.

"McKenzie? Is there a problem?"

"You know damn well there's a problem."

"I have no idea . . ."

"I got your message, okay?"

"What message?"

"The one left on my windshield telling me to mind my own business or else."

"You're making an awfully big assumption, aren't you, McKenzie?"

"Only three people knew I was at the marina. One couldn't have left the message, one wouldn't have, and the third is Brad Heggstad who told me that you told him to call the moment he found me poking around."

"Are you poking around?"

"Yeah, well, I thought I might."

"The fact that you're attempting to confirm the so-far unsubstantiated allegations that Mr. Woods was murdered only strengthens my case, you know that, right? It will help create—say it with me now—reasonable doubt; reasonable doubt as to how Mr. Woods died."

"I'm not doing it to help you."

"Which is also to my benefit. McKenzie, I want you to remember in case anyone should ask, you called me. I didn't call you."

"Which is exactly why you had Heggstad leave the message; so I'd call you."

"There you go again, making assumptions."

"I've always known you were a clever woman, Genevieve."

"McKenzie, who are you conducting this investigation for?"

I nearly answered "Nina." Instead, I said, "Nevaeh Woods."

"That's what I thought. It's even better that she's the one who is actively questioning the specious claims of criminal negligence that her stepmother has foisted upon my client."

"Specious? Foisted?"

"I subscribe to Merriam-Webster's New Word of the Day. McKenzie, can you actually prove there was a fourth car?"

"If the Stillwater Police Department has dash cams on their cruisers, Eden Stoll might have video of it; her or one of her colleagues that arrived later. If we can get an image of the license plate, we should be able to ID the driver as well. Genevieve, since you claim I'm helping you, you can help me. Contact the Stillwater PD—"

"Uh-uh, no way. As Brad Heggstad's attorney, I don't believe that it would be prudent for me to participate in this sorry witch hunt that is being undertaken solely to distract the jury from the verifiable facts of the case. Oh, by the way, I thought you did very well during the deposition. I was proud of the way you kept your temper when Toomey started leaning on you."

"Speaking of my temper—"

"It's always a pleasure chatting with you, McKenzie. Love to Nina."

By then I had found Highway 36 and was heading west through St. Paul's northern suburbs toward Minneapolis. I made another hands-free call. This time I contacted the Stillwater Police Department. After jumping through a few hoops, I spoke to an administrator who said she would make sure that Officer Eden Stoll received my name, cell phone number, and request that she contact me.

Next I called Nevaeh.

"McKenzie, have you reconsidered?" she wanted to know.

"Yes, I have."

"Oh, thank you, thank you."

"I'll try to find out what happened to your father, but Nevaeh, I'm making no promises, okay?"

"I hear you."

"Something else, and this is important—you might not like

what I discover. You might learn things you'll wish you didn't know. Have you thought of that?"

Nevaeh paused before answering.

"I understand," she said. "Thank you again, McKenzie."

"First things first—I need you to do something for me."

"Anything."

"I need you to call the Ramsey County Medical Examiner's Office. I don't have the number, but you can probably find it on their website. I want you to call and ask them to send you a complete copy of your father's autopsy report. I can't do it myself because I'm not a family member."

"Bizzy's lawyer has a copy; I know he does."

"Let's not involve either of them for now. We don't want them getting in the way."

Nevaeh paused again.

"If my stepmother . . ." she said.

"Let's not get ahead of ourselves, either," I said. "Let's not make any assumptions." *There's that word again.* "Your stepmother might be right about all of this. Just because we don't like it . . ."

"You're right, you're right. I said I wanted to know the truth. Okay, the medical examiner. I'll call him right away. It'll be our little secret."

Secrets, my inner voice said. *As if you don't have enough already.*

"Let me know when you get the autopsy report. We'll sit down and talk."

"I will. McKenzie, I really appreciate this."

FIVE

Twenty minutes later I was sitting at my desk in the office area of our condominium and staring at a computer screen. If you wanted to learn about someone these days, the first place you looked was the internet. I entered Earl John Woods's name into a search engine and the first thing that popped up was his obituary as it appeared in the *St. Paul Pioneer Press*. Unlike most I've seen, his came with two photographs. The first featured a handsome young man dressed in a U.S. Army uniform, an American flag draped behind him. The second depicted a handsome older man wearing a black suit jacket over a white shirt. The copy beneath the photographs read:

WOODS

Earl John "E. J."

Age 62 of White Bear Lake

Died unexpectedly March 25, 2023. Born June 10, 1960, in St. Paul.

E. J. served his country with distinction for 30 years in the U.S. Army.

Founder and partner of E. J. Woods Tree Care Services, he was a skilled landscaper and tree removal expert. He was loved by his employees and clients alike. E. J. was preceded in death by his parents, Jackson Woods and mother Carmen (Booth) Woods, and his first wife, Diahann (Puckett) Woods. E. J. will be deeply missed by his wife Elizabeth "Bizzy" (Beamon) Woods and his daughter, Nevaeh Woods.

Please join us for a celebration of E. J.'s life on Saturday, April 1, from 1 P.M. to 5 P.M at Potzmann-Schultz VFW banquet room in Maplewood, MN. Mass of Christian Burial 11 A.M. Monday, April 3 at Sacred Heart Church in White Bear Lake. Interment will be at Ft. Snelling National Cemetery.

I took notes on a legal pad because that's what I do, underlining *Potzmann-Schultz VFW Maplewood.*

Next, I used my computer in an attempt to access all of Mr. Woods's social media sites only to discover that he didn't have any. No Facebook, no Twitter, no Instagram, no LinkedIn, Tumblr, Snapchat, Pinterest, WhatsApp, TikTok, YouTube, or Reddit. My first thought—good for you, Mr. Woods. My second thought— not so good for me. I had a third thought, though, and searched for social media sites maintained by Elizabeth "Bizzy" Woods.

Mr. Woods's wife was everywhere and she posted about everything. The last three Instagram posts, for example, showed her sitting behind a meal she had ordered at the Ocean-aire Seafood Room, a ritzy restaurant in downtown Minneapolis, a shot of her dressed in cycling tights, a form-fitting jersey, and a bicycle helmet while leaning against a ten-speed on the path that circled Lake of the Isles, and a pic of her lounging provocatively in a blue gown in front of the grand piano at the Commodore Bar and Restaurant, a joint in St. Paul where F. Scott Fitzgerald used to hang out, above the comment #Friday #night sets the mood for the entire weekend.

I guess she's still in mourning, my inner voice told me.

I wondered if she was an influencer, or at least aspired to

become one. She had 3,691 followers on Instagram, 2.9K followers on Twitter, and 3,011 friends on Facebook. I wrote the numbers on my notepad.

'Course, they could all be the same people.

Not all of her posts were frivolous, though. She had published several rants on Facebook in which she took issue with the insurance industry for its despicable treatment of her "darling E. J.," not to mention the "criminal negligence of the Heggstad Marina."

I kept surfing back in time and examining other posts involving Mr. Woods.

A pic taken at Fort Snelling National Cemetery, Elizabeth dressed all in black and still somehow managing to look sexy, her blond hair splayed across her shoulders, while an honor guard fired a volley over her late husband's casket.

A pic of Elizabeth and Nevaeh supporting each other as they followed the casket out the front doors of Sacred Heart Church.

A pic taken at the Potzmann-Schultz VFW banquet room during Mr. Woods's celebration of life, a dry-eyed Elizabeth smiling sweetly while surrounded by her late husband's "comrades in arms."

And back further still to happier times.

Earl and Elizabeth sitting behind home plate at a Minnesota Twins game.

Earl and Elizabeth walking hand in hand on a boulevard in Paris.

Riding bikes on a path along the North Shore.

Dancing at a party.

Eating dinner.

Kissing Nevaeh, each claiming a cheek.

A sunset.

A sunrise.

My favorite was a photograph of a grinning Earl Woods wearing an orange hard hat, red earmuffs, safety goggles, orange vest, Kevlar chaps, and heavy boots, with a chain saw slung over his shoulder, above the comment He's a Lumberjack and he's okay, the line taken from an old Monty Python skit.

Yet there were no pics of Mr. Woods on a boat or a dock or standing near water of any kind, which reminded me—Maryanne Altavilla had probably seen all of this, too.

I wonder if she knows the lumberjack song.

I searched all of Elizabeth's social media accounts. In all of the pics that she had posted of them together, Elizabeth and Earl were both smiling as if there was no other place they would rather be and no one they would rather be with.

Which doesn't mean there wasn't conflict.

I wrote the word on my notepad—"conflict"—and stared at it. After a few beats, I added a question mark and stared some more. A Black man married to a white woman a full decade or more younger than he was, there must have been conflict, mustn't there? If not between them, then certainly between them and a sizeable chunk of the population. Mustn't there? I stared some more before asking myself, if there was conflict, where would it most likely be found?

We have a website here in the Land of 10,000 Lakes—Minnesota Court Records Online. Simply type "mncourts .gov," add a slash and "access-case-records," a second slash plus "MCRO.aspx," and hit execute and you'll be directed to a page on the Minnesota Judicial Branch website that will allow you to access district court criminal and civil records. I inputted "Woods, Earl John," added his birth date into the search engine, and found—*whoa*—twenty-three results.

Most of the cases were listed as "crim/traf non-mand,"

meaning the offenses were considered petty misdemeanors that carried a fine yet no jail time—speeding tickets, parking tickets, failure to stop for traffic control signal, driving after suspension, violating the open bottle law. Mr. Woods didn't need to appear in court to deal with them.

Two events reached felony status, however.

In the first, Mr. Woods was convicted of Aiding and Abetting Burglary in the First Degree and sentenced to forty-five months. Except he appealed on the grounds of "insufficient evidence of his identity." He claimed that the closed-circuit video taken of two men breaking into a tech store did not adequately identify him; that he was arrested solely because of his alleged personal relationship with the man that the video did adequately identify, another Black man named Keith Martin. The appeals court agreed and ruled that Woods should be given a new trial. The county attorney went to Martin and offered him a reduced sentence if he ratted out Woods. Martin refused. The CA subsequently dropped all charges against Woods, although Martin was sent to the Oak Park Heights Correctional Facility.

In the second, Mr. Woods was convicted of Aiding and Abetting Racketeering. It was a rather vague charge and I couldn't find anything on the website that provided specific details, although a second charge that had been dismissed offered a hint—Aiding and Abetting in the Business of Concealing Criminal Proceeds. During my time as a cop I had always been impressed by the number of people who claimed that they were given something "to hold" for a friend that they didn't know was stolen. Mr. Woods was sentenced to time served—twenty-one days in the Washington County Jail—and placed on supervised probation for five years, monitored by Washington County Community Corrections. There was a line at the very bottom of the first page of the sentencing order that made me go "Hmm," though. The question, "Was this a departure from the sentencing guidelines?" was immediately followed by the answer, "Yes."

A nod to his service record, I decided. Which made me wonder . . .

I did the math on my notepad. Mr. Woods was born in 1960. He did thirty years in the service of his country. Assuming he enlisted when he was a kid—eighteen, nineteen—he would have retired in 2008. His first brush with the system was June 18, 2008.

Are we watching a longtime veteran adjusting to the real world? my inner voice asked.

He must have finally pulled it together, I determined, because the last time Mr. Woods's name was cited on the Minnesota courts' website was in March 2010. Following that, Mr. Woods didn't receive so much as a traffic summons.

After adding all of that to my notes, I looked up Elizabeth Woods and found—nothing. Undeterred, I inputted Elizabeth Beamon's name into the search engine and *holy mackerel*! She had more results than Mr. Woods. Thirty-two by my count, most of them for parking tickets. Apparently, she had never seen a parking meter that couldn't be ignored. Among all the other cases attached to her name, though, were a couple of eviction notices, a Disorderly Conduct-Offensive, Abusive, Noisy, Obscene Behavior citation, and two felony convictions.

The first—Soliciting/Inducing/Promoting Prostitution, Sex Trafficking. According to the sentencing order she was to be committed to the Commissioner of Corrections at the Minnesota Correctional Facility in Shakopee for sixty-two months. However, the sentence was stayed for five years. Was this a departure from the sentencing guidelines? Yes.

The second felony—Identity Theft / Eight or More Direct

Victims / Combined Loss Greater Than $35,000. Once again, she was sentenced to serve a prison term in Shakopee, this time for seventy-eight months. Once again the sentence was stayed. Was this a departure from the sentencing guidelines? You betcha.

A pretty girl can get away with almost anything in Minnesota, my inner voice reminded me.

Yet something must have clicked because from that day forward Elizabeth Beamon never again had any contact with the system, either. At least not according to the website.

Don't tell me she actually started paying her parking fees.

I noticed something, though, while I was transcribing all this information. The dates. Elizabeth Beamon was summoned to the Washington County Courthouse in Stillwater for the last time on Thursday, March 11, 2010.

I checked my notes for Earl Woods. He had also been at the Washington County Courthouse in Stillwater on Thursday, March 11, 2010.

Jesus, you don't think that's where they first set eyes on each other, do you? Talk about meeting cute.

My next search led me to the website of E. J. Woods Tree Care Services. It featured a lot of photographs of Earl Woods and his people—all dressed in orange shirts and vests and wearing orange hard hats—as they removed trees that had fallen on houses and fences, that were blocking streets and alleys, and one that was leaning precariously against a bridge. In addition, there were other less dramatic pics of them simply trimming and removing trees that apparently needed to be trimmed and removed, plus a few shots of his team actually planting trees. The copy introduced:

E. J. WOODS TREE CARE SERVICES
Emergency Storm Cleanup a Specialty

E. J. Woods Tree Care Services is made up of passionate individuals, nearly all of them veterans of America's armed services, who are ready, willing, and able to meet any challenge head-on whether it's the careful removal of a tree or a major cleanup following a storm.

Starting in 2012, our mission has been to provide residential and commercial property owners with the best and most timely tree pruning, tree and stump removal, and emergency cleanup services in the Greater Twin Cities area. Our strongest asset is our people, whose combined knowledge and experience rival the largest and oldest firms around.

This is not a nine-to-five job for us, but a life commitment to be available when you need us most. This is especially true when a storm hits.

While your priority must be the care and safety of your family, your employees, and yourself, ours will be to eliminate the danger, mitigate the damage, and handle the cleanup. As a result, you can always trust E. J. Woods Tree Care Services to take care of you.

Yelp gave them four-point-eight stars based on 243 reviews. *Is this what put Mr. Woods back on the straight and narrow?* I checked the dates again. He was last seen in a Minnesota courtroom in March 2010. He started his business in 2012. *Did E. J. Woods Tree Care Services give him a purpose in life? Him and Bizzy?*

I studied the website some more. I searched for a link that might help identify the company's principals and employees and found nothing.

I wrote more notes:

Obit says Mr. Woods was founder and partner.
Who was his partner? Bizzy?
Who owns E. J. Woods Tree Care Services now?

The Office of the Minnesota Secretary of State also has a web-site. One of the pages on the website allows you to search for the name of any business in the state. I typed in "E. J. Woods Tree Care Services" and discovered the name was owned by Norfolk LLP. Next I searched for "Norfolk LLP" and learned only that it was a registered limited liability partnership and the address for its chief executive office was the same as the address for E. J. Woods Tree Care Services. I couldn't find Mr. Woods's name much less his partner's.

There must be an easy way to uncover these names, I told myself.

I strolled through the contact list on my cell phone, found the name I was looking for, and hit call. A few moments later a woman answered.

"What do you want?" she asked.

"Honest to God, H, I thought I was a valued client, yet you talk to me like I'm imposing on you."

"I've known you for a long time, McKenzie. You don't make social calls and you don't do small talk."

"I do small talk. 'Course I do. How 'bout the Wild? Could they possibly have had a worse playoff run?"

H. B. Sutton didn't respond. I could picture her sipping tea and staring out of the porthole or whatever they call windows on a houseboat.

"Minnesota Wild," I added. "They play professional hockey."

I heard a deep sigh followed by words so steeped in frustration that I nearly apologized.

"So, McKenzie," Sutton said. "What do you want?"

I shouldn't have been surprised. Sutton was the most no-nonsense person I had ever known. I blamed her flower children parents for her brusque manner and so did she. They thought they were being cute when they named their daughter Heavenly-love Bambi. Instead, they doomed her to a life of teasing and mockery.

"Try growing up with a name like that," she once told me. "Especially while wearing the peasant blouses and skirts my parents dressed me in, the flat sandals. Try going to high school or college; try getting a job; try being taken seriously by anybody."

When she reached an age where she could make her own decisions, she stopped using the name, becoming H. B. or just H to the lucky few she called friend. She also immersed herself in the business of money, the one thing that everybody took seriously. She was the financial advisor I had alluded to during the deposition, the woman who made me independently wealthy.

"I met a fellow traveler this morning," I said. "A CFP. Instead of a houseboat, he works off his yacht. He thinks you two should form a club."

"A yacht? How fucking pretentious is that?"

"Or maybe not."

"Seriously, McKenzie, what can I do for you?" Sutton asked.

"I'm trying to find out who the principals are in an LLP called Norfolk. I have the corporate address, yet nothing else."

"A little background."

"There's a company called E. J. Woods Tree Care Services.

The founder, a man named Earl John Woods, died under mysterious circumstances. His obit says he had at least one partner. I'm trying to learn the partner's name."

"I can't help you."

"You can't?"

"The information isn't public record. I mean the courts can find out. They have the power of subpoena, but the rest of us—it's kind of like a last will and testament. No one knows what it says until it's probated. I'll tell you though, if I had been advising Mr. Woods, it would have been one mother of a long and complex will. He and his partners would have a legally binding contract anticipating every possible contingency."

"Such as?"

"It would spell out in detail exactly what would happen if one of the business owners dies. Mr. Woods, say. Would the other partners inherit the entire business or would Mr. Woods's share go to one of his heirs? Is there an insurance policy?"

Insurance, my inner voice repeated.

"Would the proceeds of the policy allow the partners to buy out Mr. Woods's heirs and would the heirs even have a choice in the matter? These things can get very contentious. You need to be prepared. Was Mr. Woods prepared?"

"I don't know."

"McKenzie, you said he died under mysterious circumstances. Is this one of your cases? Are you investigating"—Sutton paused dramatically—"murder?"

"H, if you had asked me that an hour ago I would have said no. I've seen no evidence whatsoever to suggest that Mr. Woods was murdered. On the other hand, taking control of what appears to be a thriving business, that's certainly a motive, wouldn't you say? Except whose motive?"

"I have a thought."

"Tell me. I'd like to hear it."

"You could always ask."

The offices for E. J. Woods Tree Care Services were located in Washington County not far from the Oakdale Nature Preserve. They reminded me of an auto repair shop except for a sign above the door that read ASK US FOR FIREWOOD. The building had a large garage with huge doors where I was sure they stored their bucket and chipper trucks, skid steers, stump grinders, log loaders, splitters, and saws. Attached to it was a much smaller office building. I stepped inside and found a high counter. Behind the counter were a couple of metal desks that looked as though people actually sat and worked at them. Except the office was empty. There was a small bell on top of the high counter. I was about to ring it when two people stepped through a door that led from the office to the garage. They were laughing. The man was white and round and appeared to be in his mid-forties. The much younger woman was Black and slim with short hair and long fingernails.

"I hope I didn't keep you waiting," she said.

"Not at all."

She moved toward the counter.

"If you're looking for firewood—why? It's June. Are you running a Boy Scout camp or something?"

"Do I look like a Boy Scout?"

"Little bit, yeah."

I thought that was funny. My laughter seemed to increase her curiosity.

"We don't get much walk-in business," she said. "Usually when a tree falls on someone's car, we get a phone call or an email."

"Not that, either," I said.

"What can we do for you, then?" she asked.

"I'd like to speak to the owner."

The woman's expression hardened as she turned her head to look at the middle-aged man who had found a spot behind one of the desks. He was watching us, yet said nothing. When the woman turned to look at me again, she asked, "Do you know that Mr. Woods passed away a couple of months ago?"

"Yes," I said. "That's why I'm here."

The woman glanced from me back to the man again. He shrugged.

"Any questions concerning the business should be addressed to Mrs. Woods and her attorney, Mr. Garrett Toomey," the woman told me. "I can give you their phone numbers, if you like?"

"You don't know the name of Mr. Woods's business partner?"

The woman again glanced at the man sitting behind the desk as if looking for support.

"What exactly do you want?" he demanded to know.

"Just the name," I said.

"Mister . . ."

"McKenzie."

"Mr. McKenzie, we are under strict orders not to discuss our business with anyone."

"Did Bizzy issue the order?" I used Elizabeth's nickname to prove that I was just one of the family. "Or Garrett?"

This time it was the woman who answered.

"It doesn't matter," she said. "We were all told that if someone asked questions, they're supposed to contact Mrs. Woods or her attorney. I mean like in no uncertain terms, 'kay?"

Only I didn't want to do that. I didn't want either Elizabeth Woods or her attorney to know I was asking questions just yet. If I called Nevaeh—probably she'd jump to conclusions again.

"Okay," I said. "Well, thank you for your time."

"Do you want their numbers?" the woman asked.

"I have their numbers."

I turned toward the door, only I didn't reach it.

"That's it?" the man asked. "You're not going to call us names or threaten us?"

"Do you get a lot of that?"

"The last guy was pretty upset."

"Last guy?"

"He had a lot of questions, too," the woman said. "If we seem rude, it's because of him."

"What questions?"

"He wanted to know who was running the company, too; if it was going to be sold."

"Did he identify himself?" I asked.

"No."

"So, not someone looking for a job?"

The woman snorted at that.

"Or thinking of buying the company," I added.

"If he was, you'd think he'd leave his name or call Mrs. Woods or Mr. Toomey."

"You'd think," I agreed. "Listen, I don't know why this is a thing, but you won't have any problems with me. I was just looking to save myself the trouble of calling Nevaeh."

"You know Nevaeh?" the woman asked.

"Yes. She . . . Well, there's a lot going on with what happened to her father and whatnot."

"Tell us about it," the man said. "Suicide? Shit."

"She asked me to help out."

"We love Nevaeh," the woman said. "She used to work here, you know; used to have my job, all-purpose office manager. God, I haven't seen her in years. Well, except for at the funeral."

"Why did she leave?" I asked.

"I don't know. One day she was here and the next day she

was gone. E. J. said only that it was time for her to move on. I
think he fired her. Last I heard she went back to teaching."

She's a teacher? Why didn't you know that?

"That was what?" The woman was speaking to the man behind the desk. "Had to be at least six years ago. I was just starting here. I was still a kid."

"Weren't we all," the man said. "McKenzie, you claim to
know Nevaeh."

Apparently not.

"I do," I said aloud.

"Then ask her your questions."

"Why didn't I think of that?"

The woman said, "Tell her Marilyn said 'Hi.'"

I returned to my Mustang, fired it up, and started working my
way toward Maplewood, a city that resembles a hammer when
you look at it on a map. I hadn't driven far before my onboard
cell phone started playing Louis Armstrong's dazzling introduction to the jazz classic "West End Blues." The display didn't
list a name, only a phone number.

"This is McKenzie," I said.

"Mr. McKenzie, this is Eden Stoll returning your call."

"Officer Stoll, thank you for calling back. I appreciate it."

"What can I do for you, Mr. McKenzie?"

"I doubt that you remember me," I said before explaining in
detail when, where, how, and why we met.

"I do remember," Stoll said. "Quite well. In fact, I stayed on
top of the case until—I'm not an investigator, McKenzie; just
a street cop. It seemed so odd to me, though, the way the vic
was holding on to the ladder; the way the vic's wife's demeanor
kept swinging from calm to distraught. I've been asking a few
questions on my own time, something my bosses wouldn't like;

certainly the ID in Washington County's Sheriff's Office would be pissed. Only nothing came of them, my questions. A friend in the ME's office let me read the autopsy report. Undetermined, he declared. That kind of leaves it open-ended except the ME also ruled that there was no trauma, no indication of assault, so I let it go."

"Yeah, about that."

I explained again in great detail why I was working the case. Something else G. K. taught me long ago—if you don't want to talk to the cops, fine, don't talk to the cops; don't answer their questions. That's your privilege. If you do talk to the cops, though, always tell them the truth and nothing but the truth or so help you God, you're going to jail. Besides, I wanted Officer Eden Stoll on my side.

"There was a fourth car?" she asked.

"I'm pretty sure, yeah."

"In the parking lot. I didn't notice. I saw the SUV with, E. J. Woods, painted on the doors and a Mustang . . ."

"The Mustang was mine."

"Yeah. Okay. I'll ask about the dash cam footage taken from my cruiser. I know they keep it for ninety days. McKenzie, there's no evidence whatsoever that Mr. Woods's death was a homicide, is there?"

"No, Officer Stoll, there is not. At least none that I've found."

I drove at least a quarter mile before she spoke again.

"Okay, like I said, I'll ask about the dash cam footage. McKenzie, I'm not looking to boost my career, maybe get into plainclothes. It's just that, the reason I didn't let it go . . ."

"Yes?"

"This whole damn thing feels so off."

Where have you heard that before?

SIX

As the name implied, the Potzmann-Schultz VFW post had been built to honor, support, and generally celebrate those members of the U.S. armed forces who served "in a war, campaign, or expedition on foreign soil or in hostile waters." Yet it also had a comfortable neighborhood bar and restaurant vibe with video games, dartboards, and pool tables scattered throughout the clubhouse. There was a small stage where I assumed live music was occasionally played. Wide-screen HDTVs were placed hither and yon, their blank screens suggesting they were only turned on when a game was being played. A "free popcorn" machine with plenty of paper boats was pressed against the wall on one side of the front door. On the other side was a digital bulletin board with rotating notices promoting "BBQ Rib Fridays," thanking everyone who participated in last week's Memorial Day's activities, reminding members where they could go to secure the government benefits that they were entitled to, announcing that post meetings were scheduled for the first Monday of the month, congratulating a middle school student who took first place in the district's Patriot's Pen Competition, and proclaiming the return by popular demand of the "Build Your Own Bloody Mary Bar" on Saturday and Sunday mornings. Above the door was a sign that read EVERYONE IS WELCOME HERE.

I stepped inside and found a seat at the bar. There was an

older gentleman nursing a draft beer three stools down from me. Only a few of the tables were occupied, one of them by three men and one woman drinking beer from several pitchers. It was mid-afternoon on a Thursday.

I placed the bartender in his mid-forties. He had one regular leg and one made of titanium.

"What can I get you?" he asked.

The selection was fairly generic so I went with my go-to tap beer.

"Summit EPA," I said.

"Twelve or sixteen?"

"Surprise me."

He smirked at that and filled a sixteen-ounce glass decorated with the Hamm's Bear, an iconic and welcome character among Minnesota beer drinkers. He set the beer in front of me.

"Menu?" he asked.

"Too late for lunch and too early for dinner."

"But the perfect time for a beer."

"Why yes, yes it is."

"I'm Marco. Need anything, just shout my name."

"Marco . . ."

He held up an index finger.

"Don't do it," he said.

"Polo?"

"Ah, man . . ."

The older man sitting at the bar started laughing.

"You asked for it," he said.

"Just once," Marco said. "Just once."

"I'm guessing you get that a lot," I said.

"Mostly from the regulars."

He pointed at the older man who held up his empty glass.

"Marco, Marco," the older man chanted.

"See?"

The bartender moved in front of him, yanked the glass from his hand, filled it with Miller Lite, and set it in on the bar. He spoke the word as if he was spitting it at him.

"Polo."

"There you go," the older man said.

The bartender moved back to where I was sitting.

"So," he said. "Did you serve?"

"Does twelve years with the cops count?"

"Asking me? I'd say sure. Some of the regulars are nitpickers, though. They'd want to know what country you were deployed in."

"St. Paul."

"That hellhole."

"My old man was with the First Marines," I said.

"That counts, too. What brings you to Potzmann-Schultz?"

"Mr. Earl John Woods."

Marco looked up and away as if he was listening to a story he already didn't like. Apparently, the older man drinking his beer a few stools away was eavesdropping.

"Still?" he asked.

"Still?" I repeated.

"Couple of people have come in to ask about E. J.," Marco said. "Insurance investigators mostly."

"I seem to be following in their footsteps."

"You with the insurance companies?"

I raised my glass and shook my head so there would be no confusion when I answered.

"No," I said.

"Good," Marco said. "I didn't like the insurance guys, what they were saying about E. J."

"Fuckin' E. J.," the older man said. "Ever since he gone people be actin' like his shit didn't stink when it smelled just as much as everyone else's."

"Here we go," Marco said.

"Why do you say that?" I asked.

The older man waved his hand and looked straight ahead as if it was a question not worth answering.

"E. J. and J. T. used to be friends and then they weren't," Marco said.

They call him J. T.? my inner voice asked.

"How the hell would you know?" J. T. asked. "You weren't even here back then. You were still doing a tour in the sandbox."

"Hey, I work in a joint where people applaud when complete strangers win a five-dollar pull tab."

"You tell 'im the story then, you so smart."

Marco turned to me.

"E. J. used to work for J. T. cutting down trees," he said.

"Fucker was in trouble with the law," J. T. said. "Couldn't get a job, nobody would hire him; a convicted felon. I hired him, though. Taught him how to use chain saws, chippers, stump grinders—on-the-job training, you know. First time he downed a tree on his own, man, you shoulda seen how happy that made him. The look on his face; it was like he finally found his place in the world. Then what does he do? Year after I hired him, year and a half—he was running his own crew by then. Up he gets, starts his own company. Becomes my competitor after all I did for him, too."

"He gave you notice," Marco said. "Way I heard it, E. J. told you what he was going to do three months before he did it."

"Doesn't change nothin'."

"You have a tree trimming business?" I asked.

"What are we talking about?" J. T. raised his hand like a cop stopping traffic. "I had a company—J. T.'s Four Seasons Tree Removal Service. I'm J. T. Jeffrey Tribbett, 'kay? Then Earl starts his business. Calls it E. J. Woods Tree Care Services. J. T. E. J. Can't even be original about his name. 'Course, everyone called him E. J. after that like they call me J. T. Copying my life."

"You said you *had* a company," I said.

"Yeah, I retired—wait. You think E. J. put me out of business or something like that? Hell no. I did just fine without him. Better even. There're plenty of trees in Minnesota; plenty of work, believe me. Guys I sold my business to, my employees, they tell me that with this ash borer disease spreading throughout the Cities, business couldn't be better. They want me to come of retirement and help 'em."

"Then why are you so angry?" Marco asked.

"Copying my life. Weren't you listening?"

"J. T.," a man's voice called.

I spun on my stool toward the voice. It came from the table where the three men and the lone woman were drinking beer from several pitchers. Apparently, they had been listening to every word we said. The man who was speaking pointed at his crotch.

"I got some wood over here you can trim," he said.

"I told you, asshole," J. T. replied. "I'm retired."

That caused everyone at the table to laugh; J. T. and Marco, too.

They're all friends. Only friends can get away with insults like that.

A second man at the table jerked his chin at me.

"You asking questions about E. J.?"

"I'm trying to get a sense of the man," I answered.

"Why? You working for the insurance companies?"

"No."

"Bizzy, then? Bizzy's lawyer?"

"No. Nevaeh. Nevaeh Woods."

"We like Nevaeh," the woman said. "Haven't seen much of her lately."

The first man reached over and pulled a chair from an empty table and dragged it next to theirs. He patted the seat, which I took as an invitation. I grabbed my Summit and moved to the table.

"McKenzie," I said as I sat.

The man pointed at each of his companions in turn.

"Sheila, Mike, Grant; I'm Josh," he said.

Getting close, I recognized the men. "E. J.'s comrades in arms" Bizzy Woods had called them on her social media accounts. They all appeared to be in their early sixties, each suffering from varying degrees of hair loss. The woman I had not seen in any of the pics. I would have guessed that she was a decade younger than her companions, with blond hair streaked with gray, although it was possible she just took better care of herself.

"Thanks for chatting with me," I said.

"What's going on, anyway?" Mike asked. I noticed he wasn't looking at me, but over my head.

"As a wise man once said and I am fond of quoting—*the answer to all of your questions is money*," I said. "The insurance companies claim E. J. committed suicide and refuse to pay off on his life insurance policies . . ."

"Bastards," Grant said.

"Bizzy and her lawyer say that he died by accident because of the criminal negligence of the marina and are demanding everyone pay up or they'll take them all to court. Nevaeh, though—Nevaeh just wants to know the truth about what happened."

"Nevaeh," Sheila said. "'Heaven' spelled backwards. How's she holding up?"

"She seemed fine when I spoke to her this morning. Like I said, she just wants answers. She said E. J. didn't like boats, didn't like hanging around lakes or rivers, so why was her father at the marina that Saturday morning?"

"Good question," Josh said. "I never heard of him going any-where near a boat."

"Me, neither," Sheila said.

"I can tell you right off, E. J. did not commit suicide," Grant said. "He wasn't the type."

"Is there a type?" Mike asked. His voice was soft.

"I mean he never acted depressed or anything."

"That doesn't mean he wasn't."

"What I was told, the insurance companies claim he had PTSD," I said.

"We all have PTSD," Sheila said. "Those of us who saw com-bat."

Her three companions all nodded slightly as if she spoke a truth universally acknowledged.

"Was he getting therapy?" I asked.

Shrugs all around.

"It's not something people talk about," Mike said. He spoke softly again and I noticed that his companions leaned in to hear him as if this was a common occurrence.

"Some people talk about it," Grant said. "They talk about it a lot. Others, yeah, they keep it to themselves."

"Mr. Woods?" I asked.

"We're all getting therapy in one way or another," Sheila said. "Coming here; spending time with people who know your stories. You could argue that's a form of therapy."

"We all have stories," Josh added. "This is the one place where you get to tell them aloud. No one's going to judge you. In the outside world people look at you like you're—well . . ."

"Do you have a story, McKenzie?" Sheila asked. "I heard you telling Marco that you were with the cops. I bet you have a lot of stories."

"None worth mentioning," I said.

"Don't say that," Josh said. "Don't say that to us. We get a lot of people coming in here who didn't serve. Neighbors, people who just like the place, and that's cool. You wouldn't be comfortable telling them your story, we get that. But us? Tell us your story, McKenzie."

There were so many of them. Nina had been right about the dreams I had, that Bobby Dunston had. One in particular . . .

Sheila filled my glass from a pitcher on the table. I took that as a sign to begin.

I had so many stories; I picked the first of them from the time when I was working third shift out of the Phalen Village Storefront in the SPPD's Eastern District. I received the call at twelve fifteen A.M.—possible robbery in progress at the Food and Fuel convenience store. The dispatcher gave the address at the same time as the information appeared on the squad's MDT screen, along with REMARKS: alarm tripped, attempting callback at store.

Eighty seconds later, I slowly drove past the store, lights and siren off, hoping my arrival had gone undetected. I couldn't see anyone through the store windows although there were several cars in the parking lot. I drove another fifty yards and parked where I could see both the store and the lot without being clearly visible myself, taking up a position of observance, just like I had been taught at the skills academy.

I unholstered my nine-millimeter Glock and then thought better of it. I was never comfortable with the grip. Instead, I opened the door and leaned back inside the squad, hitting the button that released the standard-issue Remington 870 12-gauge shotgun from its rack. I liked the heft of it. That and its eight rounds of double-aught buck, four in the magazine.

It had been my intention to wait for backup, except a late-model sedan turned in to the parking lot of the convenience store, heading into harm's way. I jogged into the lot, carrying the shotgun in the port position. The car stopped to the left of the entrance. Two doors opened. A couple emerged—a Black man, maybe thirty, from the driver's side and a Black woman, same age, from the passenger's side.

"Police. Get back in the car." My grip tightened on the shotgun. "Get back in the car."

The couple froze; deer in the headlights.

The glass door of the convenience store swung open. The suspect came out fast, holding a paper bag with the store's logo in his left hand and a Smith & Wesson .38 in his right. I braced the stock of the shotgun against my shoulder and sighted down the barrel.

"Police. Drop the gun. Put your hands in the air." I was surprised by how calm my voice sounded. "Drop the gun. Drop it now."

He didn't drop the gun, though.

Instead, the suspect raised his hands.

I fired once.

The woman screamed. "You killed 'im, you killed 'im," she railed.

The man shouted an obscenity. "He had his hands up," he added. "You killed 'im while he was trying to surrender."

"What happened after that?" Sheila asked.

"The Ramsey County grand jury refused to indict," I said. "It ruled that I had acted properly and within the scope and range of my duties. It didn't hurt that the clerk inside the store backed up my story."

"Did you suffer from PTSD because of it?" Grant asked.

I held my hand straight out and gave it a wag.

"Did you get therapy?" Mike asked.

I flashed on Dr. Jillian DeMarais. Nina had been right about her, too. Jillian was an ex-girlfriend. Before that she was the psychologist that I was required to see by the SPPD following the shooting. I saw her once a week for three months and then stopped seeing her by mutual agreement. Six months later I asked her to dinner. I remember telling her at the time that I was calling because she was smart and pretty and not because I needed additional treatment, although I was open to suggestions. She told me that she thought I was funny. I asked if she meant funny humorous or funny peculiar. Instead of answering, she told me to pick her up at seven.

"Therapy was mandatory," I said. "I'm not sure what good it did."

"McKenzie?" Grant asked. "The suspect—was he trying to surrender?"

I looked him directly in the eyes.

"No," I said.

Sheila covered my hand with hers and gave it a squeeze.

"Damn right," she said.

I was in a hurry to change the subject.

"Earl John Woods," I asked. "What was his story?"

I noticed, though, that the mood at the table had shifted somewhat. My companions seemed more comfortable with my questions after I told my story. It was as if they no longer viewed me as a complete outsider.

"He had trouble with the law after he got his honorable," Josh said. "Truthfully, so did I although not like E. J. Then he cleaned up his act. Married Bizzy, which surprised everybody. She was a serious babe in those days . . ."

"Still is," Mike said. He was looking directly at me now and his voice was steady.

"He was what?" Josh asked. "Seventeen years older than her?"

"E. J. was Black, she was white," Grant said.

"That, too," Mike said.

"Afterward, he started his own business," Josh said. "I get why J. T. might've been pissed off about it. E. J. was his best worker. A man wants to start his own business, though, wants to be his own boss, you gotta respect that."

"It was a struggle at first," Grant said. "First five years or so. Then boom, business just took off. Looked like it, anyway. Man bought a new house, bought a new car, started traveling; Bizzy posting photos of the two of 'em in Europe and shit."

"Who was E. J.'s partner?" I asked.

"I didn't know he had a partner," Josh said. He glanced at Grant.

"Bizzy?" Grant said. "I know she helped build the business; did a lot of the marketing. The office work."

"Spent most of the money they made, too," Mike said.

"What else you gonna do with money?" Josh said. "Can't take it with you, man. Ask E. J."

"I'm just saying I heard him complain."

"All I know, whenever I saw E. J. and Bizzy together they seemed to be having fun," Sheila said. "I never saw them bickering or arguing the way some couples do, maybe most couples; the way me and my ex did."

"Could've been just for show," Mike said.

"Just for show to whom? Us?"

"Point is—did you ever spend time with them outside of Potzmann-Schultz?"

Sheila looked up and away as if she was trying to remember an occasion.

"Any of you?" Mike added.

No one had an answer.

"I mean they were our VFW buddies," Mike said. "Outside of here and the events Potzmann-Schultz sponsored, you never saw them socially. I did. It wasn't always sunshine and lollipops."

"What marriage is?" Sheila asked.

I thought of people in my own life, men and women I've played hockey with for as long as twenty years. How many of them did I know outside of the ice arena or Boogies, the bar where we hung out after the game? Five or six? Seven?

While I considered it, movement caused me to glance toward the bar. Jeffrey Tribbett had climbed down from his stool and was now chatting with Marco. A moment later he headed toward the front door. He glanced my way as he went and gave me a head nod.

"Apparently, J. T. didn't care for them," I said.

"That was goofy," Grant said. "I get that J. T. was pissed at first because E. J. quitting kind of left him in the lurch even though he knew it was coming. E. J. really was his best man. Then it got smoothed over. I worked with both of them . . ."

"You worked for them?"

"Yeah."

"Me, too," said Mike.

"E. J. had a couple of solid crews," Grant said. "Full-time crews. Arborists who spent as much time planting and caring for trees as cutting them down. Guys doing most of the trimming and pruning in the winter; that's the best time to prune and trim. Only one of the things he sold was emergency services. A hard wind like the one we had in early December, remember that? Blew trees down all over the place, branches falling on guys' cars. E. J. wanted to be the one people called to clean up the mess right now and not next week. So he had part-time crews on standby. He'd call us. 'Hard wind a-blowin', don't go anywhere.' Then we'd get out there, do the cleanup. It was a good gig. Easy money, paid in cash, for a few days' effort and you didn't need a license or extensive training, although . . ."

"E. J. was all about safety first," Mike said. "He'd get in your face about it. 'No one gets hurt, everyone goes home,' he'd say, which was—yeah."

"Anyway, I worked with both E. J. and J. T. from time to time and I didn't see any animosity between them. It started up again about a half dozen years ago. I don't know why."

"Jealousy?" Grant said. "That's about when E. J. busted out; started doing very, very well. Like I said, he bought a new house, a new car. Him and Bizzy started traveling, Bizzy posting pics of the two of them dancing in Paris."

"J. T.," Josh said. "The man doesn't like change. He's been driving the same car, a Toyota Camry, for how long? I know he bought it new after he got his honorable. It has over three hundred thousand miles on it."

"He's proud of it, too," Mike added.

"Jeffrey's idea of a vacation is driving fifty miles to the Winstock Country Music Festival for two days every year," Josh added.

"Probably the furthest he's been from home since he got back from Iraq," Grant said.

"He was in Iraq?" I asked.

"Desert Storm," Sheila said. "You might have heard of it."

"I have."

"It's starting to be a while ago," she added. "People forget."

"We all served in Iraq," Josh said. "The first war. H. W.'s war. We weren't together back then. We served in different units; different parts of the country. Came together because of Potzmann-Schultz."

"We ate a lot of the same dirt, though," Grant said.

"Sand," Sheila corrected him.

"Sure tasted like dirt."

"E. J.—he was at Norfolk," Josh said.

"I hate to reveal my ignorance," I said.

"Tank battle in southern Iraq. Us and the U.K. against the Republican Guard. Second largest tank battle in history if that matters to anyone."

"E. J. was in tanks?"

"Infantry support."

Norfolk, my inner voice said. *E. J. Woods Tree Care Services was owned by Norfolk LLP.*

"McKenzie," Mike said. "I wasn't going to say anything but, it's true, E. J. was getting therapy. I don't know if it was for PTSD. It could have been for something else. We didn't talk about it because . . . Anyway, the reason I know is because we were both seeing the same therapist."

Silence followed Mike's remarks. It could have been caused by embarrassment or respect or simple courtesy from his comrades in arms. I broke the silence.

"Could you give me his name?" I asked. "I promise not to reveal where I got it when I call."

"That's okay," Mike said.

He reached for a paper napkin and patted his pockets. I lent him my pen. I always carry a pen. Mike wrote down the contact information as well as his full name—Mike Boland—and slid the pen and napkin back to me.

"My therapist is a woman, by the way," he said.

"Of course she is," Sheila said.

"Use my name," Mike added. "Like the man said, we don't have secrets here. We have stories."

Grant pointed at the woman.

"Shields," he said.

They call her Shields?

"Tell McKenzie where you got your Purple Heart," he added.

Sheila glared at him.

"Go 'head," Grant said.

"I got it in the ass," she said.

"Wait," I said. "What?"

"Just west of Wadi al-Batin. We were rolling through a breach in the Iraqi defenses; they mounted a counterattack to close it."

"That's where our girl also earned her Bronze Star," Grant said.

"No kidding?" I said. "What did you do?"

"I was proficient in the use of the M240 machine gun," she said. "Let it go at that."

"Shields earned the star *after* Haji had already put a bullet in her behind," Grant added.

"Boys, boys, boys, no more."

I made a production of leaning over and gazing at her seat.

"Looks fine to me," I said.

Sheila grabbed the empty pitcher and raised it above her head while pointing at me.

"Marco," she called. "We need more beer at the table but you better cut off this guy. His judgment is seriously impaired."

It was all chitchat after that. We finished another pitcher of beer and I decided it was time I moved on. I thanked the group for their time and courtesy and left each person with a card containing my name and cell number in case anyone could think of something I should know. There were handshakes all around. At the same time, Sheila announced that she had to go to the ladies'. She walked in front of me. I decided I was right before. Her seat looked just fine.

She went left toward the restrooms and I went to the bar. I waved Marco over; it was getting toward late afternoon and the place was starting to fill. I handed Marco a credit card and told him I wanted to pick up the entire tab at the table. He thought that was nice of me. I told him I wanted to pick up the next tab, too. "So double the total." That caused him to smile brightly.

A few moments later, after adding a sizeable tip, I signed the receipt and headed for the door. Sheila intercepted me. Apparently, she had been waiting for my departure.

"I wanted to tell you something before you go," she said. "Only I didn't want to say anything in front of the boys."

"Tell me what?"

"The thing is, they all like Bizzy, especially Mike. They would all like to comfort her in her time of grief, if you get my meaning."

"I do."

"I like her, too. I like a woman who knows how to get what she wants. It's just that"—Sheila sighed deeply—"I wouldn't trust her as far as I could throw this building and you know what? That's not very far."

"Why not?"

"She has a roving eye. She hides it well. Hides it better than most. I have a roving eye, too, just ask my ex, and like they say—it takes one to know one. Only hers—McKenzie, what do you know about Bizzy? I mean really know about her?"

"I know she has a record, if that's what you're asking."

Sheila sighed again, this time in relief as if there were words she was happy she didn't have to speak aloud.

"I don't hold that against her, either," she said. "Given everything I've done, I'm the last person who should be judging someone else. It's just that ever since I met her I've had this feeling that something was off."

There's that phrase again.

"I don't know what else to call it," Sheila added. "A feeling. I have no reason for it, either; nothing I can point to. It's just that, this feeling, when I heard that Earl had drowned at that marina in Stillwater, my first thought was—did Bizzy drown him?"

Is that what Nevaeh wants to know but won't come out and actually say?

"It's something to consider, isn't it?" I said.

Sheila took hold of my wrist.

"Take care of yourself, McKenzie."

"Thank you for your service."

SEVEN

Rush hour usually starts at about three thirty in the Twin Cities and lasts until around six unless snow is involved in which case I hope you have plenty of gas. It took me more than twice as long to get home from Lake Elmo as it had to get there and throughout the drive I kept asking myself the same question.

"Now what?"

I had the name of E. J. Woods's therapist—Tara Brink— that Mike Boland had written on the napkin. I didn't have high hopes concerning her, though. I figured my questions about E. J. would probably go unanswered for the simple reason that therapists are like doctors and lawyers in that they're legally and ethically obligated to keep the secrets of their clients. Instead of calling her, I decided to wait until morning and confront her in her office, telling myself that it takes so much more effort to point at a door and shout "Get out!" than it does to hang up a phone.

My best bet to learn what really happened at the marina was Officer Eden Stoll's dash cam footage, although I wouldn't have put much money on that, either. The fourth car could easily have belonged to someone who had parked in the lot and simply walked across the street to get a cup of joe at the coffeehouse or a massage at the joint next to it.

"Now what?"

I would have liked to have a long conversation with Elizabeth "Bizzy" Woods starting with the request—"Tell me again
why you and E. J. were at the marina in Stillwater." I didn't
think that was going to happen anytime soon, though. Even if
Bizzy agreed to an interview, her attorney would not. "A vigilante" he had called me.

That left Nevaeh. The man at E. J. Woods Tree Care Services said if I had questions regarding the business—and who
E. J.'s partner might've been, if he had a partner—I should ask
her and he was right. Especially since I now knew that she had
worked for her father when he was first starting out. I intended
to ask those questions as soon as she called after receiving the
autopsy report from the Ramsey County medical examiner.

In the meantime . . .

I drove to our condominium in downtown Minneapolis,
parked in the underground lot, took the elevators to the seventh
floor, unlocked the door, went to the kitchen area, opened the
refrigerator, found a bottle of Summit EPA, levered off the cap,
and took a long swig.

Activity, I told myself. Ideas come to you when you're active
as opposed to just sitting around.

In that spirit, I moved to my desk in the library area, fired
up the PC, and added notes to the file I had labeled "E. J." I
had already written down everything I could remember, including impressions and feelings, from the conversations I had
at the Heggstad Marina in Stillwater that morning as well as
the results of my internet search. Now I added notes from my
conversations first at E. J. Woods Tree Care Services and then
at Potzmann-Schultz VFW. Afterward, I reread what I had
written.

"Now what?"

The answer came in the form of a phone call.

"McKenzie," Brad Heggstad said when I answered. "You

asked me to give you a call if Richard Bennett returned to the marina, Richard Bennett the guy who owns *Maverick*."

"Yes."

"Well, he's back. I just saw him topping off his tanks at the pump."

"How long is he going to stay?"

"You mean if he doesn't overnight? I couldn't say but I'd guess he'd be here at least a half hour. It would take him that long to get squared away."

Thirty-seven minutes later by my watch I pulled into the crowded lot adjacent to Heggstad Marina, expecting I was already too late. After parking my car, I encountered a locked gate and a sign declaring that from eight P.M. to eight A.M. all visitors must enter through the marina's main building. That added a few more minutes to the total.

Eventually, I began walking the length of the marina to the dock on the far side where I knew the *Maverick* was berthed. It almost felt as though I was tuning an old radio. As I passed the many luxury boats parked in their three-sided slips I heard hip-hop, rock, country and western, classical, jazz, even some reggae. None of it was particularly loud until I reached the far dock and then it became very loud indeed, pop music coming from the direction of Nelson LeMay's yacht; Taylor Swift singing about yet another ex-boyfriend who had let her down.

Daylight savings time had kept the sun in the sky so it wasn't difficult to find *Maverick*. I was relieved to see a lamp shining through the door leading to the cabin cruiser's salon. I called Richard Bennett's name. He didn't answer though and I wondered about proper etiquette. Do I knock on the hull? Do I shout "Ahoy"? I tried his name again. This time the door leading to the salon opened and a man peered out at me.

"Mr. Bennett?" I repeated.

"What do you want?"

"My name's McKenzie. May I speak with you?"

He grimaced and twisted his head. I thought he was annoyed at me until I heard him say, "Can he possibly play that crap any louder?"

"I take it you're not a Taylor Swift fan."

"I don't know the woman. I mostly listen to jazz and blues."

I saw a chance to ingratiate myself and took it.

"Buddy Guy," I said. "He just dropped an album not long ago with Elvis Costello and others. *The Blues Don't Lie*. Terrific."

"I agree."

"I actually met the man at Legends, his club in Chicago. He signed a CD for me. You remember CDs?"

"I do. I might even have a few lying around."

Bennett glanced down at my shoes. I was wearing docksiders. That seemed to impress him because he nodded his head and said, "Come aboard."

I climbed onto the boat. The salon was directly behind him, yet Bennett didn't lead me there, preferring instead to chat in the stern of the boat like a guy talking to a stranger on his porch. There were a couple of bench seats there. He sat on one, so I sat on the other. In the light of the setting sun he looked to be in his mid-sixties with thinning gray hair. I don't know why that surprised me, yet it did.

Taylor was singing, "The girl in the dress, cried the whole way home."

Bennett asked, "What do you want?"

"Earl John Woods."

"How long is this going to go on, anyway?"

"What do you mean?"

"The man died over two months ago and people are still asking questions?"

"What people?"

"That woman for one," Bennett said. "An insurance investigator. Couple of weeks ago she came by. Mary Something."

"Maryanne Altavilla?"

"You know her?"

"I do."

"Smart woman. Very serious. I liked her. She didn't waste my time."

"I hope I'm not wasting your time," I said.

Bennett answered by waving his hand, which didn't tell me anything.

"Mr. Woods," I said.

"I wasn't here when he died."

"That's what I've been told."

"I wish I'd been here," Bennett said. "I didn't know the man, but maybe I could have helped him. I wasn't here because—listen, I splashed on Tuesday when the weather was nice. I was hoping to cruise down to Red Wing for the weekend. I like Red Wing. Some nice restaurants in Red Wing. Music. Only the weather changed. Went from upper forties to low twenties in about eight hours. I battened down the hatches, as they say, and abandoned ship."

"When was that?" I asked.

"I don't know the exact time. Mid-afternoon on Friday. Woods died on Saturday."

Bennett's words were so succinct that I wondered if he had practiced them.

"That's when he was found, yes," I said. "On Saturday morning. Mr. Bennett, may I ask where you live?"

"In Stillwater. I have a small apartment about two miles from here."

"Do you walk to the marina?"

"Sometimes. Not back then, though. I had items I needed to stow on my boat that I brought in the trunk of my car."

"You didn't leave your car in the parking lot when you left, did you? Walk home?"

"No. Why would I do that?"

"Just wondering."

By then Taylor Swift had been replaced on the *Miss Behavin'*'s speakers by Shania Twain singing how unimpressed she was. Bennett looked up at the darkening sky.

"Damn, that monkey mouth drives me nuts," he said.

"Monkey mouth?" I asked aloud even as my inner voice shouted at me—*That's prison slang!*

"All LeMay does is make noise," Bennett said.

"LeMay was here when Mr. Woods drowned, too. At least his boat was. I think he told me that he splashed on Wednesday."

"The place hasn't been quiet since," Bennett said.

"Did you see him?"

"Yeah, I saw him. And heard him. I tried my best to ignore him. You know, he has this big fucking boat, likes to call it a yacht, yet I've never seen him leave the marina. I'm not kidding. Six years or more I've been moored here and not once have I seen the *Miss Behavin'* on the river."

"Did you see anyone else hanging around the marina after you splashed?"

"No one, only, McKenzie, you need to know, I wasn't looking. Some people like LeMay, they own boats so they can have a place to party, either here at the marina or out on the water. LeMay, that's all he does is party. Me? I have a boat so I can get out on the river; so I can be alone."

"I appreciate that, sir."

"The world seems so damn big and loud sometimes."

I took that as a cue to get out of his world. I thanked Bennett for his time, gave him one of my cards, and apologized for disturbing him.

"Not a bother at all," he said. "You know, I've been to Legends in Chicago, myself. Saw Buddy sitting in with the Cash Box Kings. He serves a nice catfish po'boy, too."

"I've always been fond of his gumbo."

Bennett pointed at me then like we were now best friends forever.

The moment I disembarked from the *Maverick,* Bennett ducked inside the salon, sliding the shut door behind him. I was glad. I was sure he'd disapprove if he saw me moving toward Nelson LeMay's party instead of leaving the marina and for some reason that mattered to me.

By then it was full night, yet I could easily see that there were a lot of people standing on the deck of the *Miss Behavin'* and several more lingering on the dock where the yacht was tied up. A few were wearing swimsuits, although the temperature barely touched seventy degrees. Some of them were swaying to the music if not actually dancing. Most were holding drinks in their hands.

As I approached, I found LeMay standing on the narrow wooden walkway where it intersected with the main dock. He had one arm carelessly draped around the shoulders of a woman while he gestured with his other arm as if there was something across the St. Croix River that he wanted her to see, an empty glass in his hand. The woman didn't seem to mind. In fact, she was smiling. Until she saw me. Then her body stiffened and her face took on the same terrified expression as the actresses in all those classic 1950s horror movies starring Vincent Price and Christopher Lee.

Barbara Deese rolled her shoulders to dislodge LeMay's arm. He seemed disappointed.

"Good evening, McKenzie," she said. Her voice was formal

and rose above the voices of all the people on the boat and dock; her soft blue eyes were as hard as agates.

"Hey, Barb," I said.

LeMay seemed jolted by our greetings and spun toward me. It took him a moment to recognize me.

"There he is," LeMay said. His smile never left his face. "The investigator. So, have you figured it out yet?"

"Me? I haven't got a clue." I waved at his boat and guests. "So, Thursday night at Heggstad Marina?"

"Haven't you heard? Thursday is the new Friday. All those Gen Z and Millennials working shorter workweeks."

"I don't think we fall into either category."

From his expression, LeMay seemed insulted by my remark.

"Speak for yourself," he told me. "Now, Barbie, here . . ."

Barbie? my inner voice repeated.

"She could out Z the Zers anytime," LeMay added.

Barbara closed her eyes and grimaced as if he had just revealed a deeply personal secret.

"I've always thought so, too," I said.

"Do you have more questions or are you looking for a free beer?" LeMay asked.

"Both."

"Comin' right up."

LeMay moved away from us and climbed aboard his boat. Voices rose up to greet him as if he had been too long away from his own party. A woman called "Nelsonnnnn" in a high-pitched voice. Adele sang, "My God this reminds me, of when we were young."

I glanced over at Barbara. She was wearing sandals, shorts, and a Hamline University sweatshirt, her alma mater. Her blond hair had been pulled back.

"What are you doing, Barbie?" I said.

"Don't call me that."

"Barb . . ."

"A couple of hours after you left this morning, Nels came over to the *Deese and Dose*. He said he was throwing a small party tonight and he invited Dave and me. 'It's one big happy marina,' he said."

"Where is Dave?"

"He's working late. He said he wanted to finish off a few things tonight so he wouldn't have to go into the office tomorrow."

"And you?"

Barbara shrugged her shoulders.

"I was bored," she said.

How many catastrophes have been caused by that condition, do you think?

Barbara might have been reading my mind.

"Dave knows where I am," she said. "He said he'd meet me here. McKenzie, I haven't done anything to be ashamed of."

By then LeMay had reappeared.

"McKenzie," he said and tossed me a can of Aurora Haze brewed by Castle Danger. I caught it with both hands.

He was also carrying a drink mixed in a sixteen-ounce plastic cup that he handed to Barbara.

"I thought you might want another Moscow Mule," he said.

Barbara thanked LeMay and took a sip. She looked at me over the rim of the cup.

"Yet," she said.

"Huh?" LeMay said.

"I was just telling McKenzie that my husband hasn't come home from work yet."

"Oh, him. I say a man who neglects a wife as beautiful as you doesn't deserve her. What do you think, McKenzie?"

"Object permanence."

"What are you talking about?"

"It's the understanding that things exist even though they can no longer be seen or heard."

Barbara smiled brightly. LeMay just shook his head.

"Give that IPA back," he said. "You've already had too many."

The three of us stood there drinking for a few beats while the party continued around us. Even though his practiced smile never left his face, I had the distinct impression that LeMay wanted me to depart and quickly. The tone of his voice said as much.

"What are you doing here?" he asked.

"I just had a conversation with Richard Bennett about that Saturday in March."

"Oh yeah? What did Dick have to say?"

"He says you play your music too loud."

"Fuck 'im."

"You might get on his good side if you played some blues once in a while."

"The blues is too depressing."

Okay.

"Nels, what kind of car do you drive?" I asked.

"An SUV, I told you."

"Yes, but what kind?"

"A BMW X5. Why do you ask?"

I made a mistake, then. I knew it the moment the words spilled out of my mouth.

"There was a car in the parking lot when Mr. Woods drowned and we're trying to identify the owner."

LeMay nodded his head.

"Interesting," he said.

Dammit, McKenzie. You know better than to give out information like that. Maybe you should put that beer down.

"What do the cops say?" LeMay asked.

Cops, not insurance companies.

"Who knows?" I told him. "Listen, I want to thank you for your time and patience. And the beer."

"Leaving so soon?"

"Thursdays are still Thursdays for me."

"It's time I should be leaving, too," Barbara said.

LeMay was clearly disappointed to hear her say that and knew whom to blame. He was looking directly at me when he said, "I understand, Barbie. Maybe you'll be able to stay longer next time."

I handed LeMay my empty beer can and Barbara gave him her still-full Moscow Mule.

"Thanks for inviting me, Nelson," she said. "Hope to see you again soon."

LeMay's smile broadened as if she had just made a promise he couldn't wait to redeem.

Together Barbara and I walked down the dock toward where the *Maverick* was docked. We didn't speak until we were actually passing the *Maverick*. That's when a voice called to us out of the darkness.

"Had enough?" it asked.

We paused and turned toward the boat. Rick Bennett rose from a bench seat in his stern and moved toward us. We could see him plainly when he leaned against the gunwale.

"As a matter of fact . . ." I said.

"Hi," Barbara said. She moved toward Bennett with her hand extended. "I'm Barbara Deese. My husband, Dave, and I have a boat on the other side of the marina. The *Deese and Dose*."

Bennett shook her hand.

"Rick Bennett," he said.

Barbara stepped back.

"Nelson is pretty loud, isn't he?" she said.

"Too loud."

I was wondering why she was behaving the way she was and then I realized she was making a statement.

"Well, McKenzie and I are on our way to meet my husband. It was a pleasure meeting you."

"The pleasure was mine," Bennett said.

We continued to stroll toward the far side of the marina where the *Deese and Dose* was waiting in its U-shaped slip. There were small lights lining the dock so we could see where we were going, but anything above our shoulders was veiled in shadow.

"Barb," I said.

"I know who I am, McKenzie. I know who I belong to. I wasn't going to do anything stupid."

"LeMay certainly seemed like he wanted you to."

"He wouldn't have been the first."

"The man is a predator. You know that, right?"

"Yes, I know that. He's just better at it than most. Nels has a way of making you feel . . ."

Barbara sighed deeply and stopped walking. I was two strides past her before I noticed. I turned to look at her looking at me. From Nelson LeMay's yacht we could hear Alicia Keys singing that she was on fire.

"McKenzie, have you ever done something dumb that you knew was dumb even while you were doing it yet kept doing it anyway?" Barbara asked.

"Frequently."

"I haven't. Only tonight—tonight I came awfully close. So, thank you."

"For what?"

"For being here. For making it easy for me to walk away."

"You're welcome."

"For a few moments . . ."

Barbara never finished her thought. Instead, she shook her head and linked her arm to mine, and we continued walking toward the *Deese and Dose*. We didn't speak until we reached the intersection that connected the maze of docks with the concrete steps leading to the marina's main building.

"About Dave," Barbara said.

"What about Dave?"

"What are you going to tell him?"

"Concerning what?"

"McKenzie, don't be vague. Please."

"I'm not going to tell him anything, Barb. Why would I?"

No harm, no foul. You don't call a penalty on a player if you don't see the player actually committing a penalty.

"He's your friend," Barbara said.

Exactly.

"So are you," I said aloud.

Barbara's grip on my arm tightened. It loosened a few beats later, though, when we heard footsteps on the concrete steps. We looked up to see Brad Heggstad approaching. He shook his head when he saw us.

"Nelson LeMay is at it again," he told us. "It's not even the weekend yet."

I tilted my head and listened to the music drifting across the marina. It was barely above a whisper where we were standing.

"Is that Aretha?" I asked. "Not even Richard Bennett can complain about Aretha Franklin, can he?"

"He can if it's after ten P.M. And now I have to be the bad guy breaking up the party, ruining everyone's fun."

"Maybe that's LeMay's plan. He throws a party, lets it

get out of hand, and then leaves it to you to break it up so he doesn't have to do it. He can play the good guy and still go to bed early."

"Possibly with a woman who volunteers to help him clean up," Barbara said.

Heggstad and I both turned to look at her.

"That could be part of the plan, too," she said.

"I have to go," Heggstad said.

He continued walking toward the *Miss Behavin'* at a brisk pace. Barbara glanced at her smartwatch.

"Ten twenty P.M. and Dave isn't home yet," she said. "You know, McKenzie, it's enough to make a girl do some misbehaving herself."

"Give him hell, sweetie. Give him hell."

I nearly hung around to see what kind of hell Barbara would give her husband, yet decided not to.

That's someone else's marriage, my inner voice told me.

I left Stillwater with the idea of driving to Rickie's. I changed my mind, though, at the intersection where Highway 36 met I-35E. Instead of going south toward St. Paul, I went west toward Minneapolis. The words "monkey mouth" that had been blinking softly in the back of my head were now shining brightly, so I drove back to the condominium, popped open yet another Summit Ale—*that's an even half dozen for the day if you're keeping track*—and turned on my computer.

I accessed Minnesota's court records once again and followed the prompts. Where directed, I typed the name "Bennett, Richard," hit execute, and damn, but there were a lot of Richard Bennetts committing crimes and misdemeanors in Minnesota. I didn't have a middle name, birth date, case number, or even a county to narrow the search, so I had to review them all one at a time—eighty-five cases according to the results. I stopped at sixty-four, though. That's when I found "Case Title: State of Minnesota v. Richard Peter Bennett. Case Type: Crim/Traf Mandatory. Charges: Attempted Murder—2nd Degree—With Intent—Non-Premeditated."

Using the state's websites and the archives of the *Minneapolis Star Tribune,* I was able to piece together Bennett's story.

What happened, Bennett owned and operated a medical supply company. He was pretty successful, too, according to what I read. When his daughter started applying to colleges and universities, he decided to make some changes to his investment portfolio in order to help pay for her tuition. That's when Bennett discovered that his financial advisor had been embezzling from him. His financial advisor also happened to be his brother-in-law, which is why he didn't immediately contact the police. Instead, Bennett confronted his brother-in-law in his brother-in-law's offices. Unfortunately, he brought a gun with him. Fortunately, he didn't kill his brother-in-law, only wounded him.

Do you think that's part of the reason why Bennett dislikes Nelson LeMay so much, because the financial planner reminds him of his brother-in-law?

Bennett was arrested and charged with Attempted Murder Two. The Hennepin County attorney had him cold, so he took a deal, plead guilty, and was sentenced to twelve years, instead of a possible twenty, at Oak Park Heights, Minnesota's only Level Five maximum security prison.

As a side note, the brother-in-law was released from the Hennepin County Medical Center just in time to be arrested himself. He was charged with seventeen counts of embezzlement, fraud, and forgery; it turned out that Bennett hadn't been the only client he had cheated over the years. Unlike Bennett, he decided to roll the dice, claiming in court that he didn't actually intend to steal from his clients, plus he was acting under duress. The jury either didn't believe him or didn't care. He was convicted on fourteen of the seventeen counts, and was sentenced to fifteen years to be served at the minimum-security prison located in Faribault.

The brother-in-law was still doing time when Bennett was finally released for good behavior after serving eight years. By then, his business had been sold and his wife had divorced him, eventually moving to North Carolina. I couldn't discover how much money he had left following the divorce, yet apparently it was enough to afford both a thirty-six-foot Carver worth approximately $150,000 and live the life he was enjoying now.

I was careful about the times and places as I compiled my notes.

E. J. Woods was convicted of his crimes in 2010 in Washington County, yet did not serve a day in prison. He went to work for Jeffrey Tribbett soon after, eventually starting his own business in 2012.

Richard Bennett was convicted of his crime in 2008 in Hennepin County. He did eight years and was released in 2016.

E. J. was Black and a veteran.

Bennett was white and did not serve.

As hard as I tried, I was unable to discover even a trace of a suggestion that the two men somehow met, much less had a relationship.

Which proved—what?

Nothing at all, my inner voice said. *Although . . .*

Although what?

Maybe when E. J. went to the marina that Saturday morning, he made too much noise and Bennett tossed him in the river.

It sounded even less likely when I repeated it out loud to Nina when she came home after closing Rickie's.

I had another beer.

That night I dreamt of shooting a man who was trying to surrender while standing on a dock in the middle of the ocean. I didn't even try to figure out what that meant.

EIGHT

Red Wing is a river town known mostly for its arts, historical sites, scenic views, and overall charm. Founded in the 1850s, it's located on the Minnesota side of the Mississippi River approximately twenty river miles south of Prescott on the Wisconsin side; Prescott is where the St. Croix and the Mississippi merge. Red Wing is also about an hour's drive from St. Paul, which made me go, "Huh?"

According to the internet—how did we ever get along without it?—Tara Brink, LPCC, was located in downtown Red Wing. Her offices—Brenda Smieja/Tara Brink Counseling Services—were housed in an eighty-five-year-old building not far from the St. James Hotel. I checked the website. It claimed:

> Our mission at Smieja/Brink is to promote the health and well-being of individuals, families, and couples by offering comprehensive counseling and therapy services. We work with a wide variety of issues including: anxiety, stress management, depression, trauma, couples counseling, perinatal and postpartum support, and more. We offer individual therapy, couples counseling, and family therapy—all while emphasizing the importance of compassion, trust, autonomy, and respect. We are in network with all major insurers.

Yet nothing on the website suggested that Brink and her colleague offered therapy off-site in, oh, I don't know, the Twin Cities, for example. That's where the "huh" came from. I had a hard time believing that E. J. Woods and Mike Boland would drive an hour to receive therapy and another hour back home, making it what? A three-hour round trip counting the time they spent on the couch? I understood that they might not want people, even their own families, to know that they were receiving help. Yet a three-hour absence would have been harder to explain than a much quicker trip to a location in the Twin Cities.

I arrived in mid-morning and found a parking space on the street not far from the Uffda Gift Shop. I ignored the building's elevator and used the stairs to reach the third floor. The lobby of Brenda Smieja/Tara Brink Counseling Services was comfortably furnished and had large windows providing a view of Bush Street. A young woman sat behind a wooden reception desk with a low counter in the corner of the lobby; a computer with three screens suggested that she did much more than greet visitors and book appointments.

She smiled at me.

"Good morning," she said. "May I help you?"

"I would like to see Tara Brink, if that's possible."

"Tara is counseling a client at the moment and can't be disturbed." She glanced at one of the computer screens. "Do you have an appointment?"

"I don't," I said. "I was hoping I could steal a few minutes of her time to ask about one of her patients."

The woman tilted her head and stared at me as if she had never heard such a request before.

"Please have a seat, Mr. . . . ."

"McKenzie."

"Please have a seat, Mr. McKenzie. I'll tell Tara that you're here when she's finished with her session."

"Thank you."

I took a seat and glanced at the artwork hanging in identical frames on the lobby walls. It was all clearly designed to be calming to the eye. There was a painting in the shape of an egg; three quarters of the egg was sky and the bottom quarter was water. Another was a painting of a high-backed wooden chair with a pot of flowers on the seat. Another simply had the words EVERY THING WILL BE OKAY stacked on top of each other. I decided I preferred the window where I could watch people going about their lives in the morning sun. I wondered what that said about me.

A half hour passed before a door to the left of the young woman opened and a man with thinning hair stepped out. He was accompanied by a slender thirtyish woman wearing a white lab coat over a tasteful blue work dress and blond hair that was pulled back. The two of them were laughing. After the man passed through the office door and down the hallway, the woman stopped laughing, though. Her face took on a severe expression as if she was attempting to digest important information.

"Tara," the young woman said.

Brink waved at her as she moved past.

"Just a sec," she said. "I need to write something down."

Brink hurried through the door behind the young woman. She returned ten minutes later.

"What do you need?" she asked.

The young woman pointed at me.

"Mr. McKenzie," she said.

Brink moved toward me, her hand extended, as I rose from the chair. We shook hands.

"Yes, Mr. McKenzie, what can I do for you?" she asked.

"If you have a moment, I'd like to ask a few questions."

Brink glanced behind her.

"You're good until eleven fifteen," the young woman said.

Brink smiled at me as if she meant it.

"What questions, Mr. McKenzie?" she asked.

I noticed that she didn't invite me into her office.

"I'm here to ask about Mr. Earl John Woods," I said. "I believe he was a patient of yours."

"We call them clients."

"Were you aware that Mr. Woods died"—the smile disappeared—"a couple of months ago?"

"Yes, I was aware that Mr. Woods passed," Brink said. "I found it tragic. What is your relationship to Mr. Woods?"

"It's complicated."

"Make it simple, then. Whom do you represent?"

"Ms. Nevaeh Woods."

From the way her blue eyes widened, I was sure that the name was clearly familiar to her.

"I wasn't aware that she knew that her father was receiving therapy," Brink said. "Earl was adamant about keeping it a secret, something that I actively counseled against."

I could have dropped Mike Boland's name, only I didn't want to toss him on the barbie unless I had to. Instead, I shrugged my reply, hoping that Brink would accept the gesture as evidence that I knew more than I was saying.

"You asked who I represented," I said. "Has someone else contacted you about E. J.?"

"No. Why would they?"

"I don't know if you appreciate that there is much controversy surrounding E. J.'s death." I deliberately used his initials again to give the impression that I was his friend. "Insurance companies are involved; lawsuits have been filed in court. Some claim E. J. committed suicide. There's even an allegation of murder."

That last word caused Brink's eyes to open even wider.

"Nevaeh is simply searching for answers," I added. "She's hoping that you might be able to supply them since you were her father's therapist."

"I honestly wish I could supply them. Perhaps give his family closure. Unfortunately, I cannot."

"You can't?"

"We take client confidentiality very seriously here, Mr. McKenzie. Mr. Woods, of course, was free to speak about his therapy with whomever he pleased. I am not."

"In this case—"

"In all cases. Confidentiality isn't a choice, Mr. McKenzie. It's a legal construct which prevents us, prevents therapists and counselors, from disclosing the events of therapy to anyone without the client's express permission. It gives the client the assurance they can share whatever they want with us. We couldn't possibly do our jobs without it."

"There are limits."

"No," Brink said.

"You are obligated to breach confidentiality in the name of public safety or your client's health."

"That doesn't apply here."

"You're allowed to speak up if your client was contemplating suicide."

"He wasn't."

So, there's that, my inner voice said. *On the other hand . . .*

"Are you saying that because you believe it's true or because you don't want to admit that you failed to recognize the signs?" I asked.

Brink's eyes narrowed. She knew I was challenging her integrity yet refused to challenge mine.

"There is a comprehensive inventory of behaviors that indicate suicide ideation," she said. "Should I list them for you? In any case, Mr. Woods did not display any of those behaviors."

"His wife, Bizzy, and daughter, Nevaeh, don't believe E. J. committed suicide, either . . ."

Mentioning both names caused Brink's eyebrows to curl. She seemed to communicate a lot with her eyes.

"They might have trouble proving it in court, though," I added.

"I've already revealed much more than I should."

"Ms. Brink—"

"If a court issued a subpoena, I suppose I could be compelled to turn over all my notes concerning Mr. Woods; I could be forced to testify. Honestly, it's never come up before. I'd have to ask my attorney. Until then, my clients have a right to privacy and I have a duty to respect that right even after the client dies."

"When a person is killed, that person loses his right to privacy."

Brink paused.

"Was Mr. Woods killed?" she asked. "Was he murdered?"

"We don't know."

"Then we have nothing more to discuss. Look, clients share their most intimate problems with their therapists, and they do so with the understanding that their comments will not leave the room. Without that legal guarantee I believe most clients wouldn't be attending therapy at all. Confidentiality serves to protect clients from the outside world."

"You keep saying that and I get it, believe me," I said.

"Then why are we having this conversation?"

"E. J.'s family wants to know what you were treating him for."

"We don't treat clients," Brink said. "We treat mental health problems—anxiety disorders, such as obsessive-compulsive disorder, phobias, panic disorder or post-traumatic stress disorder, mood disorders, such as depression or bipolar disorder. We help clients deal with these problems."

"Was E. J. using prescription medications?"

"I'm a therapist, not a psychiatrist. I am not allowed to prescribe drugs."

And there's that, too.

"That's not what I asked," I said.

"Mr. McKenzie, go away."

This time I smiled. I had nothing against Tara Brink despite her refusal to be more forthcoming. Truth is, I admired her professionalism. I thanked her for her time and moved to the door. Before I reached it, though, I spun back and gave her my best Peter Falk playing *Columbo.*

"One more thing." I actually said that. "Why would Earl Woods drive all the way to Red Wing and back to get therapy that he could easily have received in the Twin Cities?"

"My partner and I used to work out of the Cities," Brink said. "We decided to come down here three years ago when we realized that rural Minnesota was grossly underserved."

And presented less competition for your services?

"Mr. Woods, as well as a few of our other clients, decided to follow us," Brink added.

"Ms. Brink, who paid your fee?" I asked. "Earl Woods or E. J. Woods Tree Care Services?"

"Good day, Mr. McKenzie."

I left the offices of Brenda Smieja/Tara Brink Counseling Services, descended the two flights of stairs, and went out the front door of the building, hanging a left on Bush Street. All the while my inner voice spoke to me.

Tara Brink, a licensed professional clinical counselor, did not believe that her client, one Earl John Woods, committed suicide, it insisted. *You'd think that would be a particularly useful tidbit of information, something that might sway a jury in a lawsuit filed against a bunch of heartless and greedy in-surance companies that were bullying a poor widow and her fatherless daughter.*

Except Bizzy—and especially her attorney—hadn't asked Brink for her opinion, I told myself. Which meant they were either afraid of what her answer might be or . . .

Could Bizzy have been holding out on her own attorney, afraid that the information would hurt her claims that E. J. died by accident? If whatshisname Garrett Toomey knew E. J. had been receiving counseling, he would have contacted Brink, wouldn't he? Plus, he would have been legally and ethically obliged to disclose that information with the attorneys repre-senting the insurance companies; with G. K. Bonalay and Brad Heggstad. I mean, that's the way it works, right?

Unless Bizzy honestly didn't know that E. J. was receiving treatment. From my conversations with her, it was apparent that Nevaeh didn't know.

Which raises another question: What are you going to do, McKenzie?

Nothing.

Nothing?

Unless a court forces me to raise my hand and tell the truth, the whole truth, and nothing but the truth, I have no legal obli-gation to tell anybody anything.

Cutting it a little thin there, aren't you, pal?

We'll see, I told myself. In the meantime . . .

Yeah?

I'm hungry.

One of my favorite places, the 150-year-old St. James Hotel—or the Historic St. James Luxury Hotel, depending on who you talk to—had aged well. It featured sixty-seven Victorian rooms all in different sizes, shapes, and décor, some that might even be haunted (shhh, don't tell anyone), meeting rooms, wedding facilities, a miniature shopping mall, several bars—Nina and I especially liked the one in the basement—and a couple of four-point-five-star restaurants. What interested me most, though, was the patio just off the Scarlet Kitchen and Bar where I ordered an early lunch consisting of a muffuletta sandwich and an iced tea. Yes, I said tea.

From the patio you could see much of what was worth seeing in Red Wing—the He Mni Can-Barn Bluff, Red Wing Overlook, the Marine Museum, the train station, Bay Point Park, and the mighty Mississippi as it looped down toward Lake Pepin. Across the river was Wisconsin, of course, and the unincorporated community of Pucketville and Mud Lake and—marinas. I could see two marinas on the Wisconsin side of the river. At the same time, I wondered if there were marinas on the Minnesota side and then asked myself what difference does it make? I bet there must be a thousand marinas on the Mississippi River.

Well, since we're here . . .

It turned out that there were eight marinas serving greater Red Wing, three on the Wisconsin side of the river and five on the Minnesota side. Freedom Island, Trenton Island, Harbor, Red Wing Marina, Red Wing Yacht Club, and the two Ole Miss marinas were not helpful. The final marina was named Sunset even though it faced northeast and was located about a mile walking distance from Red Wing's downtown bars and restaurants, something the marina owners promoted extensively.

I found two guys standing behind a high counter. One of them greeted me with a familiar, "Hey, there. What can I do for you?"

"Afternoon," I said. "I'm looking for a friend who said he

would be coming down to Red Wing. Richard Bennett; his boat is called *Maverick*?"

The first man looked up and away.

"*Maverick*," he repeated. "Lot of boats named *Maverick*."

"But you're talking about Rick, yeah, yeah, yeah," the second said. "You missed him, though. Missed him by a day." The second man was looking at the first man when he added, "Rick Bennett. He left yesterday around noon."

The first man waved a finger at the second.

"That's right," he said. "Where did Rick say he was going?"

"Stillwater, I bet," I said.

The first man turned and waved his finger at me.

"I messed up," I said. "Got my dates wrong."

"It happens," the first man said. "Rick, he's one of our best transients. Docks for one night, maybe two, and then he's on his way. But he keeps to no schedule. Never know when he's going to be here till he calls in a reservation usually the day of. 'Hey, you guys have a slip for me?' Yeah, we always have a slip for Rick."

"Do you know if E. J. Woods was with him on this trip?"

The two men glanced at each other.

"Black guy," I added. I raised my hand a couple inches above my head. "Tall."

"Not that I can say," the first man said. "But you know, I'm not sure I've ever seen Bennett hanging with anyone."

"Mostly he keeps to himself," said the second.

"There was that one time we saw him—not here at the marina but at the Barrel House. Last summer, wasn't it?"

"That's right. That band that you like was playing . . ."

"We walked in and saw Bennett sitting in a booth with this other guy and we went up to say hi."

"He wasn't a Black guy, though. He was a white guy. What was his name?"

"I don't know. Coleman? Bowman?"

"Boland?"

"Yeah, yeah, yeah. Mike Boland."

I tried to keep my voice calm and well-modulated.

"Well, thanks, fellas," I said. "Sorry to waste your time."

"It's cool," the second man said.

"Next time you see Rick, tell him McKenzie said, 'Hi.'"

The first man waved his finger at me.

Okay, okay, let's not get crazy, my inner voice cautioned me.

"Who, me?" I asked aloud.

By then I was driving north on Highway 61 toward the Cities and telling myself that life is full of coincidences. That's why Merriam-Webster's had a citation for it. Think it through, I told myself. You knew that Richard Bennett liked boating to Red Wing; he told you so. That's why you dropped his name at the marinas. You know that Mike Boland came down to Red Wing to get therapy. He all but told you so when he gave you Tara Brink's name.

But that they know each other? That they both knew E. J. Woods, one in life and the other in death? What are the odds?

There's a game, I reminded myself. Six Degrees of Kevin Bacon. I once won a slice of pizza by connecting the actor to Greta Garbo in five moves. Hell, I connected him to myself in three moves. Bacon worked with Tom Cruise in *A Few Good Men.* Cruise worked with Paul Newman in *The Color of Money.* I got Paul Newman's autograph when I was a kid and he was racing Trans Am sports cars at the Brainerd International Raceway in northern Minnesota.

The question is—were Richard Bennett and E. J. Woods connected? If they knew each other, that might explain why Woods was at the marina that cold Saturday morning.

Or not. Bennett said he didn't know E. J.

That's what he said all right.

I found the Potzmann-Schultz VFW post even more inviting the second time I visited there than the first and far more
crowded. It was late afternoon on a Friday after all, and those
of us who weren't Gen Z or Millennials were just starting to
shake off the workweek.

Marco was behind the stick mixing drinks and setting them
on a tray carried by a woman who didn't look old enough to
drink. Hell, I wasn't sure she was old enough to drive. After a
few minutes, I caught Marco's eye and he slid in front of me.

"McKenzie," he said. "Don't tell me that you're becoming a
regular."

"I don't know. The service seems kinda wobbly."

"Ho, ho, ho, wobbly he says. Whaddya have?"

"Maker's Mark on the rocks, but only because I decided I've
been drinking too much beer lately."

He served the bourbon in less than a minute.

I told him I was impressed by his professionalism.

Marco said I was just trying to make up for the "wobbly service" crack.

"Has Mike Boland been in?" I asked.

"Not yet but I expect to see him and a few of the others. It's
Barbecue Rib Fridays starting in"—Marco glanced at the clock
on the wall behind him—"about a half hour and Mike likes his
baby backs. Gotta say they are pretty good. But the coleslaw—we
make the best coleslaw in Minnesota."

"That's a pretty grandiose claim, pal," I said. "I just might
have to call you on that one."

"We don't start serving until four thirty, but half the people here already put their orders in, so . . . If you wait until five or later, it might take you an hour or more to get served."

"Then put me in," I said.

Marco didn't leave, though. Instead, he stood behind the bar and smiled as Sheila walked up behind me and hugged my shoulders.

"Marco," she said.

"Polo," he said.

"There you are," I said.

"Thanks for picking up the tab last night," Sheila said. "That was awfully generous of you."

"What can I say? I'm an eccentric millionaire. Are you here for the ribs, too?"

Sheila claimed the stool next to mine.

"Yep," she said. "Although, I don't usually eat this early. It makes me feel like an old woman lining up for the over-fifty-five menu at Perkins."

I pointed at her.

"Marco, put her order in with mine," I said.

"Are you trying to buy my affections, McKenzie?" she asked.

"If they're for sale, sure, why not?"

Sheila thought that was funny.

Marco moved away. A few minutes later he returned and set a tap beer in front of Sheila, although I hadn't heard her order one. She thanked him and he left to take care of his other customers.

Sheila and I chitchatted for a few minutes, mostly about the weather, because that's how Minnesotans break the ice, but also about the Twins; Sheila was a fan. Finally, I said, "Tell me about Mike Boland."

"What about him?"

"Were he and E. J. Woods pretty tight?"

"Yeah, I think so. I know they hung out together outside of

Poztmann-Schultz. Of course, Mike had worked for E. J. on and off over the years cutting down trees. He also worked in E. J.'s office, although I'm not sure what he did there. When E. J. died—E. J.'s death seemed to hit Mike harder than the rest of us. It was like he felt guilty that E. J. was gone yet he was still here. Believe me, I get that. I didn't know they were seeing the same therapist until yesterday, though. I didn't even know E. J. was seeing a therapist. That surprised me a little bit. Mike, I get. He's—well, he's had his issues over the years. I have a friend who has a friend who claims that Mike has symptoms of an anxiety disorder. He has difficulty making eye contact with people he doesn't know, speaks with a very soft voice so it can get hard to hear him, sometimes sweating when it's not hot, or trembling . . ."

That's how he behaved when you met him yesterday, my inner voice reminded me.

"My friend's friend says it's because he's self-conscious; because he's afraid people will judge him negatively," Sheila added. "Yeah, like everybody doesn't feel that way at one time or another. Anyway, probably that's why he's seeing a therapist. But what do I know?"

"What does he do?" I asked. "Does he have a job?"

"Mike? I guess you would call him a freelance accountant only I don't think he works a lot of hours, at least not anymore. I know he's busy during tax season. He did my taxes. I know he was busy during COVID, too—helping people that were quitting their jobs and starting their own businesses. Mostly, I think he treats it as kind of a side hustle, though. Something to do when he gets tired of hanging out in bars. He receives his army pension like the rest of us so it's not as if he needs the money."

"Have you ever heard of Richard Bennett?"

Sheila gave it a moment and shook her head.

"He owns a boat called *Maverick*," I added.

"I don't think so," she said.

"Did Mike or E. J. ever mention his name?"

"Not that I recall. Why?"

"Just someone I came across who might not have anything to do with anything."

"So, you're not going to tell me. Fine, keep your secrets."

It was nearly five before we were served our ribs; Sheila and I ate at the bar. The ribs were better than most; extremely tender with a nice rub and BBQ dipping sauce on the side. Marco was right about the coleslaw, though. If it wasn't the best I've ever had, it was easily in the top three.

We were just finishing up our meal when I felt a hand on my shoulder and Grant's head dipped between mine and Sheila's.

"Mmm, that looks good," he said.

"Is good," Sheila said.

"I don't suppose you could spare a bone until my order comes up. I promise to pay you back."

"Hit the head, soldier."

I guessed that meant no, because Grant turned to me.

"McKenzie?" he asked.

I might have given in to his request, except I only had one bone left.

"*I am not in the giving vein to-day*," I told him.

"Giving vein?"

"Shakespeare. Richard III to Buckingham."

Sheila smiled brightly.

"Buying me drinks, buying me dinner, and now he quotes Shakespeare," she said. "Grant, I do believe this man wants to seduce me."

Grant massaged her shoulders.

"We all do, Shields," he said. "We all do."

A few moments later, Mike Boland appeared.

"You guys didn't wait for me?" he asked.

"Not only that," Grant said, "they're quoting Shakespeare."

"To be, or not to be, that is the question," Mike said.

We all turned to look at him.

"Once more unto the breach, dear friends, once more, or close the wall up with our English dead."

We looked some more.

"But, soft! what light through yonder window breaks? It is the east, and Juliet is the sun. That's it. That's all the Shakespeare I know."

"Well, I'm impressed," Sheila said.

"Me, too," said Grant.

"Mike, do you have a minute?" I asked.

"Yeah, sure," Mike said, and the two of us stepped away from the bar. I wiped my fingers with a cloth napkin while we hovered in an empty space near the door.

"Have you spoken to Tara?" Mike asked.

I nodded my head.

"I was surprised to learn that she had offices in Red Wing," I said. "Seems like a long way to go to get therapy."

"Not for me. I'm actually from Red Wing; it's where I lived before I joined the army. I still have people down there, my mother. Going back once a week isn't a problem."

"What about E. J.?"

"It was tougher for him because he had a business to run," Mike said. "Only staying with Tara after she moved there—we both liked Tara and neither of us wanted to start over with someone new; someone we might not like or trust as much as her."

"How long have you and E. J. been seeing her?"

His expression suggested that Boland thought that was an

intensely personal question and I had no business asking it. He answered it anyway.

"I've been with her on and off for eight, nine years," Boland said. "E. J.—he asked if I was seeing someone and if she was helping and if I could introduce him. That was five years ago."

"Did he tell you why he wanted to see someone?"

Boland gave me the same look; this time he didn't answer.

"I drove down to Red Wing this morning and spoke to Tara," I said. "She refused to tell me much. Apparently, she likes to keep all her interactions with clients strictly confidential."

Mike nodded his head as if he was glad to hear it.

"Did you mention my name?" he asked.

"No."

He nodded again.

"For what it's worth, Tara does not believe that E. J. committed suicide; she kind of let that one slip."

"I don't believe it, either," Mike said.

"While I was having lunch, I met a couple of guys who run Sunset Marina. I asked them if they knew Richard Bennett."

Mike reached up with his right hand and started rubbing his suprasternal notch, the part where his neck met his clavicle. According to the body language courses I took when I was with the cops, he was subconsciously telling me that he was suddenly feeling stressed.

"Bennett, they said, sometimes stays at their marina when he's boating up and down the river," I added. "They also said that they met you . . ."

"I don't remember that," Boland said.

"They said you were with Bennett at a joint called the Barrel House last summer."

"Yes, I do remember now. Rick was a friend of one of my Red

Wing friends; that's how we met. I haven't seen or spoken to him for at least a year, though. Why do you ask?"

"Bennett stores his boat at the Heggstad Marina in Stillwater."

"I didn't know that. I only know Rick from Red Wing."

"His boat *Maverick* was one of the few boats in the water the day E. J. drowned."

Mike paused for a long time before he asked, "Do you think he had anything to do with that?"

"Honestly? I haven't found a shred of evidence to suggest that he was even there at the time. He says he wasn't. We know he wasn't at the marina when E. J.'s body was discovered; the cops checked. I just thought that it was an odd coincidence."

"Coincidence?"

"That you two know each other."

"I don't—I don't . . ." Mike paused as he gathered his thoughts. "I don't know what that has to do with anything."

"Probably nothing. Still, I'll talk with him again."

"I'd be curious to hear what he has to say."

Boland kept rubbing his neck.

I glanced at my watch. It was pushing six P.M. and the VFW was now wall to wall with customers. Sheila and Grant were still at the bar; Grant had commandeered my stool. I was convinced that Nina was probably wondering where I'd been all day, so I paid the bill and thanked everyone for their time. Sheila seemed disappointed that I was leaving.

"I thought you might ply me with alcohol and take advantage of me," she said.

I didn't know if she was joking or not.

"You know I'm married, right?" I held up my hand so she could see my wedding ring to prove it.

"That never bothered my ex," she said.

Only the way she was smiling, yeah, I told myself, she was joking.

"Take care," I said.

This time when I reached the intersection of Highway 36 and I-35E, I headed south toward downtown St. Paul and Cathedral Hill, which hovered above it. I was halfway there when my onboard computer told me I had a phone call.

"Where have you been all day?" Nina wanted to know.

"Doing what you asked me to do, trying to learn what happened to E. J. Woods."

"Do you have anything?"

"His therapist does not believe that E. J. committed suicide, for what that's worth."

"It has to be worth something."

"We'll see."

"Will you be here for dinner?"

"I'm on my way to Rickie's right now, only not for dinner. I've already eaten."

"You did?"

"It's a long story. I'll tell you about it when I get there. Oh, by the way, if you're looking for a really good coleslaw recipe, I know a guy."

NINE

It was late Saturday morning and my cell was lying face down on the island in our kitchen area. Nina was on one side eating the last slice of chocolate chip banana bread that I'd made from a recipe I found online. I was on the other side eating a bowl of cereal because someone had taken the last slice of chocolate chip banana bread before I could get to it. From the phone's speaker I could hear Louis Armstrong playing the opening bars to the jazz classic "West End Blues." I turned it over.

"It's Dave Deese," I said. I put the cell on speaker before I answered. "D. D., what's going on?"

"Hey, are you and Nina busy?"

Nina shook her head vigorously.

I got the message.

"Nina is," I said.

"Too bad. I thought you guys might want to come down to Stillwater. I have a story to tell you."

"About what?"

"Your murder investigation."

I was staring at Nina when I replied.

"You can't tell me over the phone?"

"It'll be more fun in person," Deese said.

"Do you have any decent beer?" I asked.

"You'll drink what I give you and like it."

"I'll see you in an hour or so."

I hung up the phone yet continued to look at Nina.

"You don't want to go to Stillwater with me?" I asked.

"I don't want to go to the marina. At least not yet."

"Understood."

"I really appreciate that you're doing this," she told me. "I know it's silly."

"It isn't silly. I wish I could give you more than what I have so far."

"What do you have so far?"

"The same as the Ramsey County medical examiner—undetermined."

An hour later I was on Highway 36 heading east when my on-board cell phone rang.

"McKenzie," Stillwater Police Officer Eden Stoll said. "I'm sorry I didn't get back to you sooner. You asked about our dash cam videos?"

"I did."

"According to the tech guys it's sixty to ninety days. The SPD usually retains nonevidentiary video from dash and body cams for sixty to ninety days. Unfortunately . . ."

"No," I said.

"It's been over sixty days since the incident. Seventy-eight to be exact."

"Dammit."

"Sorry about that," Stoll said.

"It's not your fault."

"If I had thought about it sooner . . ."

"Not your fault," I repeated.

"Also, I figure you should know in case it goes any further—the tech guys also work with the Washington County Sheriff's

Office and the detective sergeant in charge of the Investigations Division somehow heard that I had asked about the cam footage. He wanted to know why. I told him."

Of course she did, my inner voice said. *Why wouldn't she?*

"He was not happy," Stoll added. "This was yesterday. He actually had me report to his office at the LEC after my shift so he could tell me that I had no business putting my nose where it doesn't belong; that the last thing he needed was some female beat cop checking his homework. He said it was a Washington County case and not Stillwater PD, and besides, the case was closed. He said if I didn't mind my own business he'd have a word with my captain."

"I'm sorry, Officer."

"Don't be. He's not the first jerk to get in my face for doing my job. The way I look at it, I am doing my job whether he likes it or not. The only reason I'm telling you this is in case you run into him or more likely he runs into you."

"What's his name?"

"Sergeant Stephen Holmes."

"Holmes?"

"They call him No Shit Sherlock in case you're wondering what kind of guy we're dealing with."

"Thank you for the heads-up," I said.

"Something else, McKenzie. I checked you out."

I would have, too.

"When I discovered that you were with the SPPD I reached out to a friend of mine."

"Who?"

"Detective Jean Shipman in the Major Crimes Unit."

No, no, no, no, no.

"How do you know Shipman?" I asked aloud.

"I met her when she gave a lecture at the academy a couple of years ago and we stayed in touch."

Oh, man.

"What did she say?" I asked.

"First, Jean called you a lot of names."

That sounds like the Jean Shipman you know and love.

"She said you were a subpar investigator."

Uh-huh.

"Jean also said I should listen to you; that I shouldn't blow you off as some kind of buff. She said whether or not I act on what you have to say is entirely up to me, but I should always listen. She said that if you had a reason to call her, she would listen, too."

Wow.

"Sometimes, Jean said, you get lucky," Stoll told me.

"Shipman and I have a complicated relationship," I said.

"I gathered that. I also think she likes you more than she's willing to admit. McKenzie, if you turn up anything about Mr. Woods's death I expect you to call me and not Washington County."

"I promise, Officer Stoll."

"My friends call me Edie."

I'm embarrassed to admit that the first thing I noticed when I climbed aboard the *Deese and Dose* was Barbara Deese dressed in a one-piece bathing suit and lying on a blue mat rolled out on top of the bow's hardtop near the front hatch, her hair fanning her head, her arms at her side, her leg bent provocatively. She was wearing sunglasses so I didn't know if she could see me seeing her. Dave could, though.

"Hey, pal, you want to stop perving on my wife?" he asked.

"I bet you say that to all the guys."

Barbara laughed at my remark.

"And girls," I added.

She thought that was funny, too.

I managed to pry my eyes off of her body and slumped on a bench seat in the stern of the boat where I couldn't see her. Dave handed me a cold can of Leinenkugel's before claiming the captain's chair, which he swiveled toward me. I opened the beer and took a long pull without complaint. It was very warm for June in Minnesota, about eighty-two degrees on the deck where Barbara was sunning herself.

"What do you want to tell me?" I asked.

"There was a fight last night."

"Where? Here?"

"On the other side of the marina, two guys going at it. I would have told you yesterday; I was going to call, except, well, I was distracted."

From the front of the boat I heard Barbara's voice.

"You might say something came up," she said.

It took me a few beats before I realized what she was telling me.

"Too much information, Barbara," I said.

She laughed again.

"What happened, we were invited to a party on a yacht," Dave said. "Guy named LeMay, first name Nelson—he insisted everyone call him Nels. You believe that?"

"I do," I said.

"That's right, you met him. By the way, Barbara told me what happened last Thursday. Thanks for rescuing her."

I wonder if she told him everything.

"She didn't actually require rescuing," I said.

At that moment I was glad that Barbara and I couldn't see each other. That way no guilty glances could be exchanged.

"I figured," Dave said. "On the other hand, I barely know LeMay and I wouldn't trust the man with any unaccompanied females, you know? Anyway, we went to his party; figured it'd be nice to meet our neighbors, people who hang at the marina, when this fight broke out."

"It was your friend Richard Bennett and another guy," Barbara said.

"He's not actually my friend," I said. "You know, you could come down here and talk to us."

"Do you promise to behave yourself?"

"No. No, Barbara, I do not."

"Okay, then."

A few moments later she appeared carrying her blue mat. Dave watched every step she took as if he had never seen her before. I sipped my Summer Shandy and pretended not to watch.

"I'm going inside to change," Barbara said. "Do you guys promise not to peek?"

"Nope," Dave said. "Can't promise that. McKenzie?"

"What's happened to you two?" I asked.

Barbara laughed some more and descended the narrow companionway into the salon, closing the door and the blind behind her.

"It's like I've been saying, McKenzie," Dave said. "You gotta get a boat."

"Tell me about this fight," I said.

"The reason I bring it up was because they used your name."

"My name?"

"Barb and I were standing on LeMay's yacht and I hear this guy yell, 'Rick. Where the hell are you, Rick?' My name's not Rick, only the guy sounded so close that I actually thought for a second that he was talking to me. I turn and I see the guy standing on the dock in front of a boat with MAVERICK painted on the bow, his hands on his hips. 'Dammit, Rick,' he yells. LeMay was standing next to us; he never seemed to stray too far from Barb."

Barbara's voice rose up from the salon.

"You're exaggerating," it said.

"You think I don't know when a guy is lusting after my wife?"

"McKenzie's been lusting after me for years and you've never noticed."

Deese turned to stare at me.

"Have you, McKenzie?" he asked.

"You two need counseling," I said.

"I heard that," Barbara said.

"You were meant to. The fight, tell me about the fight."

"Anyway, the guy, Rick Bennett, I found out his last name was Bennett—Barb told me."

"It was the man I met last week, remember?" Barb said.

"Anyway, Bennett appears on the stern deck and he says, 'What are you doing here? You know you're not supposed to be here.' And the other guy says way loud so we can all hear him—this is where he used your name—he says, 'You've been talking to McKenzie? What are you doing talking to McKenzie?'"

Mike Boland, my inner voice said.

"And Bennett yells back, 'How do you know McKenzie?'"

Huh.

"And the first guy says something to him, to Bennett, that I didn't hear but it caused Bennett to jump out of his boat onto the dock and shove the first guy hard. The first guy fell backward, only he didn't fall off the dock. Instead, he bounced off the bow of a boat parked in the slip across from Bennett's. There was some struggling after that, only it stopped when Bennett looked up and saw all the people on LeMay's yacht watching them. He grabbed the first guy by the arm and pulled him down the walkway and onto his boat, onto *Maverick.* They disappeared inside and LeMay says 'I bet they're gay' and a couple people laugh and everybody else just shakes their heads and goes back to partying. Then LeMay tells Barb and me, 'Rick and your friend McKenzie are buddies.' And I'm like, 'What?'"

"This happened Friday night?" I asked.

"Yeah, about nine o'clock."

I wonder if Boland got his baby back ribs?

Barbara left the salon. She was wearing jeans, a sleeveless top, and flip-flops, only I kept thinking swimsuit.

"The sun had just about set," she added.

"That's it?" I asked.

Barbara sat on Dave's lap.

"That's it," Dave said. "We went back to the party and about a half hour later we came here. I really meant to give you a call but like I said, I was distracted."

"I can't imagine why," I said.

"Hey," Barbara said.

I was talked into a second beer. Afterward, I left the *Deese and Dose* and moved to the far side of the marina. Even before I reached it, I realized that the U-shaped slip where the *Maverick* had been parked was empty. I kept walking though, finally halting in front of the open slot. With hands on my hips, I considered my options.

"McKenzie," a voice called to me.

I spun to find Nelson LeMay standing on the bow of his yacht, his arm draped over the shoulder of a young woman dressed in a lavender bikini that left little to the imagination. If I were a bartender I would have carded her. I walked toward the *Miss Behavin'*.

"If you're wondering, Dick and his boyfriend left early this morning," LeMay said.

"They were both on the boat?"

LeMay gestured with his right arm. He kept his left arm

around the woman's shoulder as if he was afraid if he removed it she would disappear.

"Ah, well, to be honest, I'm just guessing," he said. "I don't know if the boyfriend was with Dick or not. *Maverick* was gone before I got up. Isn't that right, honey?"

The young woman shrugged.

"Have you ever seen the two of them together before?" I asked.

"I haven't seen Dick with anyone before," LeMay said. "Seriously. Man nor woman. Oh, and thanks for siccing Barbie girl's husband on me."

"I didn't, actually. But do you blame him for wanting to keep a sharp eye on you?"

"Doesn't matter. There are plenty of fish in the river, am I right?"

LeMay turned his head and nuzzled the young woman's temple. She grimaced at the gesture. I don't think she liked being referred to as a fish.

"Gonna be another party tonight," LeMay said. "You should come. Bring Deese and his honey. I promise to be on my best behavior."

I think we've already seen him at his best.

A few minutes later I was driving the St. Croix Trail south toward downtown Stillwater. Once again I was considering my options and once again I was distracted, this time by a white SUV with a red, white, and blue light bar, a push bumper, and the words SHERIFF WASHINGTON COUNTY painted on the doors.

My gaze moved from my rearview mirror down to my speedometer. I was actually driving the speed limit for a change, yet I tapped my brakes anyway. When I did the deputy moved his vehicle so close that its push bumper nearly banged my rear.

The SUV backed off quickly, though. The light bar was turned on and the siren activated.

C'mon, man, my inner voice said. *That's not necessary.*

I angled the Mustang onto the shoulder and slowed to a stop. I turned off the engine and rested my hands on top of the steering wheel where they could easily be seen. I thought about my wallet and the laminated card I kept next to my driver's license proclaiming that I was a proud member of the St. Paul Police Department, "retired," that I had occasionally used to get out of speeding tickets. Only I suspected this stop had nothing to do with my adherence to the existing traffic laws. Using the side-view mirror, I watched the deputy exit the SUV. There were golden sergeant stripes pinned to the collar of his shirt.

Kinda knew it was him, didn't you?

The sergeant approached my Mustang on the driver's side instead of hugging the body on the passenger side, swinging his arms like he was marching in Stillwater's Lumberjack Days parade. Normally, I would have called that sloppy, except I knew that he knew I wasn't a threat to him.

When he reached my open window I said, "Good afternoon, Sergeant Holmes. Is there a problem?"

He didn't seem nonplussed at all that I had guessed his name.

"Speeding," Holmes said. "Reckless driving. Failure to stop. Open bottle. I don't see a seat belt."

I pulled the strap off my chest and let it slide back into place. Holmes sniffed the air.

"Is that marijuana I smell?" he asked.

"Is smoking grass still illegal in Minnesota?"

"It would be if I was king."

"What are the chances that you'll let me off with a stern warning?"

Holmes rapped the roof of my car with his knuckles.

"Why don't you step into my office and we'll talk about it," he said.

Homes opened my car door and stood behind it until I slipped out. I walked to his SUV while he walked behind me, probably out of habit. I went to the passenger side and he went to the driver's side. Once we were both comfortable on the front seat of the SUV Holmes said, "After chatting with Eden Stoll, I checked you out."

"Yeah, I get that a lot."

"I thought I had heard your name before only I wasn't sure. Now I remember. You're the SPPD who recovered all that cash some embezzler siphoned; returned it to the insurance company for fifty cents on the dollar. How much was that, anyway? I heard ten million."

"Closer to three million and change."

"Long time ago. What? Ten years? Half the guys thought you had won the lottery at the time, lucky you. The other half thought you sold your shield."

"Yeah," I said just to let him know I was listening.

"Don't care about that, though. Why would I? What I care about—McKenzie, I don't like it when someone interferes in an ongoing investigation."

"I was under the impression that the investigation was closed."

"Is that what Stoll told you?"

I was impressed that Holmes didn't use any adjectives to describe her. On the other hand, he didn't use her title, either.

"That's what Officer Stoll told me," I said.

"It's not closed."

"Was it reopened before or after she told you about the fourth car?"

Holmes didn't answer my question. Instead, he asked one of his own—"Why are you involved in this?"

I answered, repeating pretty much the same words I had used when I explained myself to E. J. Woods's friends at the Potzmann-Schultz VFW post. I didn't tell him that Nevaeh Woods thought her father might have been murdered.

"So, not working for the lawyers or the insurance companies," Holmes said.

"Just the daughter."

Holmes watched the cars that automatically slowed down as they passed us.

"I didn't know about the fourth car," he said. "If I had, I would have looked into it way back in March."

"Now that you do know?"

"I did what Stoll did, I had our tech guys check the dash cam and body cam footage taken at the scene by our deputies, even the county's Water, Parks, and Trails Unit. Unfortunately . . ."

"It's all been erased," I said.

"Yes."

"Because the case was closed."

Holmes glared at me.

"Except now the case has been reopened again," I added. "That's why you were at the marina just now. That's why you stopped me."

"I hate loose ends. They vex me."

Vex? This is the guy they call No Shit Sherlock?

"Me, too," I said aloud.

"You think because you were on the job you get to still play cop?" Holmes said. "I could give you a lecture, McKenzie; tell you that it doesn't work that way. I'm not going to, though. Partly because I know you won't listen. Mostly because I want you to play cop. The daughter, Nevaeh Woods, she wants to know what happened to her old man. So do I. She thinks you can help. Then help. Only McKenzie . . ."

"Whatever I find out, you expect me to share."

"Is that asking too much?"

"Will you be sharing with me?"

"I believe in a quid quo pro relationship."

"Fair enough."

To prove that we were both on the same page, and to avoid telling Holmes that I had made the same promise to Officer Eden Stoll, I said, "There was a fight at the Heggstad Marina last night."

"Not a fight, just a dustup, I heard."

Who's his source? Brad Heggstad? Nelson LeMay? Do you think he'll tell you? Yeah, when the Minnesota Vikings finally win the Super Bowl.

"The two men," I said aloud. "You should know about them."

I revealed everything I knew about Richard Bennett and Mike Boland including the facts that Boland was a Desert Storm veteran receiving therapy in Red Wing and Bennett was an ex-con. Holmes transcribed much of what I said in a notebook.

When he finished, I said, "Your turn."

"My turn?"

"Did you check E. J.'s phone messages from that Saturday?" He didn't reply.

"Quid pro quo?" I asked.

"'Course I checked. Nothing on Saturday. Friday his last phone call was from his wife at three thirty-three P.M. His last text was also from his wife at five fifteen. He wrote, 'Heading 2 PS now.' She texted back, 'Tell everyone I said hi.' Nothing after that."

"What about Bizzy's phone?"

"Are you referring to Mrs. Woods?"

"Yes. Elizabeth. They call her Bizzy, I don't know why."

"Under the law, the dead no longer have a legal right to privacy. Being very much alive, Mrs. Woods does. Unless we have just cause, there's no way a judge allows us to see her phone records. It doesn't matter, anyway. Whoever she spoke to or texted after five-fifteen, it wasn't him."

"Thank you."

"Bennett and Boland, though—I don't like coincidences," Sergeant Holmes said.

"They vex me, too."

Holmes stared for a half dozen beats.

"Don't fuck with me, McKenzie," he said. "I'll fuck back."

"Fair enough," I repeated.

I returned to my car, not knowing exactly what to think about Sergeant Stephen "No Shit Sherlock" Holmes. I started up the Mustang and drove off. He followed for a half mile before turning off the St. Croix Trail. By then I was in downtown Stillwater.

Once again, I considered my options and decided I had only two at the moment—talk to Rick Bennett or talk to Mike Boland. I already knew that Bennett was on his boat and cruising the river to parts unknown. That left Boland.

I drove to Potzmann-Schultz, parked, and went inside.

"McKenzie," a voice called to me and suddenly I was in an episode of the TV series *Cheers* and everybody knew my name. Or at least Jeffrey Tribbett did. He was sitting at the bar. I sat next to him. Marco wasn't working the stick so I gave my order to a woman who told me to call her Scooter. J. T. nudged me when she stepped away.

"Scooter drove an M60A1 tank in Afghanistan," he said.

"And they call her Scooter?"

"What should they call her?"

"Ms. Scooter."

J. T. thought that was funny and repeated the joke to Scooter when she returned with my Summit Ale.

"I like it," she said before moving away to serve other customers.

I glanced around. None of the other vets I had met previously at Potzmann-Schultz were there.

What? Did you think Boland, Sheila, and the others lived here?

"By the way," J. T. said. "I'm sorry if I gave you the wrong impression about E. J. the other day. Truth is, I liked the man. We were all friends at one time. I was pissed when he left me to start his own business. I had trained him, you know. Taught him everything he knew. Kinda made me think that he owed me something. Only he didn't. Not really. Gotta admit, the man was the best worker I ever had. Ah, you should tell people things like that when they're alive, am I right?"

"Yes, sir."

"Bizzy, too. Mighta said a few things to her I wish I could take back. If I ever see her again, I will. Woman's a beauty; guys hittin' on her only she never hit back from what I saw. A good woman."

"Did that happen a lot, men hitting on Bizzy?"

"Not a lot but you know how some guys are."

I flashed on Nelson LeMay.

"Yes, I do," I said.

"E. J. wasn't someone to put up with that, though. I never seen him have anything but a smile for Bizzy, but those guys who thought they might have a chance with her, he soon taught them different."

"You're saying he was a jealous man?"

"I don't know if 'jealous' is the right word. Just sayin', E. J.—he didn't like it when you messed with what was his. His wife. Anything. Everything."

So, he was a nice guy, yet only to a point? What does that tell you?

"Undetermined," I said aloud.

"Huh?"

"Mr. Tribbett, let me buy you another beer."

TEN

Nevaeh Woods received her father's autopsy report in the mail early Monday morning and called me as promised. She swiveled patiently in a chair behind the desk in her office while I studied it. The door was open, only there was little traffic in the elementary school corridor. It took me a long time to read the entire report; it was twenty pages long and included the Washington County Sheriff's Office Investigator's Narrative signed by Sergeant Stephen Holmes. What I discovered was that the Office of Ramsey County Medical Examiner was damn thorough during the autopsy:

DECEDENT: Woods, Earl John
AGE: 62
SEX: Male
RACE: Black
CITY: White Bear Lake
STATE: MN

The ME examined the man's chest/abdominal cavity, cardiovascular system, musculoskeletal system, respiratory system, liver and biliary system, gastrointestinal system, urinary system, genital system, and on and on, listing systems that I had never even heard of. From what I was able to decipher with my questionable grasp of the language of forensic pathology, E. J. was pretty healthy when he died. On the first page of the autopsy report, the ME noted:

Evidence of therapeutic intervention: None
Evidence of external traumatic injury: None
Evidence of internal injuries: None

The ME even provided a detailed summary of the clothes the man was wearing when he was dragged out of the St. Croix River onto the pier—boots with a faux fur liner, jeans, thermal shirt, heavy down parka with fur-lined hood, leather gloves, and a knit hat—from which the ME concluded that Mr. Woods had not drowned while going for a swim.

In the medical examiner's opinion:

The decedent died as a result of drowning with hypothermia as an associated significant condition. A complete autopsy examination showed no evidence of trauma and toxicology studies did not show acute drug or alcohol intoxication. Police investigation did not show evidence of foul play or obvious signs of an accidental mishap. A full review of the circumstances of the case and appropriate consultation do not support intent to harm oneself. The manner of death is therefore classified as accident-homicide-suicide-undetermined.

None of this surprised me; Maryanne Altavilla had told me what I would find in the autopsy report nearly two months ago. Except two details caught my eye and held it.

The first:

Date and time of death: Found March 25, 2023 (1130 hours)

This was the legal time of death, the time when the body was discovered by Nina and myself; the time that was listed on the death certificate. However, while noting the nearly negligible decomposition of the body, bloating, skin slippage, and other factors associated with drowning in an icy cold river, the ME suggested

> The victim drowned from 1–16 hours before his body was discovered.

This was the estimated time of death.

One to sixteen hours, my inner voice said. *The timing would certainly fit Elizabeth Woods's story. She said she had arrived at the marina a half hour before she started looking for her husband and that was a half hour before Nina and you arrived. 'Course, the estimate could easily be made to fit a lot of other scenarios, too. Sixteen hours meant E. J. could have been in the water as early as seven thirty P.M. the night before Nina first found him.*

Nevaeh must have caught something in my manner.

"What?" she asked.

"Just thinking."

"Tell me."

"Do you know where your father was the night before he died? It would have been a Friday night."

"He was at the VFW."

"Potzmann-Schultz?"

"Yes."

"Are you sure?"

"When we did Dad's celebration of life there, a couple of people told me how shocked they were when they heard that he had died; how they had been eating barbecue ribs with him just the evening before. They said he had seemed so happy and full of life."

Funny how no one ever says things like that about you when you're alive.

"Okay," I said.

"Okay? What does that mean?"

"It means I now know that your father was eating baby back ribs the night before he died."

"McKenzie . . ."

"I also know that the medical examiner found no evidence whatsoever to suggest that your father was killed and I have found no evidence to prove that the ME was mistaken."

Nevaeh leaned back in her chair and turned her head so she could look out of the window. A couple hundred kids aged kindergarten through fifth grade were running around an asphalt playground adjacent to the Kingfield Middle School located more or less in the center of Minneapolis. She smiled slightly as she watched them, only there was a touch of sadness to it.

"School lets out on Thursday," she said. "So many of these kids will have nowhere else to go then; no free meals; parents working. I've long thought year-round school would be a good idea. In England, the school year runs from early September to late July with plenty of breaks. We should do that. Our school year was established two hundred years ago to appease the damn farmers. Is that still a thing we need to do? How 'bout we think of the kids for a change?"

"How long have you been teaching?" I asked.

"I've been at Kingfield for six years now; assistant principal for a year and a half."

"You started right after your father fired you then."

"That's when I started teaching here. I used to teach—wait. Who told you that?"

"A woman named Marilyn."

"Marilyn? Marilyn Staples? At E. J. Woods Tree Care Services, sure. I love her. When did you see Marilyn?"

"Last week."

"She told you that Dad fired me?"

"Is it true?"

"Yes, it's true. He came over to my apartment one day with a check. Severance pay. You believe it? He said I was done making sacrifices for him. He said he knew my first love was teaching and it was time I went back to teaching instead of dedicating my life to his needs. He said I was fired.

"McKenzie, I was so angry. Those two—Bizzy was standing beside him at the time. Those two didn't know anything about running a company. Well, that's not entirely true. They were very good at taking care of customers; good at taking care of business. Simple bookkeeping, though, managing cash flow, paying taxes, paying employees, renting equipment, my God, paying their electric bills, buying health insurance—it messed with them. They were still living solely off of Dad's army pension because even though they had plenty of work, they couldn't seem to make the business pay. That's when I stepped in—me and my bachelor's degree in education.

"I put my career on hold because I wanted to help them. I did, too. I got their finances under control and found people who could run an office and they started making serious money and five years later they fired me. Just like that. I told them they'd be bankrupt by the end of the year and not to come crawling back to me for help. Only they did quite well without me. Better even. Which was irritating. Then they bought me a new car. A hybrid. Bastards."

Nevaeh started laughing after that. I couldn't help but join her.

"Yeah, they sound pretty ruthless," I said.

"You could argue that Dad was doing what he thought was

best for me. Probably he was right. Only I missed it. I missed working with him every day. Our relationship—ah, you don't need to hear that."

"Yes, I do."

"Dad was in the army when he married Mom, when I was born. We followed him around from base to base until I was old enough to go to school and then Mom insisted that we, that she and I, stay in one place. So, she moved us back to St. Paul where she was from; where Dad was from.

"Growing up, McKenzie—it was like they were preparing me for the worst. We often talked about what Dad did for a living; how he served his country. We talked about the danger. We talked about the possibility that one day he might not come home. Only we never talked about the possibility that Mom, that she . . ."

Nevaeh leaned forward, propped her elbow on her desk, and rested her head in her hand.

"Cancer," she said. "Such an emotional word. Filled with fear and anger and grief and resignation. Dad came home for the funeral. The army gave him five days. Then he was gone again. I was eleven at the time. The following year was Dad's twentieth in the service. He could have retired with a nice pension. Instead, he reenlisted. He was afraid of raising a child alone. Even at the tender age of twelve I understood that. He didn't abandon me, though. Not completely. I saw him. He'd come home on leave. When he was stationed in Germany, I went to visit him. He'd call. Send money. Send emails. Send presents. After serving another ten years, he finally retired. Could be the army pushed him out, I don't know. He was forty-eight. I was twenty-two. We barely knew each other.

"It wasn't like I didn't feel loved, McKenzie. My grandmother took care of me. I had aunts and uncles and cousins, mostly from my mother's side. And I knew that my father loved me. It's just that we were strangers to each other. We'd spend time together but that's all we did, spend time. He was adjusting, trying to adjust to life in the real world and not doing a very good job of it. He drank, did drugs, got involved with people my grandmother said were gangsters, some of them actually his childhood friends. Keith Martin. God, how my grandmother hated Keith Martin. I tried to help Dad. Gave him advice about what he should be doing with his life. Imagine. Me. The daughter providing guidance to the father, like he was one of my students. Finally, he was busted for burglarizing a store with Martin, which he swore he didn't do, and for concealing stolen property, which clearly he did.

"Then a miracle happened. Looking back it seems like a miracle. Dad hooked up with Bizzy, who at the time was just as fucked up as he was. I was so angry, both at him and his white bougie slut who was seventeen years younger than he was; who was only nine years older than me. Yet somehow the two of them seemed to solve each other, gave each other a reason—I wanted to hate her so much. I tried so very hard. The two of them together, though, the way they fashioned this unlikely partnership and started maneuvering through the world around them; they just rose up.

"Bizzy treated me—not once did she try to be my mom. Instead, she treated me like a kid sister. It didn't take long to figure out why. Turns out her family was even more fucked up than she was. She went to the street when she was sixteen because the street was safer than her family. At the same time, Bizzy desperately wanted a real family. Wanted a sister. Someone she could talk to; someone she could trust. Suddenly, we were a real family. Like I said, McKenzie, it was a miracle.

"That's why I was so upset when Dad fired me. I missed—I missed the family. It's not like I didn't see him and Bizzy. I saw them all the time. Bizzy would take me shopping. No one loves to shop more than Bizzy. Only it wasn't the same."

A bell rang. The kids came inside all at once; the corridor was filled with their playground noise. Nevaeh didn't shut her office door, though. She seemed to enjoy the noise; took pleasure in watching the kids as they stomped past her office.

"Let's talk about money," I said.

"The root of all evil."

"Not all evil; just most of it."

"You want to know about the insurance policies," Nevaeh said. "I was surprised when I heard how much they were worth."

She shook her head abruptly.

"No, I wasn't. McKenzie, when my mother died, my father knew he wasn't going to be there for me yet he wanted me to know that I was going to be okay living with my grandmother, my mom's mother. The words he kept repeating—'You'll be all right; you'll be taken care of.' To prove it he sat me down before he went back to base and showed me an insurance policy, a life insurance policy with my name listed as beneficiary. He told me the policy was worth $500,000. He told me that if anything ever happened to him that I would get this money plus the money from a service-members group life insurance policy offered through the Department of Veterans Affairs worth another $400,000. Plus, there was other money, he said. I would be a millionaire if something happened to him, he said. Imagine telling that to your child. 'If I die you'll be rich.' I know now that this was his way of showing that he loved me, yet at the time I wanted to slap his face. I might have, too, if my grandmother hadn't been holding my hand. 'Just come home, Daddy,' I said. 'Please come home.' I begged him."

Nevaeh rose from her chair and went to the window, looking out at the now empty playground. The noise in the corridor outside her office door had slowly faded to silence like someone turning down the volume on a radio.

"Anyway, there was an accident at a worksite," Nevaeh said. "A near accident. What I was told, a log slipped out of the grapple attached to an excavator that they were using, bounced off the side of a bucket truck, and missed my dad's head by this much."

Nevaeh held her thumb and index finger an inch apart.

"Dad said he could feel the air brushing his face as the log passed it. That was the nearest anyone had ever come to being seriously hurt on the job since Dad started the company; he was very keen on safety."

"That's what I was told," I said.

"Bizzy was in his face, telling him that he shouldn't be out there at job sites anyway. Let his employees do the heavy lifting, she told him. Like that was going to happen. Half of Dad's workforce were veterans and half of those came from Potzmann-Schultz. No way he was going to let them do the work while he watched. No way he was going to appear less capable than them. This was only a couple of years ago, too. I think he had just turned sixty and was feeling it. Old man can't step up anymore? C'mon, now. What he did do, though, was start buying up life insurance policies."

"E. J. did this," I said. "Not Bizzy."

"That's what I was told."

"Who sold your dad the policies?"

"I have no idea. I doubt it was one guy, though. From what I was told when the lawyers became involved, insurance companies frown on what Dad was doing."

"It's because your dad bought so many policies in such a short period of time before he passed that the insurance companies believe they have a reason to deny coverage."

"My father did not commit suicide, McKenzie."

"His therapist agrees."

Nevaeh spun away from the window to face me. Her eyes flared and her mouth opened as if she was about to shout at me.

"I'm sorry," I said. "I did warn you, though, that if we continued to do this you might learn things that you didn't want to know."

"Tell me."

"Your dad was receiving therapy from a woman named Tara Brink. She has an office, Brenda Smieja and Tara Brink Counseling Services, in Red Wing. E. J. had been seeing her for at least five years. I haven't been able to pin down exactly why he was seeing her. Ms. Brink refused to breach client confidentiality. At least with me."

Nevaeh moved to her chair, sat down, and swung the chair to face me.

"I didn't know this," she said. "That he was receiving therapy."

"Did Bizzy know?"

Nevaeh shook her head slowly. "If she did she never said." She shook her head some more. "McKenzie, Red Wing is like a hundred miles from here, isn't it?"

"Closer to fifty," I said. "Southeastern corner of the state."

"Why would Dad go all that way to see this Tara?"

"Apparently, he became a client when she had offices here in the Cities. When she moved her business to Red Wing three years ago he followed because he liked her, because he trusted her and he didn't want to start over with someone new."

"Is she hot?"

"Excuse me?" I asked.

"Tara Brink. Have you seen her?"

"We've met, yes."

"Well then?"

"I guess she's attractive. I hadn't thought of her that way."

"Dad liked what was hot. He was a connoisseur of what was hot. Trust me. He especially had a weakness for white women with blond hair. Gentlemen prefer blondes, tell me it ain't so. You'll notice that Bizzy has blond hair. What about this Tara?"

"She has blond hair, too . . ."

For some reason I flashed on Barbara Deese.

She's also a blue-eyed blonde.

I shook the thought from my head.

"You can't believe your father was having a sexual relationship with his therapist," I said.

"I'm saying she wouldn't have been the first," Nevaeh told me. "I don't know if Bizzy ever cheated on Dad. I want to say no. Just a feeling I have. Dad, though, oh yes, he cheated on Bizzy. I don't think he could help himself. Some men can't. You need to remember, he literally grew up in the army surrounded for thirty long years by high-testosterone guys just like him who were trained to take it to the limit. Once he hit on a close friend of mine. A fellow teacher. And yes, she was a blonde. This friend? She spent a weekend with him and later told me she'd be happy to do it again."

"Does Bizzy know?" I asked.

"Bizzy knows everything. She knows the who, the what, the when, and probably the where. You know what else she knows? The why. Should I tell you what Bizzy used to do for a living?"

I flashed on the thirty-two citations I found beneath her name on the Minnesota court records website including the felony for Soliciting/Inducing/Promoting Prostitution, Sex Trafficking.

"Yes, I know what she did for a living," I said.

"Bizzy understands human nature. If nothing else, she knows why men do what they do."

"I was told by several people that she and your father got along famously; that no one ever saw them bickering. I was told by people who knew them well that E. J. and Bizzy always seemed to be having fun."

"That's true."

"If he was cheating on her . . ."

"I have a hard time wrapping my head around it, too; why she didn't freak," Nevaeh said. "I think that's because we're taught to demand all or nothing from our partners. Only Dad and Bizzy, they were both damaged people when they hooked up. Yet, somehow they managed to seize the best of what each had to give and ignore the rest. Somehow it worked. When they were together, they were together. In the things that mattered most—McKenzie, in the things that mattered most they were intensely loyal to each other."

"Comrades in arms."

Nevaeh wagged a finger at me.

"That's one way of looking at it," she said.

"I've seen some of Bizzy's social media posts. She doesn't seem—excuse me, but in her social media posts, at least the most recent ones, she doesn't appear particularly grief-stricken. The one where she's dressed in a blue evening gown at the Commodore in St. Paul . . ."

"How long should a person grieve after someone dies, McKenzie? A wife, a lover, a friend, a daughter—how long should they wear black? If you see them going about their lives as best they can, maybe even looking happy and prosperous, does that mean they're not grieving? You don't always smile because you're happy or laugh because you're having fun. Sometimes you smile and laugh because it's the only way you can deal with the pain."

"I appreciate that," I said. "I really do. The only reason I bring it up, I was wondering who took the photos of her that Bizzy posted."

Nevaeh stared at me as if I had just asked her to explain quantum physics.

"I don't know," she said.

"Who was your father's business partner?" I asked.

"You mean besides Bizzy?"

"Yes."

"He didn't have a partner."

"Yes, he did. In his obituary, it said 'founder and partner of E. J. Woods Tree Care Services.'"

"That was just a figure of speech," Nevaeh said.

"I checked with the Office of the Minnesota Secretary of State website. It says that E. J. Woods Tree Care Services is owned by Norfolk LLP."

"You must have misread it. Norfolk is an LLC—limited liability company. McKenzie, I'm the one who set it up."

"I don't know what to tell you," I said.

"Are you serious?"

"Norfolk is definitely listed as a limited liability partnership."

"Why would Dad take on a partner? When would Dad have taken on a partner?"

"I'm guessing it must have been sometime after you left the company."

Nevaeh picked up her cell phone and started tapping the screen.

"What are you doing?" I asked.

"I want to know about this."

I jumped from my chair, reached across her desk, and pushed the cell against the leather desk mat.

"Who are you calling?" I asked.

"I'm calling Bizzy."

"No. I told you, we don't want to involve her or her lawyer in this. Not yet."

"I want to know who inherits my father's business. If it isn't Bizzy . . ."

"I wanted to know, too, but there's someone else we can contact."

"Who?"

"I have no frickin' idea," Marilyn Staples said. "I didn't know E. J. had a partner, I mean besides Bizzy."

Maybe Bizzy is listed as a partner on the LLP? my inner voice said.

"Who's running the business now?" I asked.

"Bizzy is. Well, actually me and Jack Matachek are. You remember Jack."

"I do," Nevaeh said. "How is he?"

"The same. As long as he has something to complain about he's good."

Nevaeh and I had arranged to meet Marilyn at Neumann's Bar and Grill, which claimed to be the oldest bar in Minnesota, after both she and Nevaeh finished work. While she was under orders not to discuss E. J. Woods Tree Care Services with strangers, Marilyn had no problem talking to the woman she called "sista" and "girlfriend."

Marilyn took a deep swallow of the expensive cognac she was drinking while we sat on the patio adjacent to the 106-year-old building located not far from E. J. Woods Tree Care Services, but that was on me. Even as she ordered the drink I could hear my father's voice in the back of my head telling me, "Never offer to pick up the tab until *after* people place their bets."

Even during happy hour.

"Bizzy's in charge," Marilyn added. "Except it's been me and Jack running the place since your dad passed. Bizzy and her lawyer came in a couple of days after he passed; right before the funeral it was. They said not to worry, the business wasn't going to close; they said that we would keep operating as usual. A lot of people were worried that it would close. I was worried. Anyway, we stayed open and, you know, everything is going along pretty much the way it was going before except it's not as much fun. Your dad made it fun."

Nevaeh nodded her head as if that's what she had expected to hear.

"How does the business work?" I asked.

"It's a simple system," Marilyn said. "Customers call us, send us an email, sometimes walk through the door like you did, but not often. They explain what they need, trees cut down or trimmed or planted or even moved, and then we send a guy to check it out, either Benny, Lucas, or Tom—you know those guys."

Nevaeh nodded some more.

"They're in charge of our crews. We have three full-time crews. We also have emergency crews on standby only we haven't had much work for them lately. Anyway, we send a foreman out and he reviews the job and gives the customer an estimate. The customer contacts the office. That's me. They accept the estimate and we schedule the job. That's me, too. The crew goes out, completes the job, and we send the customer an invoice. Mostly this is done electronically or over the phone. The customer can pay by cash, check, credit card, Venmo, sometimes a bank transfer. The crews do not accept payment, though. Not ever. Often when they do the job, the client won't even be there."

"Do you do the bookkeeping?" I asked.

"No. I keep track of everything, you know, make sure the client pays on time. That's never been a problem. But the bookkeeping—we have a guy who comes in who does the books and writes the checks; been doing it ever since Nevaeh left to become a teacher. How's that working?"

"It's mostly great," Nevaeh said. "I love the kids; the school district not so much."

"Anyway, the guy always comes in on Friday to write the checks and Bizzy signs them and off they go, usually on Monday. Used to be E. J. signed everything. Should I be telling you this? The only reason I am is because you're family."

Marilyn turned to gaze at me across the small table.

"Nevaeh, she's family," Marilyn repeated in case I was confused.

Afterward, she held up her now empty glass.

"Can I have another one of these?" she asked.

"Sure."

I waved a waitress over and placed Marilyn's order. The waitress returned a few minutes later.

"Why is this all such a deep, dark secret?" I asked.

"I told you about the guy."

"What guy?" Nevaeh asked.

"Bizzy didn't tell you about the guy?"

"No."

"It was like a week after they buried E. J.," Marilyn said. "Actually no, more like two or three weeks. This brother comes in and demands to speak to the owner. We tell him that the owner just died and he says he already knows that. He wants to know who's running the place now. He was very loud and very angry and my first thought, one of our crews musta accidentally dropped a tree on his house or something. So, we're trying to calm him down, Jack and me, and figure out what's going on. Guy keeps asking who's in charge here and I keep telling him that I am, sorta. He doesn't want to hear that. He's yelling 'I want my money,' and I'm thinking what? Is he a vendor or somebody that we forgot to pay? Only he's not giving us nothin'. Finally, Jack says, 'Sir'—he actually called him 'Sir' because you know what? The brother never told us his name. Anyway, Jack says if he doesn't get out of here he's going to call the cops. So the guy left. He stared at Jack for a minute, turned around, and walked away. Just like that. So we call Bizzy and tell her what happened and she says not to worry, she'll take care of it."

Brother? Does that mean he was Black?

"Did Bizzy take care of it?" I asked.

Marilyn shrugged her reply.

"I don't know," she said. "I only know that the next day Bizzy and her lawyer come in again and tell us not to discuss our business with anyone and if anyone should ask, to tell them to contact either Bizzy or the lawyer. Which is what we told you. Besides you, no one else has asked about our business except once in a while a long-ago customer might wonder if we're still cutting and planting."

"Did you tell Bizzy and her lawyer that I came in to see you?" I asked.

"Sure we did. Is that a problem?"

Marilyn was looking at Nevaeh when she asked that question.

"I don't know why it would be," Nevaeh answered.

"We miss you, sista."

"I miss all of you guys, too."

"Marilyn." I asked her the same question that I had posed when we began our conversation. "Do you know who E. J.'s partner is?"

"Like I said before, I have no frickin' idea unless—I'm still thinking Bizzy. Who else could it be?"

Good question.

Does the answer even matter? I asked myself.

Inheriting the business could be a motive for murder.

So is flirting with another man's wife and apparently E. J. wasn't above that. Or maybe he was. I don't know.

The total amount of what you don't know is staggering.

"Anything else?" Marilyn asked.

"What's the name of the person who comes in and does your books?"

"You know him." Once again Marilyn was looking at Nevaeh

when she answered me. "He was your dad's VFW buddy. Mike Boland."

Nevaeh and Marilyn were happily reminiscing about the good old days when I left Neumann's Bar and Grill, but only after I settled the tab, of course. I headed to my Mustang.

My first thought was to track down Mike Boland again. Except he told me when we first met at the VFW that he didn't know that Earl John Woods had a business partner.

No, he didn't. The others, Grant and Josh, said they didn't know if E. J. had a partner. Mike didn't say a word.

Which means either he didn't know or he deliberately chose not to give up the name.

Do you think anything has changed since then?

Do you think you can stop talking to yourself?

My cell was in my hand by the time I reached my car. I tapped H. B. Sutton's name on my contacts page. She answered the phone just as I was opening the door.

"McKenzie." Sutton sounded nearly breathless. "I can't decide. Should I wear red?"

"Red?"

"It's such a sultry color. A sensual color. I'm afraid it'll send the wrong message. 'Course black—what does a black dress say?"

"Depends on who you're talking to."

"You know what? I'm going to wear blue. God, what is wrong with me? You'd think I was sixteen years old again."

"What's happening?" I asked.

"I'm going on a date. Is that so hard to believe?"

"No, not at all."

"McKenzie, I'm fifty-four and I'm going on a date. It *is* hard to believe."

The voice in the back of my head reminded me that Sutton

had not once spoken of a relationship with anyone at any time in the ten years that I had known her, only I wouldn't let it speak.

"Truth is, any man who dates you is one lucky S.O.B.," I said.

"Why would you insult his mother like that?"

"Oh, for God's sake."

"He's so sweet, McKenzie, and so kind and why am I telling you this? What the hell do you want, anyway?"

That's my girl.

"Would the bookkeeper of a business know who all the partners were?" I asked.

"Yeah, most likely. The bookkeeper would probably be the one doing the business tax filings, the K-1s. The bookkeeper is probably also writing the checks. Are the partners taking a salary; are they actually working as an employee?"

E. J. was.

"Are they taking their money in quarterly payments, semi-annually, yearly?" Sutton added. "The bookkeeper would know all that."

"Then I should talk to the bookkeeper."

"You could, but if he was my bookkeeper and he answered your questions, I would fire his ass on the spot. A bookkeeper is expected to protect confidential information. Is this guy a licensed CPA? Is he a member of the Institute of Certified Bookkeepers?"

"I don't know. Does he need to be?"

"No, but if it were my business he'd be licensed up the ying-yang. McKenzie, I don't have time for this. I need to get dressed."

"When's your date?"

"I'm going to meet him—oh, not for two hours yet."

"Can I give you some advice?"

"You can try."

"Have a drink—not alcohol. Alcohol is for later. Have an iced tea, coffee, whatever. Relax on one of those chairs on the roof of your houseboat facing the sun and just chill. Listen to some tunes. Then in an hour, slowly get up, slowly get dressed, slowly head out to where you need to be. Remember, you're not dating him, he's dating you."

"He is?"

"And H, wear red."

"You think?"

"If you're going to bet, bet big. Besides, what if your date is also wearing red?"

"Oh, God."

Nina Truhler had propped her elbows on Rickie's downstairs bar, rested her face in her hands, and leaned toward me while I nursed a Maker's Mark on the rocks. It seemed as if we had been doing that a lot lately, talking to each other across a bar.

"I'm so happy to hear that H is dating," she said. "I've always liked H even though I don't think she's ever called me by my first name."

"You've only known her for about a year and a half."

"True."

"I wonder what her red dress looks like," I said. "I wonder if it looks anything like that shimmering red number you wore to the old Minnesota Club."

"You mean the night I pushed that guy who was threatening you down a flight of stairs?"

"The night I fell hopelessly in love with you."

"Ah, memories."

My cell phone began playing Louis Armstrong again. I glanced at the name on my caller ID. Something in my expression must have alerted Nina.

"Who is it?" she wanted to know.

I responded by tapping the green telephone icon.

"Good evening, Sergeant Holmes," I said.

"McKenzie, I said I would share if you did the same."

"Yes, sir."

"Tell me more about Michael Boland."

"I already told you pretty much everything I know about the man except I learned just a couple of hours ago that he works as a freelance accountant for E. J. Woods Tree Care Services and has been doing so for the past five or six years."

"You said he was a veteran," Holmes reminded me.

"The first Gulf War. H. W.'s war, they called it. He hung out at the Potzmann-Schultz VFW post in Maplewood along with Woods."

"You also said he was receiving therapy for post-traumatic stress disorder."

"No, Sergeant, I did not," I told him. "I said he was receiving therapy, but I didn't say why. I don't know why. His therapist is named Tara Brink. I suppose you could ask her."

"Probably doesn't matter."

"Why doesn't it matter?"

"He's dead."

"Excuse me?"

"Boland is dead. They believe he committed suicide."

I came off of the stool in such a hurry that it wobbled and nearly fell. I heard Nina call my name.

"What are you talking about?" I asked.

"Based on what you told me Saturday, I reached out to the Goodhue County Sheriff's Office to see if they had anything on Boland; Red Wing, where he used to live, is the county seat. Captain Follmer runs the Investigations Division down there. She said at the time that she didn't have anything on Boland. An hour ago she called back. Seems a couple of tourists just found our boy's body at the bottom of a cliff. Goodhue ID is pretty sure that Boland jumped. Telling them what you told me about Boland seeing a therapist only confirmed their theory."

"I don't believe it."

"Seems pretty cut-and-dried from what Captain Follmer told me."

"Where was Richard Bennett when this happened?"

"Do we care?" Holmes asked.

"As far as we know he's the last person to see Boland alive."

"On Friday night. It's Monday, McKenzie."

"Aren't you the least bit curious?"

"You're going to make a big deal out of this, aren't you?"

I almost said it—"No shit, Sherlock"—only I didn't. Instead, I said, "Loose ends vex me."

Holmes thought that was funny.

"Keep in touch," he said.

Nina became distraught when I revealed the contents of my conversation with Sergeant Holmes.

"Am I responsible for this?" she wanted to know.

"Of course not. Why would you be?"

"If I didn't make you go out and ask questions . . . I just wanted to find out what happened to Mr. Woods. I didn't want to make things worse."

"No, honey bunny." I reached across the bar and took hold of both of her hands. "Yes, I called you honey bunny in public. This has nothing to do with you. I was told that Mike Boland had issues; he was receiving therapy because of them. Probably they just caught up to him."

"I don't know," Nina said.

Neither do I.

I comforted my wife as best I could; it wasn't something I was particularly good at. When she was called away, I reached for my phone again. I found a number on my contacts list and placed a call. Brad Heggstad answered on the second ring and for a brief moment I wondered if he was always at his place of business.

That would make him a member of Nina's tribe.

"Brad," I said. "Is Richard Bennett at the marina?"

"No. I checked just a little while ago. Rick pulled out early Saturday A.M. and I haven't seen or heard from him since. McKenzie, like I told you before, that's not unusual behavior for him. If I don't see him again until the end of the month, I wouldn't be surprised."

"Do me a favor," I said. "Same as before—if you see him, let me know."

"A couple of hours ago a guy from the sheriff's department asked me to call them, too."

"Sergeant Stephen Holmes?"

"Yes."

Okay, Sherlock. I see you.

"McKenzie, what's going on?" Brad asked.

"What makes you think something's going on?"

"C'mon."

"Give G. K. my love," I said.

After thanking Heggstad for his time, I found yet another name on my contact list. It took Nevaeh Woods five rings before she answered.

"McKenzie," she squealed. I heard the instruments of a rock and roll band in the background yet could discern no melody. "Where are you?"

"It doesn't matter. Listen—"

"You should join me and Marilyn at Bunkers, Dr. Mambo's Combo is rockin' the house."

Apparently, they were rocking the house very loudly because Nevaeh had to practically shout to be heard.

"I'm going to pass," I said.

"No. Come dance with us."

"Some other time. Listen, Nevaeh . . ."

"What?"

"I changed my mind. I think it's time we had a very serious talk with your stepmother."

ELEVEN

I was sitting at a table on the second floor of Dunn Brothers Coffee in downtown Minneapolis, about a fifteen-minute walk from the condominium I shared with Nina. From the window I watched the heavy traffic moving along Central Avenue and crossing at the intersection with Washington. Meanwhile, the ancient building across the street that sheltered the U.S. Department of Housing and Urban Development, the National Labor Relations Board, and the Minneapolis Passport Agency didn't seem to have any traffic at all.

Despite my surveillance, I didn't see Garrett Toomey enter Dunn Brothers. I didn't even know he was there until he climbed the stairs and slowly crossed the room toward me. He was fifteen minutes late, which didn't surprise me at all. I had expected him to keep me waiting; would have been surprised if he hadn't.

Toomey's secretary had called me at exactly eight A.M. I was in bed with Nina at the time. She often didn't get to bed before two—she ran a jazz joint after all—and seldom rose before ten. I had left my cell phone plugged in to its charger on my desk in the office area. However, my smartwatch was synched to it and began to vibrate. The vibration not only woke me, it woke Nina who demanded to know who was calling at that ungodly hour. I read the caller ID.

"Not Erica," I said.

Learning that it wasn't her daughter was enough for Nina. She rolled over, said, "Well, then," and went back to sleep. I slid out of bed and made my way to the office area. The phone had stopped ringing by the time I reached it. I called the number that had been left.

"O'Hara, O'Hara, and Thomas," a woman said. "How may I direct your call?"

"My name is McKenzie. I just received a call from this number. I presume it came from Garrett Toomey."

"Please hold, Mr. McKenzie."

A moment later another woman spoke to me.

"This is Mr. Toomey's legal secretary," she told me. "Mr. Toomey requests that you meet him in his office at exactly nine A.M. this morning to discuss a matter of some importance."

"Tell Toomey that I'll meet him at Dunn Brothers Coffee at exactly ten A.M. Tell him not to be late."

The woman began to protest. I hung up the phone.

Now Toomey was sitting across from me dressed in a suit that cost more than my car and glaring over his white cardboard coffee cup. I made a production of looking at my phone, swiping through pics Bizzy Woods had posted on her social media accounts.

That'll teach him, my inner voice said.

Eventually, I set my cell face down on the table.

"You know how some people say 'This ain't my first rodeo' when they're dealing with an issue they've dealt with before?" I said. "Well, I've never been to a rodeo; not once in my life. Yet I have sat in the luxurious offices of several attorneys while they attempted to intimidate me into doing something that wasn't necessarily in my best interest. Which, of course, is what you intended to do. I thought I'd try something different this time."

I held up my coffee cup.

"Besides, have you tried the caramel mocha?" I asked.

Toomey was clearly not appeased by my explanation for demanding that we meet at the coffeehouse.

"You will immediately cease involving yourself in the affairs of Mrs. Elizabeth Woods," he told me.

"See, I knew you were going to say that, only it sounds much less threatening when you're sipping a cup of joe and watching a beautiful woman jogging outside the window."

Toomey's eyes darted outside and slowly found mine again when he realized that there wasn't a beautiful woman jogging outside.

Gotcha.

"If we need to take legal action—" Toomey began.

I interrupted him, reciting from memory, "Minnesota statute 609.50, Subdivision 1: Whoever intentionally hinders, or prevents the lawful execution of any legal process, civil or criminal, may be sentenced to imprisonment for not more than ninety days or to payment of a fine of not more than $700, or both."

Toomey raised an eyebrow, which I took to mean I had scored a point.

"Remember what you called me during the deposition?" I asked. "Well, I've been a vigilante for a long time, counselor."

"Is that what this is about? I damaged your pride? Is that why you insist on involving yourself in something that is none of your business?"

"I was asked to help; that's what made it my business."

"Not. By. Elizabeth. Woods." Toomey emphasized each word by jabbing a finger at me. "I received a very disturbing phone call from Mrs. Woods last night. It came immediately after she spoke to her stepdaughter who, in a drunken rage, all but accused my client of murdering her husband."

"Really? I wonder what prompted that. Nevaeh sounded both sober and happy when I last spoke to her."

"What prompted the altercation is your insistence that Mr. Woods was killed—"

I raised my hand like a referee calling a penalty in a hockey game.

"Who says?" I asked.

That caused Toomey to pause before adding, "Mrs. Woods said that Nevaeh said that you said—"

"You call yourself an attorney? I'd pay real money to hear you repeat that in a courtroom."

"McKenzie—"

"I did not tell Nevaeh that E. J. was murdered. In fact, I keep repeating to her that there isn't a scintilla of evidence even suggesting that he was murdered. Why she would believe otherwise has nothing to do with me."

"Then what is this about?" Toomey wanted to know.

"Questions. We have questions. Nevaeh and I wanted to speak to her stepmother to see if she could answer some of our questions."

"There. Is. No. Way." Toomey was jabbing his finger at me again. "Mrs. Woods. Speaks. To. You. Ever."

"Well, that makes it harder."

Toomey stood up, rested his hands on the small table, and leaned toward me.

"You will no longer insinuate yourself into these proceedings, McKenzie." His voice was stern, the words coming out in a slow hiss, and for a moment he reminded me of the assistant principal in charge of discipline at my high school who once heatedly berated me about underage drinking. "You claim that this isn't your first rodeo. It isn't mine, either. I know how to deal with people like you. I have been doing it my entire career. Do you understand me? As for Nevaeh Woods—Mrs. Woods chose to involve her stepdaughter in these matters strictly as a courtesy. That courtesy is revoked as of now."

Toomey spun away from the table and moved toward the staircase. I called to him.

"Hey, Garrett."

He glared at me over his shoulder as if his name was an insult.

"Don't you at least want to hear the questions?" I asked.

He didn't answer, yet he did pause.

"I bet G. K. Bonalay would like to hear them," I added. "Not to mention the insurance companies."

Toomey raised his head toward the ceiling and sighed deeply, not unlike my old man when he heard about the underage drinking. He slowly returned to the table and sat across from me. His coffee cup was still there. He picked it up and took a sip.

"What questions?" he asked.

"Can we stop putzing now?" I asked. "Can we get down to business?"

"What questions?"

"Why was E. J. Woods at Heggstad Marina that Saturday morning?"

"That has already been asked and answered."

"Not once do we see E. J. on a boat or a dock or near a lake or river in any of the hundreds of pics Bizzy had posted to her social media accounts. Plus both Nevaeh and E. J.'s friends at the Potzmann-Schultz VFW claim that they had never heard of him going anywhere near a boat. Personally, I don't think Bizzy's claim that E. J. wanted to look at the boats and at the river, that he liked boats and the river is going to hold up to scrutiny. 'Course, that's none of my business."

"No," Toomey agreed. "It's not. None of this is."

"Speaking of the marina, there were four cars in the parking lot when I arrived that Saturday morning. One belonged to Brad Heggstad, one belonged to my friend Dave Deese, one belonged to E. J. Woods. Who owned the fourth car?"

Toomey paused before he asked, "Does it matter?"

"I don't know. Does it matter? In any case, the Washington County Sheriff's Office is looking into it."

"Let me guess—it's because of you?"

Instead of answering, I took a sip of my coffee because—drama—while Toomey waited impatiently for the next question.

"Who was E. J.'s business partner?" I asked.

This time it was Toomey who remained silent.

"Your refusal to answer, is that because you don't know or because you don't want me to know?" I asked.

Toomey responded by taking a long sip of coffee. It was like we were taking turns.

"All right," I said. "Why was E. J. receiving therapy?"

Toomey tried hard not to show it, yet the way his eyes widened and his grip on the cardboard coffee cup tightened, I knew the question had jolted him.

"Nothing?" I asked just to be a tease.

Nothing is what he gave me.

"Bizzy didn't tell you, did she?" I said. "Don't worry, counselor; she's not necessarily holding out on you—that would have been my first thought, too. It's entirely possible that she doesn't know. Nevaeh didn't know, either. E. J. had been receiving therapy from an LPCC named Tara Brink on and off for five years, first here in the Cities and for the past three years in Red Wing. She's a principal in Brenda Smieja and Tara Brink Counseling Services in that town. I spoke to her last week only she refused to answer my questions except to state that she didn't believe E. J. committed suicide. Perhaps you can do better."

Toomey picked up his coffee cup again, realized that it was empty, and set it back on the table.

"What else?" he asked.

"Who sold E. J. all those life insurance policies?"

"That's easy enough to find out."

"It should all be easy to find out, yet it isn't. Why is that?"

Toomey didn't reply.

"I have something else for you, more of a statement than a question. About six years ago, E. J. fired Nevaeh. She had been running his office and taking care of his books. Nevaeh told me that he fired her so she could go back to teaching. Afterward, E. J. hired a freelance accountant named Mike Boland to take care of his books. Boland and E. J. knew each other through the VFW post. Tara Brink was Boland's therapist, too. Apparently, E. J. started seeing her at Boland's recommendation."

"You're telling me this because . . . ?"

"Did you know this? Did you know that Boland was keeping E. J.'s books?"

"Answer my question."

"Why? You haven't answered mine."

Toomey set his hands on the table and pushed himself upward.

"Yesterday, they found Boland's body in Red Wing," I said. "The Goodhue County Sheriff's Office believes he committed suicide."

Toomey lowered himself back to his chair. As he was an attorney with decades of experience, I didn't believe he would be prone to making what the legal profession labeled an "excited utterance," yet he threw one at me just the same.

"Jesus, you can't possibly believe that this has anything to do with the death of Mr. Woods," he said.

I didn't know if he was speaking to me or to himself.

"You seem distressed by the news," I said.

Toomey paused before answering.

"I know Mrs. Woods will be distressed," he said. "Losing a friend and valued employee in such a manner."

"It gets better," I said.

"How?"

"Boland was acquainted with a man named Richard Bennett. Bennett owns a boat named *Maverick*. It was one of the very few boats that were moored at Heggstad Marina when E. J.'s body was found by my wife. Full disclosure, there is no evidence proving Bennett was at the marina when E. J. died, nor is there any evidence indicating that he and E. J. actually knew each other. Bennett said they didn't. Still, all these unanswered questions, they vex me. That's my new favorite word, by the way—'vex.'"

Toomey gazed out the window at, well, nothing that I could see. Perhaps he was watching the traffic moving below us. Or perhaps he was waiting for a beautiful woman to jog past. He watched for what seemed like a long time. I gave him the time without interruption because I was sure I knew what he would say once he stopped watching. Toomey didn't disappoint me.

"McKenzie, if you could prove that Mr. Woods was murdered or at least provide a convincing argument to that effect, the result would be the same," he said. "Accident or murder, the insurance companies would be compelled to honor their contracts."

"You would lose your lawsuit against the marina."

"A small matter."

I doubt that Brad Heggstad would agree.

"I am aware of E. J.'s life insurance policy with Midwest Farmers—half a million bucks plus a double indemnity rider," I said. "What about the other policies?"

Again, Toomey chose not to answer my question. I was beginning to lose patience.

"C'mon, man," I said. "Here I thought we were becoming friends."

"There are three additional life insurance policies, each for a half million dollars, each with a DI rider."

"Four million total," I said.

"Yes, a lot of money. E. J. was in the process of gaining a fifth policy; he liked the idea of five million dollars. A round number. He was talking to a financial advisor, someone Bizzy knew, when—"

Bizzy, not Mrs. Woods.

—"these unfortunate events transpired. Mr. McKenzie . . ."

Mister?

"I apologize for my earlier outburst. I was premature in my criticism of you. I realize now that all of your activities to date have been undertaken solely to help Nevaeh Woods deal with the grief of losing her father . . ."

Here it comes.

"If you wish to continue, at Ms. Woods's behest, of course, I certainly would have no objection. Possibly we might be able to help each other. If you have additional questions for Mrs. Woods for example, I'd be happy to pass them along."

"I appreciate that," I said.

Only we won't hold our breath.

"I wonder, though, if I may rely on your discretion," Toomey said.

"Not even a little bit. I haven't volunteered any information to anyone involved in this except for you and I don't intend to. However, you know how it works even better than I do. If I'm called to make a statement, I'll spill my guts."

"I understand entirely. If you were my client, I would encourage you to do just that."

You would?

Toomey glanced at his watch, which I took as an indication that the meeting had concluded. He rose from his chair. I had a couple more questions for him before he could rush off, though.

"Bizzy has been posting a lot of pics on social media these days." I picked up my cell from the table and turned it over. "There's a shot of her in a very short skirt sitting on a leather sofa while she adjusts the strap on one of her high heels—nice legs, by the way—with the line, 'Hello #Friday #night! I've been waiting for you.' There's another of her in a sexy red dress with the tag, 'Happy International Women's Day.' Here she's walking across a hotel lobby in that same red dress while Whitney Houston sings 'I Wanna Dance with Somebody.' In this one we don't see Bizzy at all, just a few logs burning in a fireplace with 'The Night Is Young' by DJ Smash playing in the background. In this one—"

"What's your point, McKenzie?"

"Who was taking the pics and the videos, the ones that clearly weren't selfies, I mean?"

Toomey glanced at his watch again. I thought he would leave without answering. Instead, he said, "I took several of them."

Just several?

"Mrs. Woods and I have become—close—during this ordeal."

Really? A guy sipping a caramel mocha in a downtown coffeehouse might consider that to be unethical behavior. On the other hand—four million bucks.

"Let's say, just for argument's sake, that E. J. was murdered and your client is somehow implicated," I said. "What would happen next?"

"My client would not be implicated. There is no evidence—"

"I know that," I said. "Speaking hypothetically, though, if Bizzy were implicated, what would you do?"

Instead of becoming upset, Toomey answered smoothly.

"We would defend her as vigorously as the law allows," he said.

"If she were convicted?"

He paused a few beats before answering that one.

"Under the 'slayer rule,' a murderer or someone who is directly tied to a murder cannot retain a property interest in their victim's estate," he said. "In that case, all death benefits, such as insurance claims, would be paid to the victim's contingent beneficiaries. As the attorney for Mr. Woods's estate, I would insist on it."

I bet you would.

"Who is E. J.'s contingent beneficiary?" I asked.

"His daughter, Nevaeh Woods."

It took me all of fifteen minutes to walk back to the condominium and another ten before I settled myself in front of my computer on the desk in our office area. I used the computer to call up the newspaper that served the residents of Red Wing in the hope of learning more about Mike Boland's death than what Sergeant Stephen Holmes told me. Unfortunately, I discovered that the *Republican Eagle* was published only two days a week—Wednesday and Saturday.

It's Tuesday, my inner voice reminded me.

"No shit, Sherlock," I said to the empty condo.

I wondered what the chances were that I could see a copy of the Goodhue County Sheriff's Office incident report.

Holmes could get one. He might already have it. Do you think he'd share?

"No."

What else is there to do?

I used the computer to find the website of the Sunset Marina in Red Wing. Its phone number was conveniently placed at the top of the page. I called it.

"Sunset Marina, how may I help you," a male voice answered. I thought I recognized one of the men I had spoken to earlier.

"Hey," I said. "My name is McKenzie. I was down there last Friday asking about Rick Bennett. He owns the boat *Maverick*."

"Yeah, yeah, yeah," a male voice said. "I remember. You had missed him by a day."

"Right. I just wanted to make sure I got my dates right this time. Have you seen Rick?"

"Not since last week."

"Really? I know he left Stillwater on Saturday. I thought he was stopping in Red Wing on Monday."

"Haven't seen him."

"Huh. Well, if you do, could you tell him McKenzie was looking for him; that I wanted to talk to him?"

"Do you want to leave a number?"

"Rick has my number."

I threw out that last part because Bennett did have my number—I had given him my card—*hopefully, he kept it*—and because I wanted to leave the impression that he and I were friends.

"Do you have his number?" the voice asked. "You could call him yourself."

Uh-oh. Explain why you don't have your "friend's" cell number.

"Rick usually turns off his phone when he's not using it. He claims the world is too damn big and loud."

Man, you can lie with the best of them.

"Yeah, that sounds like him," the voice said.

See?

I completed the phone call and leaned back in my comfy swivel chair.

Now what?

Bennett wasn't in Red Wing when Mike Boland died. At least he wasn't parked at the marina.

Yeah, I got that.

Yet even so, what does this have to do with E. J. Woods drowning in the icy water of the St. Croix River while holding on to a ladder that could have taken him to safety?

Probably nothing.

What was it you told Nina—we might never find out what actually happened on that dock?

Is that where you're going to leave it?

As it turned out, I wasn't given much choice in the matter.

It was late afternoon and I had just finished a heavy workout in the gym located on the second floor of the condominium. I try to get to the gym at least three times a week, either here at the condo or at Gracie's Power Academy, a martial arts training center located in a St. Paul neighborhood they used to call Frogtown. Partly it was to maintain my girlish figure but also because I have on occasion been compelled to engage in physical activity that required hitting and being hit. Jogging three miles along Mississippi Boulevard, which I also did a couple times a week, wasn't enough to cut it, especially at my advanced age.

The phone call came after I had stepped out of the shower.

"McKenzie," the voice said.

"Nevaeh," I said.

"McKenzie, I want to thank you for everything you've done for me. You've been so kind and generous . . ."

I hear a "but" coming.

"But . . ."

There it is.

"I've just had a long talk with Bizzy and her lawyer at Bizzy's place and—they told me about Mike Boland. I can't believe it. Suicide?"

"That's what I was told."

"That's just so awful."

"It is," I agreed.

"It just makes me wonder about all of the people who have risked their lives to serve our country; how much we could do for them that we don't."

"You're making assumptions that Mike was suffering from post-traumatic stress disorder. So did the Goodhue County Sheriff's Office. Only we don't know if that's true."

"Does it matter?"

"The insurance companies are saying the same thing about your father," I reminded her.

"My father did not commit suicide. It was an accident that he fell into the river."

Wait. What?

"You're satisfied that it was an accident now?" I asked.

"You've said yourself many times that there isn't any evidence to even suggest that Dad was—that he was killed. McKenzie, I'm sorry. I have no reason to snap at you. You've been such good people, only enough is enough."

"I don't understand."

"I was upset about Dad's death, about how he died, and I was thinking—I don't know what I was thinking. I suppose you could say I wasn't thinking. That's why I asked you to help me."

"And now?"

"Now I just want it to stop. I want you to stop. This investigation isn't helping anyone. Not me. Certainly not Bizzy."

"You said you just met with her and her lawyer?"

"Yes."

"What did they tell you?"

"They told me about Mike, about what happened to him. Mike was Dad's accountant. You know that. Now that he's gone, Bizzy has asked me to take over the job; to keep the books for the company. Not forever. Just during the summer while school is out. We'll decide next September what we're going to do. It's possible I could teach and still work for Bizzy. We'll see."

Is that all they told her?

"Okay," I said.

"Bizzy and I, even though we're not related, we're family. You see that, don't you?"

"Sure."

"Thank you, McKenzie. Thank you for everything. If there's ever anything I can do for you . . ."

"Nothing at all. But, Nevaeh . . ."

"Yes."

"Remember what I told you when this all began—you might learn things you'll wish you didn't know."

"I hear what you're saying, McKenzie, only this is something I need to do."

"Need to do?"

"I need to move on."

"If things don't work out, you have my number."

"Thank you, McKenzie."

We ended the call. Afterward, I stared at the screen of my cell phone. My reflection stared back.

I'll ask again—now what?

Nevaeh gave me cover. Only I didn't get involved in this because of Nevaeh.

That doesn't answer the question.

I turned my phone over.

TWELVE

I stood at the bottom of a cliff, using the flat of my hand to shield my eyes from the sun as I gazed upward. The sheer rock wall was two hundred feet high according to the Red Wing *Republican Eagle*. At least that's how far the newspaper estimated that local resident Michael Boland fell to his death.

That wasn't the headline, though. The headline read:

AFTER FATAL FALL, RED WING OFFICIALS
CONSIDERING NEW SAFETY MEASURES

Apparently, Boland had fallen from a trail on the He Mni Can-Barn Bluff that had been closed ever since another hiker had plummeted to his death ten years earlier. The mayor said he expected the city to have a long discussion about additional safety measures to prevent more tragedies. The city administrator echoed that sentiment, though she called it a difficult issue with no clear solution other than to post more signs and increase public education.

"We can't put up a fence along the entire Mississippi River," she said. "It's just not practical."

At no point did the newspaper story suggest that Boland, a decorated veteran of Desert Storm, committed suicide. Instead, it said that he fell from a steep and narrow and difficult section of the scenic North Trail. It did not state why he was on the trail, nor were any members of the Goodhue County Sheriff's Office or the Red Wing Police Department quoted in the story. There was only this line:

> "It's a very dangerous hiking path," said Cpt. Roger Knutson of the Red Wing Fire Department. "The best advice we can give people is, you know, the signs are there for a reason."

My first thought was the *Republican Eagle,* being a small-town newspaper with a circulation of 5,200, was more respectful of a family's grief than, say, the *Minneapolis Star Tribune* with its 580,000 readers.

My second thought—*You don't think Sergeant Stephen "No Shit Sherlock" Holmes is messing with you?* my inner voice asked.

I examined the railroad tracks where Boland's body had been discovered, not by tourists as Holmes had claimed, but by employees of the nearby wastewater treatment plant. I didn't know what I was looking for. Blood? Bone fragments? Brain matter? All I found was gravel and wooden ties and steel tracks.

I looked at the cliff some more.

> The 340-foot-high He Mni Can-Barn Bluff is considered one of the jewels of Red Wing, drawing hikers of all ages to its natural beauty and providing exceptional views of the Mississippi River, Lake Pepin, and the city of Red Wing.

I didn't need the newspaper to tell me that, though. He Mni Can-Barn Bluff—it translated to "hill, water, wood" in the language of the Mdewakanton Dakota people who had lived in the area long before Europeans arrived—has enticed everyone from Zebulon Pike to Henry David Thoreau to yours truly.

I wasn't dressed for it—I was dressed for a funeral—yet I decided to hike the bluff and take a look at the trail myself.

I drove until I found the small gravel parking lot just off of East 5th Street where Nina and I had started our climb when we were last in Red Wing. Across the street was a long flight of concrete stairs. At the top of the stairs was a kiosk where I found a map. I used the map to guide me along the South Trail.

The South Trail was wide and more or less hugged Highway 61; I could hear the noise of traffic far below me. I followed the South Trail to the Prairie Trail. Along the way I passed several groups of hikers, including couples holding hands. They looked at me like I was certifiable. Possibly because they were dressed in shorts, T-shirts, and hiking boots while I was dressed in black dress shoes, black slacks, and a black sports jacket over a white shirt. I took off the sports jacket and draped it over my shoulder because of the heat.

I followed Prairie Trail as it looped around the west side of the bluff and morphed into the North Trail. I encountered a sign. TRAIL CLOSED KEEP OUT. I ignored it just as Mike Boland must have. The trail narrowed considerably, yet the dirt was well packed down, suggesting that Boland and I weren't the only ones who had a problem with authority.

I kept moving until I felt I was more or less in the approximate location where Boland must have fallen, jumped, or been pushed. *You're starting to sound like the Ramsey County ME.* I searched carefully, as the sheriff's deputies must have done, and discovered nothing to indicate that a man had met his fate up there much less what introduced him to it. I went as close to the edge of the cliff as I dared and glanced at the train tracks.

Jesus, that's a long way down.

I backed away from the edge until I could no longer see the ground. Truth be told, I was frightened by heights; one of the things I had discussed with Dr. Jillian DeMarais all those years ago.

A couple approached from my right. Girl and boy, early twenties; they were talking and laughing until they saw me and then they ceased doing both. From the expressions on their faces as they passed me I wondered if they thought that I was going to jump. They kept walking, although the girl glanced back at me several times before disappearing down the trail.

I told myself that if I was desperate enough to commit suicide, I'd sure as hell find a better way to do it than leaping off of a cliff.

Apparently, Mike didn't agree with you.

"Who says?" I asked aloud.

It was a good question. Once again I found myself wondering why Sergeant Holmes was convinced that he had jumped.

It can't be just because he knew Boland was seeing a therapist, could it?

I let the thought bounce around in my head as I hiked down the mountain—it felt like a mountain to me. A quick reading of my map told me it would be easier to go back the way I came, so I did, following the North Trail to the Prairie Trail and finally to the South Trail again. Not once did I look over the edge.

When I finally reached my Mustang, I glanced at my watch.

Plenty of time, I told myself.

My two friends at the Sunset Marina were standing behind the high counter exactly where I had left them a week earlier. The first man waved his finger at me.

"McKenzie, right?" he asked.

"Yep."

"What are you dressed for? A funeral?"

"As a matter of fact, I am," I said.

"Oh God, man, I'm sorry. I didn't mean to—"

"It's okay."

"Who died?" the second man asked.

"Remember the last time I was here, you mentioned meeting one of Rick Bennett's friends—Mike Boland."

"I'm sorry. I didn't know. Wait. Isn't he the guy who went off the bluff?"

"Oh man, that, that, that just sucks," the first man said.

"Does anyone know what happened? I never heard what happened."

"I don't know," I said. "I'm hoping someone will tell me."

"This friend—was he a good friend?" the second man asked.

"I didn't really know him very well," I said. "Listen, the reason I'm here with you guys—no one has been able to get hold of Bennett. The S.O.B. just won't answer his damn phone."

"Can you believe that?" the first man asked.

"I was wondering if you heard from him and if you were able to give him my message."

"Not a peep," the second man said.

"If you do, have him give me a call. He has my number. You know what?" I reached into my jacket for my wallet and pulled out a card printed with my name and cell number. "In case he lost it, give him this."

"I will," the second man said.

The first man waved his finger at me again.

"You know, the reason people carry phones with them wherever they go these days is so shit like this won't happen," he said.

"Tell me about it."

He Mni Can-Barn Bluff could easily be seen from the parking lot of the funeral home. It was a large parking lot, yet only a few spaces were filled. I parked my Mustang in the shade at the far

end and went inside. One of the things that always impressed me
about funeral homes was how quiet they were. I climbed the carpeted stairs and moved along the corridor without hearing even
the sound of my own footsteps. There were several large viewing
rooms. A sign outside one read BOLAND. I stepped inside.

The first thing I noticed was the casket mounted on a mahog-
any stand in the front of the room. It was black with a high-gloss
exterior and silver hardware. The hardware was embellished
with the seal of the United States Army against an American
flag. The casket was closed with three red roses set on top. There
were also vases filled with flowers positioned around the casket.
The sash wrapped around one said it was from "Mike's friends
at E. J. Woods Tree Care Services." Along with the flowers were
dozens of photographs of Michael Boland taken at various stages
of his life from his birth until just a few weeks ago. Many of them
showed him in uniform. In the earliest of those photographs he
was smiling. In the later pics not so much.

There were rows of chairs set in front of the casket, yet no
one was sitting in them. Instead, the people gathered in the
room stood in small circles. I counted five circles totaling about
twenty people, their voices no more than a murmur. I didn't
know anyone in four of the circles. The fifth, though, consisted
of veterans from the Potzmann-Schultz VFW post. I recognized
Josh, Grant, and Sheila. Sheila was wearing black, her blond-
and-gray hair grazing her shoulders. It was because of Sheila
that I had made the trip to Red Wing.

She had called me Thursday evening; asked if I was planning on attending Mike Boland's funeral. I hadn't actually
given it any thought. Since my conversation with Nevaeh
Woods on Tuesday evening, I had all but abandoned my investigation into E. J.'s death.

"There's nothing to learn and no way to learn it," I had told
Nina.

She was not happy about it. Neither was I.

"Think about it, though," I said. "E. J. could have just as easily slipped, tripped, lost his balance, and fell into the river as any of the other scenarios."

"I get that," Nina said. "The way I figure it, though, if we knew why he was at the marina in the first place, the rest would explain itself."

Good point, my inner voice said.

Except I could see no way of moving forward. Bizzy was never going to answer my questions and neither was Garrett Toomey, despite his promises. Nevaeh had blocked me. And Rick Bennett had all but disappeared somewhere on the Mississippi River.

Sheila's phone call had revived my interest, though.

"Some of us are going down to Red Wing for Mike's funeral service," she told me. "They're not burying him in Red Wing. They'll be burying him with full honors at Fort Snelling on Tuesday, but we were talking about how the family might enjoy seeing some of his friends from the Cities, friends that served like he did. I don't know how close he was to people down there."

"This is kind of quick, isn't it?" I asked. "Boland died on Monday and they're conducting services four days later? Usually it takes a week or more."

"I know. It's like they're just trying to get it over with as soon as possible. Mike deserves better than that. Anyway, would you care to join us? I know you didn't know him very well."

What did Mike say the last time you saw him? "Once more unto the breach, dear friends, once more, or close the wall up with our English dead."

"Yes," I said. "I'll go to Mike's service, only I'll have to meet you down there. I have a few things I need to do."

"Investigation things?"

"Yes."

"Do you think Mike's death has anything to do with E. J.'s death? That's what we've been asking ourselves—what's going on?"

"I don't know, Sheila," I said. "It's entirely possible, even probable, that nothing's going on. That it's just life happening and there's no rhyme or reason or story or melody to it."

"One thing I learned at Wadi al-Batin, McKenzie; probably the only thing I learned in that shitty place—there's always a reason. It might be nothing more than one enormous cluster-fuck, yet there's always a reason."

Now I was approaching her in the funeral home. Sheila saw me and reached out a hand that ended up resting on my wrist.

"You guys know McKenzie," she said.

Handshakes were performed between me and Josh and Grant and two other men who knew Boland from Potzmann-Schultz.

"It was nice of you to come," Grant said. He gestured meekly at the room. "Not a big turnout."

"Something my old man used to say—if you have one good friend, you're rich." I gestured at the veterans. "I'd say Mike did all right for himself."

Sheila's hand returned to my wrist.

"Meet Mike's mother," she said.

She led me to the circle closest to the door.

"Mrs. Boland," Sheila said.

A woman spun toward me. If someone told me she was taller than five feet I would have argued with him. Her hair was white and her eyes were red.

"Mrs. Boland, this is McKenzie."

I offered my hand to the woman. She didn't shake it; merely held it.

"I am so sorry for your loss," I said.

"Were you a friend of Michael's, too?" she asked.

"I knew him at the VFW."

"You people from Potzmann-Schultz. Such good friends. Coming all this way. Mike's friends from Red Wing." Mrs. Boland glanced around the viewing room. "I guess it was too far to go. Or not. Some people, when they heard how he died. Such a terrible thing. We all thought he was doing so much better."

She thinks he jumped, too.

"It was the war, you see," Mrs. Boland added. "The war changed everything. Did you see the war? I know Sheila did."

She reached out and took Sheila's hand even as she continued to hold mine.

"I wish it was you," Mrs. Boland said.

"Me?" Sheila asked.

"The blond woman."

Blond woman?

Mrs. Boland spoke to a woman who was standing almost directly behind her.

"Mary," she said. "Tell her about the blond woman."

"What blond woman?" Mary asked.

"At the hotel."

Mary moved up next to us. She was about to speak, only Mrs. Boland cut her off.

"It was—it couldn't have been more than a month ago, isn't that right?" she said. "Michael and the blond woman."

"Six weeks, maybe," Mary said.

"Mary saw Michael walking into the St. James with a blond woman. Michael and her were holding hands—Michael and the blond woman," she added in case we were confused.

"They were holding hands," Mary confirmed.

"She called to them. 'Michael Boland,' she said."

"Michael looked directly at me and he kind of smiled," Mary added. "Only he didn't say anything; just went inside. Do you think he was embarrassed?"

"I think he was embarrassed," Mrs. Boland said. "He was always shy around girls. Anxious around girls. In high school, too. His prom pictures. He could barely smile. So nervous. It wasn't you, was it?"

"Me?" Sheila asked again.

"At the hotel."

"No," Mary said. "The woman at the hotel was prettier. Her hair was golden."

If Sheila was offended by Mary's remarks, she didn't show it. Mrs. Boland gave her hand a shake and released it.

"I still wish it was you," she said. "You understand. The rest of us, we don't understand. I don't understand. I never have. War. I tried to talk to Michael so many times. Only I didn't understand."

"You did your best," Mary said.

"We all thought he was doing better. The past couple of years. He seemed happy. At least happier than he was. He came home once a week. Came home to see his mother. Then he'd leave. Go to see his friends."

"What friends?" I asked.

"Just friends. He'd go to see his friends. Go to bars, I guess. I knew when Michael was drinking. Even when he was in high school. The way his eyes became shiny. He'd come home and the next morning he would have breakfast with his mother and then he'd leave. These last few months especially, I thought he seemed happy."

Last months? Since E. J. died?

"He seemed fine when I saw him at the VFW last Friday," I said.

It was an innocuous thing to say, I know, only I wanted to draw the woman out without her noticing.

"He seemed fine when he came home on Sunday, too," Mrs. Boland said.

Sunday, not Saturday, the day Rick Bennett left the marina in Stillwater.

"We spent the day together," Mrs. Boland added. "Monday, too. After dinner, he went to see his friends. Last thing he said to me, 'I'll see you later. Love you.' Two hours later the police called me, said . . ."

Mrs. Boland never finished the sentence. Instead, she seemed to draw into herself. It was as if she was shrinking before my eyes.

"It was the blond woman," Mary said.

"What about the blond woman?" Mrs. Boland asked.

"Maybe he was in love. Michael."

Mrs. Boland glanced around the room.

"The blond woman isn't here," she said.

"Maybe they broke up. Maybe that's why . . ."

Mary didn't finish her thought. Mrs. Boland stared straight ahead. I could only imagine what pictures she was seeing.

Finally, "I wish it was you," she said.

"So do I," Sheila said.

Mrs. Boland was distracted by the arrival of additional mourners. It gave Sheila and I the opportunity to slip away without seeming rude. We moved back toward the VFW circle.

"Wasn't it you who told me that Mike had feelings for Bizzy?" I asked.

Josh overheard me.

"We all had feelings for Bizzy, even Shields," he said. "You know what I'm talking about."

"No, I don't," Sheila said. "Explain it to me."

"Animal lust—am I right?"

The other vets didn't say if he was or wasn't.

"Fuckin' jarhead," Sheila said.

"The night before E. J. died, I was told he was eating ribs at Potzmann-Schultz," I said.

"That's right," Grant said. "BBQ Ribs Friday."

"Was Bizzy there, too?"

"No, but Ribs Friday is kind of a club thing. I doubt I saw her more than—I'm going to say a couple dozen times over the years."

"Something like that," Josh said.

"When did E. J. leave?" I asked. "Do you remember?"

"About nine?" Grant glanced from Josh to Sheila while he answered as if he was looking for someone to correct him.

"Don't look at me," Sheila said. "I left early, too."

"Nine sounds right," Josh said. "I remember he was chatting with Mike before he left. The two of them standing alone at the bar before he headed for the door. I remember calling to him, 'Leaving so soon?'"

"What did he say?" I asked.

"He said it was getting late and he wanted to go home to see what Bizzy was up to. We all thought that meant—well, you know what we all thought."

Sheila glanced at the ceiling and shook her head.

"Did Mike leave with him?" I asked.

"No, why would he do that?" Josh said.

"Mike was at Potzmann-Schultz until closing along with the rest of us," Grant said. "Wasn't he?"

"I walked out with him," Josh said.

"Okay," I said.

"What are you thinking, McKenzie?" Josh asked. "Mike and E. J. got into it over Bizzy, E. J. drowns, and Mike jumps off a mountain because he can't live with the guilt?"

"It's a nice story," Grant said. "Not nice, but at least it's better than the story we have now."

"What story do we have now?" Sheila wanted to know.

"We don't have a story, that's the thing."

"Everyone assumes that Mike jumped," I said.

That quieted the group for a few beats.

"No one wants to say it out loud," Sheila said. "There but for the grace of God go I."

Grant gave it a half beat more before asking, "Are you one of those conspiracy nuts, McKenzie, seeing crime and corruption wherever they look?"

"Are all cops like that?" Josh asked.

"Just thinking out loud," I said.

"I'm like Nevaeh," Sheila said. "I just wish I knew what happened."

Except Nevaeh no longer cares, my inner voice reminded me. *Or maybe she already knows.*

Loud voices caused us to turn our heads toward the circle that included Mrs. Boland.

"No," she said. "No. No."

Tara Brink was standing in front of her, her head bowed as if she was attempting to conduct a private conversation with the older woman. The way Mrs. Boland's friends crowded around her, though, I didn't think that was possible.

"You were supposed to help him," Mrs. Boland said.

Brink replied, although I couldn't hear her voice.

"All those sessions, all that money," Mrs. Boland said. "You were supposed to help him."

Brink kept leaning forward and speaking softly. Her hands were clasped together at the waist of her blue dress. The tension in her arms suggested that she was gripping them tightly.

"I don't believe you," Mrs. Boland said.

Mary was at her side.

"Go away, just go away," she said.

"I don't want you here," Mrs. Boland said.

Brink nodded her head and said something else that I couldn't hear. Afterward, she turned and made for the door.

"Who's that?" Sheila asked.

"Excuse me," I told her.

Brink was nearing the steps that led to the front entrance of the funeral home by the time I reached the carpeted corridor. I called her name. Either she didn't hear or chose to ignore me.

"Tara, please," I said.

She kept walking.

"Tara."

She stopped, both of her hands resting on the door handle.

I was on the steps now and descending to where she stood. She turned her head to look at me. There were tears in her eyes.

"Do I know you?" she asked.

"Are you okay?"

"Yes. I remember. McKenzie."

"How can I help you?"

"Do I need help?"

"What you just did took real courage. You had to know how Mrs. Boland and her friend would treat you, yet you came here anyway."

"I felt . . ."

Brink closed her eyes.

I waited.

She opened them again.

"Walk with me," Brink said.

She pushed open the door and we stepped outside. Instead of heading for the parking lot, she led me to the sidewalk and we slowly strolled together side by side, our backs to He Mni Can-Barn Bluff. We walked in silence for several blocks until we reached Central Park. There was a band shell in the park and several picnic tables scattered across the lush green grass in front of it. Brink led us to one of them. She sat on one side and I sat on the other.

"One of the signs of good emotional intelligence, McKenzie, is empathy," Brink told me. "An example of empathy is the individual's ability to resist interrupting when someone is talking—or not talking. That's because the minute you speak is the minute when you stop listening; stop learning. Not only that, when you interrupt, you're telling your partner that you aren't really interested in them; that you don't care about what they have to say. Tell me—were you taught this, or did you come by it naturally?"

"I'm a disciple of Steve Martin," I said.

"The comedian?"

"He once said that sincerity is everything. If you can fake that you've got it made."

Brink thought that was funny.

"Actually, I think George Burns said it first," she said. "McKenzie . . ." Brink seemed to be searching for something in my eyes. "You don't look away much, do you? That's to your credit, too."

I said nothing.

"Ah, McKenzie," Brink said. "I've lost two patients in three months. I'd never lost a patient before. I'm told that they both committed suicide, but I can't believe it. I can't believe I didn't see it coming. There was no ideation, no—should I provide you with a list of behaviors and warning signs that might indicate suicidal thoughts? Mike Boland didn't display any of them. His personality didn't change. He didn't start using alcohol or drugs. He didn't have erratic moods swings. He didn't say he wished he were dead or that he wished he had never been born. Neither did Mr. Woods. You need to believe me."

"I believe you."

"Yet I keep searching my notes for clues; keep trying to remember if there was something I missed."

"Tara, how often did you see Mike?" I asked.

"Usually once a week. I say usually because sometimes we would take a break for a month or more and then reconnect."

"I was told Mike had anxiety issues."

Brink didn't reply. Instead, she gazed off to the side at a group of kids and one adult lingering on a terrace at the top of a limestone brick wall. The wall had been built into the side of a hill and surrounded by a row of small columns topped by a rail, what they call a balustrade. Again, I waited.

"It would be against the rules for me to reveal that Mr. Boland did, in fact, have anxiety issues, although they were not severe," Brink said. "It would be a breach of confidentiality to say that even though those issues were exacerbated by his experiences while serving in the military, they most probably began in childhood. As much as I would like to, I am ethically forbidden to tell you that I believe some of Mr. Boland's issues also stemmed from his relationship with Mr. Woods, whom Mr. Boland claimed was his best friend, and whom Mr. Boland repeatedly maintained that he was more than happy to help."

"Would it be improper of me to ask what Mr. Boland did to help Mr. Woods?"

"Yes, Mr. McKenzie, it would be improper. Almost as improper as me providing you with the answer, if I knew the answer, which I don't. Sometimes clients keep secrets from their therapists . . ."

And their friends, my inner voice reminded me.

"For example, a client, whom I will not identify, once confided in me that he felt exceedingly guilty about the deep personal feelings that he had slowly developed for his best friend's wife, yet when I pressed him, he refused to declare one way or another if he had ever acted on those feelings."

"What do you think?"

"If you're asking me to speculate, I would say no."

Huh.

"About Earl John Woods," I said.

"I told you in my office last week that I will not discuss Mr. Woods's therapy with you. As I said, we take client confidentiality very seriously here."

"I understand."

"Do you, McKenzie?" Brink asked. "In my experience most people have serious misconceptions concerning therapy."

"In what way?"

"They fail to realize that therapy isn't only for people who are in the middle of a major life crisis or who are suffering from a debilitating mental illness. Often people will see a therapist simply because they need someone to talk to, someone who will help them sort out their feelings and release pent-up emotions or secrets that they haven't felt free to share with anyone else.

"Just talking about the things that are bothering you can help you to feel less burdened or overwhelmed, McKenzie. Talking to a therapist gives you the additional opportunity to open up to someone in a safe and confidential environment. Because a therapist isn't personally invested in what's going on in your life, she can be objective and simply listen. She can give you her undivided attention during your appointment time.

"Of course, you may feel that you could get just as much out of talking to a trusted friend, except there are times when your friends may be distracted by their own issues and problems or they may be very opinionated about what you should do and who you should be. They might be judgy. Most people would like to avoid that.

"I had one client—again, I won't identify him by name—whom I had worked with for more than five years. Sometimes I saw him once a week, sometimes once every two weeks, sometimes just once a month or more. It all depended on how he was feeling and mostly he was feeling fine."

"Not at all suicidal?"

"Not at all."

"If I may bring up E. J. Woods again . . ."

"Please don't."

"His daughter Neaveh told me that he had a particular fondness for blue-eyed blondes, especially blue-eyed blondes who were hot—that's the word she used."

"Are you deliberately attempting to provoke me?" Brink said.

"Yes."

"I'm sure you have a reason."

"When people become angry because, oh let's say someone questioned their personal integrity, they are more likely to lose control of what they're saying."

"You mean like I have been doing for the past fifteen minutes, oh my God."

"Tara . . ."

"My relationship with Mr. Woods was strictly professional. Our meetings lasted approximately forty-five minutes and every single one of them was conducted in my office. That he might have thought I was 'hot,' as you say, never once came up in conversation."

"Have you been contacted yet by Mrs. Woods or her attorney, Garrett Toomey?"

"No."

"The Goodhue County Sheriff's Office?"

"Why? Should I have been contacted?"

"I would have thought so."

So why wasn't she?

I considered the possibilities while we both sat quietly at the picnic table. The kids and their adult chaperone had left the terrace. Residents and tourists of all sizes, shapes, and sexes moved through the park, yet no one settled at any of the other picnic tables. They all seemed to be on the move.

"I need to get back to my office," Brink said. "Review my notes some more."

I stood with her.

"Goodbye, McKenzie," she said.

"Ms. Brink, may I?"

I didn't wait for her to reply, yet stepped forward and wrapped my arms around her shoulders in a hug.

"Should I ever have a friend who needs to speak to someone they can trust, I will recommend you."

I released her.

"Thank you, McKenzie," she said. "Or is that just Steve Martin talking?"

"Take care, Tara."

"You, too."

I walked back to the funeral home. Along the way, I let a theory bounce around inside my head. *E. J. Woods was a jealous man,* it said. *If he thought Mike was messing with what was his . . . Except, he wasn't here to act on his jealousy. Could someone else have acted on E. J.'s behalf? Who would that be?*

I found the driveway leading into the funeral home's parking lot. At the same time, the building's doors opened and people began leaving, including the circle of VFW friends. Among them was Sheila, her blond-gray hair splayed across her shoulders. I stopped to watch her. She saw me and smiled. She gestured toward Josh and Grant and moved alone toward where I was standing.

"There you are," she said. "We were wondering what happened to you."

"I took a walk with Tara Brink. She was Mike Boland's therapist."

"I gathered that from what Mrs. Boland had to say after they chased her out of the funeral home. I can't remember the last time I heard the words 'hussy' and 'trollop' used in the same sentence."

"For the record, I don't think she's either."

"I appreciated the insult, though," Sheila said. "It seemed so much nastier than 'slut' or 'whore,' at least the way Mrs. Boland used it. Did the therapist tell you anything interesting?"

"She doesn't believe that Mike jumped off the bluff."

"Or did she screw up like Mrs. Boland says and now doesn't want to admit it?"

"Who knows?"

"Listen, the boys and I are going to stop off at the Treasure Island Casino on the way back home. Would you care to join us? You can put a stopwatch on me; see how long it takes to lose a hundred bucks playing blackjack."

"Thank you, but I have a few things left to do."

"Okay. Well, thanks for coming, McKenzie. We all appreciate it. Don't be a stranger."

Sheila began to move away. I called to her. She stopped and looked back at me.

"This is where I run the risk of insulting you," I said.

"Insult away."

"Nevaeh Woods told me that her father had an appetite for blue-eyed blondes who were hot. She said E. J. made every effort to satisfy this appetite as frequently as possible."

"My eyes are brown," Sheila said.

"Yes, they are."

Sheila moved toward me.

"Are you asking if I'm free with my favors, McKenzie?"

I didn't reply. By then she was standing directly in front of me. She leaned in and whispered in my ear.

"Yes." Sheila backed away. "In case you're interested."

She smiled brightly before making her way back to her companions.

I turned and started walking across the emptying lot toward my Mustang, which was now parked in the bright sunshine. I stopped when I noticed the woman who was half sitting on and half leaning against the front bumper. She was wearing a dark blue business suit over a light blue shirt and I tried to remember if I had seen her inside the funeral home. Her arms were folded and her head was tilted down so that her chin was nearly resting against her chest. Brown hair—*brown, thank God*—caressed her face. She seemed to be deep in thought. Either that or she had mastered the ability to sleep while standing up.

She slowly lifted her head as I approached as if I were a mechanic she had summoned to fix her own car.

"McKenzie?" she asked.

Who wants to know? my inner voice replied.

"Yes," I said aloud.

"I'm Captain Debra Follmer, Goodhue County Investigations Division. Please don't make me reach into my bag for my badge and ID."

"Perish the thought."

"Just so you know, we're not having this conversation."

"You have no idea how nervous that makes me feel."

"Steve Holmes up in Washington County says you used to be on the job so you know how it works."

"That's what makes me nervous. How did you know I was here?"

"Holmes said you'd probably make a big deal out of Michael Boland's death since it might be connected to a possible homicide in his county . . ."

Possible homicide?

"I had a deputy checking out the funeral home during Boland's service in case you showed." Captain Follmer rapped the hood of my Mustang with her knuckles. "Nice ride."

"It was a birthday gift from my wife."

"Oh, yeah? What did you give her?"

"A Steinway grand piano."

"It's good to be you."

"I've always thought so, Debra. Do your friends call you Debbie?"

"No."

"Debra, then."

"Captain Follmer. Or just Captain if you want to be friendly."

Friendly—that's your middle name.

"Captain," I said. "I have questions."

"What a coincidence. So do I."

"Would you like to get a drink? I could use a drink. There's a joint not far from here called the Barrel House."

"I'm familiar, but no, McKenzie. It's easier to not have a conversation in a parking lot than to not have a conversation surrounded by customers in a bar. Besides, I'm on duty."

"So you'd rather stand outside in this heat?" I dangled my key fob in front of her. "We could slip inside my car. I'll turn on the air-conditioning."

"Do you know how many men have asked me to do that over the years?"

"Probably none while you're in uniform. Only you're not wearing your uniform, are you?"

"There's a very thin line between what's charming and what's obnoxious, McKenzie."

"Yes, and I keep crossing it. The reason I mentioned the Barrel House, Captain, is because it's part of my story."

"Do tell."

"Mrs. Boland told me earlier that Mike came home to Red Wing once a week. To see his mother, she said. She also told me that he would go out with his friends. Only none of his friends seemed to be at the funeral. However, we know that at least one friend—a man named Richard Bennett—met with him at the Barrel House. Bennett owns a boat called *Maverick*. *Maverick* was docked—"

"At the Heggstad Marina in Stillwater when Earl John Woods drowned. I'm aware. I also know that Bennett did serious time for attempted murder."

"Holmes told you?"

"Occasionally, law enforcement will communicate across jurisdictions."

"Who woulda thunk it? The *Maverick* is currently cruising somewhere on the Mississippi River. I checked with the boys at the Sunset Marina where Bennett usually stops—"

"So did I. They expect to see him when they see him."

"Captain Follmer, I was under the impression that the sheriff's office had ruled Michael Boland's death to be a suicide; that the case was closed. Yet you seem to be very active."

"Who told you the case was closed?"

"Sergeant Holmes."

Follmer shook her head at that.

"I've known Steve for a long time," she said. "Sometimes he's Sherlock Holmes and sometimes he's Watson, and not the smart Watson in the remakes but the dumb Watson in the Basil Rathbone films."

"Are you a fan of Turner Classic Movies, too?"

"I live in Red Wing. There's not that much to do unless you're a tourist, which brings me to the point. I'm leaning toward suicide because, one—Boland has been receiving therapy nearly every week for years and because, two—Boland was not a tourist climbing the hill to look at the sights. He was a native. He grew up here. He's seen the sights. And three—he didn't hike, at least according to his mother. He wasn't dressed for it in any case. So what was he doing up on the bluff? Alone?"

"Are you sure he was alone?" I asked.

"There's no evidence to suggest that he wasn't. Have you been up there?"

"Yes."

"I figured. What did you see?"

"That it was a long way down to the railroad tracks."

"What else?"

"Nothing."

"Nothing," Follmer repeated. "Nothing to suggest that there was an altercation of any kind. Nothing to suggest that he fell."

"He could have fallen. It's been done before."

"Yes, it has. That's why—Goodhue is served by the Southern Minnesota Regional Medical Examiner's Office. The ME hasn't released its autopsy report yet, but I suspect that he'll rule—"

"Let me guess. Accident-homicide-suicide-undetermined."

"There isn't enough evidence to prove anything one way or the other."

Where have you heard that before?

"For the record," I said, "Boland was seeing a therapist named Tara Brink, an LPCC working here in Red Wing."

"I know."

"If you had bothered to question her you might have learned that she doesn't believe that Boland was suicidal."

"Her professional opinion carries a lot of weight, only it doesn't explain what Boland was doing on the bluff at dusk on a Monday evening."

"When you found his body, did you recover his cell phone?"

Follmer gave it a few beats before she answered.

"No," she said.

"No cell phone?"

"Not on him, not in his car, not in his room at his mother's house."

"Could it have fallen out of his pocket when—"

"We searched. Thoroughly. No cell phone."

"That's—that's unlikely."

"Now you know why I'm not having a conversation with you in a parking lot of a funeral home instead of a nice cool bar. Anything you can give me on or off the record, McKenzie, I'll take."

"I have no answers for you, Captain. Only questions."

"Such as?"

"The same ones you've been asking. What was Mike Boland doing on that mountain? What was E. J. Woods doing at the marina?"

"I changed my mind, McKenzie. I'll have that drink with you after all."

THIRTEEN

G. K. Bonalay and Maryanne Altavilla approached my table at Kincaid's in downtown St. Paul without knowing that they were both at the restaurant to see me. They didn't meet until they reached the table, gazed at me, at each other, and then at me again. Bonalay seemed confused. Altavilla was clearly suspicious. She dropped her black bag, which was three times as large as the one Bonalay carried, on the table.

I stood up.

"Ladies, thank you for coming on such short notice," I said. "G. K., this is Maryanne Altavilla. Maryanne, this is G. K. Bonalay."

They nodded at each other without smiling. Afterward, Bonalay crossed her arms over her chest and Altavilla set both of her hands on the back of a chair and looked at me some more. About a half dozen quick jokes buzzed through my head, yet I didn't give voice to any of them.

"Gen, Maryanne is my friend," I said instead. "She is also chief investigator for the Midwest Farmers Insurance Group's Special Investigative Unit. Midwest Farmers had insured Earl John Woods for a million bucks and she was assigned to the case. Maryanne, Genevieve is also a friend and my personal attorney. The reason I asked her here, though, is because she is representing Heggstad Marina in a wrongful death lawsuit filed against the marina by Elizabeth Woods, widow of Earl John Woods."

The second introduction clearly had an impact because they were both smiling when they shook hands.

"My pleasure," Altavilla said.

"The pleasure is mine," Bonalay replied.

"So, ladies," I said, "would you care to sit down?"

"Oh, I absolutely want to sit down for this," Bonalay said.

The two women wordlessly negotiated over which chairs to seize. Altavilla went left, Bonalay went right. As they took their seats, a waiter appeared.

"Would either of you ladies care for something from the bar?" he asked. "I recommend any of the selections listed on our happy hour drink menu."

Both Altavilla and Bonalay glanced at me.

I raised my glass.

"I'm drinking bourbon," I said.

"I'll have a mojito," Bonalay said.

Meanwhile, Altavilla was scanning the menu on the table in front of her.

"I'll have a glass of your La Luca Prosecco 2020," she said.

"Wait," Bonalay said. "Change my order. I'll have the same as her."

"Very well," the waiter said and moved away.

"I like a good sparkling wine," Bonalay said.

"My mother told me that when the sun is shining you should only drink something light," Altavilla said. "She never specified if it should be light in alcohol or light in color."

"Mine said to drink whatever you like but only two—only two. Oh, and sip. Always sip."

Is this how women bond? my inner voice wanted to know. *When are they going to start talking about hockey and baseball?*

"Are you buying food to go with these drinks, McKenzie?" Bonalay asked.

"I'm starving," Altavilla said.

"Order a couple of appetizers if you like," I said.

They did. Altavilla ordered mushroom bruschetta and Bonalay asked for coconut shrimp that they shared with each other. While they ate, Altavilla asked, "Are you going to tell us why you're being so generous, McKenzie?"

"Generous is right. You both should be picking up the tab considering that I've been doing your jobs for you for the past two and a half weeks."

"I hadn't noticed," Bonalay said. "Have you?"

Altavilla merely shook her head, but that was because she was biting into a slice of bruschetta at the time.

"Seriously, McKenzie," Bonalay said. "You've kept us in suspense long enough. What's on your mind?"

"Ladies," I said. "It is my intention to misbehave."

Bonalay glanced at Altavilla.

"I hate it when he talks like that," she said.

"What form of misbehavior are you contemplating?" Altavilla asked.

"For one thing, I mean to become a gossip," I said.

"A gossip?"

"A person who engages in unconstrained reports about the personal and private affairs of others."

"I know what a gossip is."

I let my voice rise a couple of octaves.

"Did you know that Bizzy Woods was having an affair with her attorney?" I asked. "Why, I do declare, have you ever heard of such unethical behavior? All those pics the poor grieving widow has been posting on her social media sites—who do you think is taking them?"

Bonalay leaned back in her chair.

"Interesting," she said. "Not necessarily useful."

"Ever since Nevaeh Woods claimed during my deposition that her father was murdered—"

"Excuse me," Altavilla said. "She did what?"

Bonalay reached across the table and rested her hand on top of Altavilla's. Maryanne didn't seem to mind at all.

Hmm, my inner voice hummed.

"I'll explain, I promise," Bonalay said. "McKenzie, please continue."

"I've been investigating the possibility that E. J. Woods was murdered ever since Nevaeh made her allegation. She's the one who actually convinced me to do so. Along the way, I have come across a cache of facts that are interesting yet not necessarily useful. It is my intention to become somewhat boisterous about them."

"Why?"

"Partly to see how the people involved react. Partly because so many others seem to want me to, including members of the Washington County and Goodhue County Sheriff's Offices."

"I don't understand," Altavilla said.

"For example, did you know that E. J. Woods was receiving therapy from a licensed professional clinical counselor named Tara Brink in Red Wing?"

"No, I didn't."

"Did Garrett Toomey know?" Bonalay asked.

"Who's Garrett Toomey?" Altavilla asked.

"Elizabeth Woods's attorney. Did he know, McKenzie?"

"He might not have known then but he knows now."

"Since when?"

"Since I told him on Tuesday morning."

"He hasn't disclosed that information, but it's only been a couple of days."

"Here's the thing, Genevieve," I said.

Altavilla interrupted.

"Your name is Genevieve?" she asked.

"Yes," Bonalay said. "Most people call me Gen or G. K., though."

"Genevieve Bonalay—that's a beautiful name."

"Thank you."

What's going on here?

"If I may continue," I said.

"Please," Altavilla replied.

"Gen, Garrett Toomey all but told me to spill my guts to whoever would listen. Why would he do that?"

"So he doesn't have to," Altavilla answered for her. "He doesn't want to reveal his client's secrets yet keeping them might be construed as unethical if not illegal behavior. This way the information gets out, leaving him in the clear. Or am I being naïve?"

Bonalay patted the younger woman's hand before withdrawing her own.

"No," she said. "That works. McKenzie, what else?"

"This is where it gets complicated," I said.

"I'm going to need another drink."

"Two, only two," Altavilla said.

"You're too young and pretty to be my mother."

"Well, in that case . . ."

The two women flagged down a waiter who refilled both of their glasses.

Are they flirting with each other?

"At the risk of being a monkey mouth—" I said.

"Monkey mouth?" Altavilla asked.

"It's prison slang for someone who talks and talks and talks without having anything to say."

She stared at me with a quizzical expression on her face.

"I'll explain," I said.

I took my time reciting in specific detail everything that I'd done, everyone I'd met, and everything I'd heard since Nina found Earl John Woods in the icy water of the St. Croix River, concluding with a recap of the conversation between Captain Follmer and myself in the funeral home parking lot earlier that afternoon. While I spoke, Altavilla removed a pen and notebook from her enormous black bag and began taking notes. Both women asked questions. Altavilla and Bonalay were particularly interested in what Tara Brink had to say, in her purposely roundabout way, about E. J.'s sporadic therapy sessions.

"I wonder if she'd be willing to go on the record without being forced to answer a subpoena," Altavilla asked.

"Unfortunately, if McKenzie is correct, Brink's testimony would be detrimental to both of our cases," Bonalay said.

"I don't look at it that way. I'm genuinely sorry if it goes against your interests, only my job is simply to gather the facts. What Midwest Farmers does with it after that is entirely up to the lawyers."

"What do you make of Michael Boland and Richard Bennett?"

"There is no evidence to suggest that either of them were present when Mr. Woods died; quite the contrary. While I find their relationship with Mr. Woods very curious, as McKenzie does, I don't believe it's pertinent. However . . ."

"Yes."

"The fact that both the Washington County and Goodhue County Sheriff's Offices seem to be conducting an ongoing investigation—I could see how that might support your argument."

"What's my argument?"

"That a conscientious jury couldn't possibly conclude that Mr. Woods died by accident any more than the Ramsey County medical examiner had."

"I wish you were on my jury."

"I'd like that."

Holy mackerel.

"None of this explains—McKenzie, why are you telling us this, anyway?" Bonalay asked.

"I'm easily ignored," I said. "But you two have standing. The people who won't talk to me can be compelled to speak to you on the record. Bizzy Woods, for example. Tara Brink for another. That will bring pressure to bear and people do the most amazing things when they're under pressure."

Bonalay smiled at Altavilla.

"Do you get the impression that we're just props in a Rushmore McKenzie production?" she asked.

"It wouldn't be the first time. Did he ever tell you how he found the Countess Borromeo for us?"

"The missing Stradivarius? I actually advised him not to go after it."

"He didn't mention that."

"He didn't mention you, either. Tell me, it's Friday night. Do you have plans?"

"Sadly, no. I thought I'd just hang around the apartment and watch *Bridgerton* again."

"I love that show."

"You're welcome to join me."

Wait. Netflix and chill?

"May I buy you dinner first?" Bonalay asked.

"I would like that very much," Altavilla said.

What have you done?

"What have I done?" I asked.

"You mean besides introducing two people who seemed to hit it off right away?" Nina asked.

We were sitting in her office at Rickie's and having Chef Monica's daily special for dinner—miso-marinated sea bass with Yukon gold potato puree and sweet corn and roasted red

pepper succotash that went for forty-two bucks on Rickie's
menu. The meal had come with a lecture from Monica Meyer
on how difficult and expensive it was to get fresh fish from the
East Coast to Minnesota "while it's still fresh!"

"Have you thought of having it sent in from the West Coast?"
I asked.

"Are you trying to be funny?" Meyer asked.

"Yes, a little bit."

"Very little."

A moment later, Meyer was gone.

"How long have you two been squabbling?" Nina wanted to
know.

"I don't know. When did you hire her? Four, five years ago?"

"It's starting to get old."

"We just like teasing each other."

"Is that what you call it?"

I pointed my fork at the sea bass.

"I have to admit, this is amazing," I said.

"You might tell her that. Monica owns ten percent of the
business, remember? I don't know what I'd do without her."

"That's right. Rickie's is an LLP."

"Just like E. J. Woods's business," Nina said. "See, I listen to
you. Not always convinced that you listen to me."

"A licensed therapist told me today that I have good emotional intelligence."

"I'm sure her credentials are impeccable."

I waved my fork some more.

"See?" I said. "We're teasing each other. That doesn't mean
we're not madly, passionately in love, right?"

This time it was Nina who used her fork as a prop, pointing
it at my plate.

"Eat your dinner," she said.

Only that was after I told her I couldn't believe that G. K. Bonalay and Maryanne Altavilla were hooking up.

"Having dinner together doesn't mean that they're hooking up," Nina said. "We're having dinner. Does that mean we're hooking up?"

"Well, yeah, eventually, I hope. Anyway, I didn't know that G. K. was a lesbian."

"She's not. She's bi. Get your terms right."

"How do you know that? I've known her for eight years and I didn't know that."

"If she thought it was important, she would have told you," Nina said.

"Yes, but how did you know? And Maryanne, did you know that she was—is she bi, too?"

"No, she's a straight-up lesbian."

"I've known her for three years," I said. "She never told me."

"Why would she?"

"She told you."

"No, she didn't, but I knew and she knew I knew. There was no reason to talk about it."

"How did you know?"

"McKenzie, if you and I weren't together she would have been all over me like a cheap suit."

"That's my line."

"That's why I used it."

"No, I don't believe it."

"Don't believe what?" Nina asked. "You don't think I'm desirable to other women? Huh."

"No, what I meant—I'm just surprised that I could have been friends with these women for so long and not know something as personal as this about them."

"Does it matter?"

"To me? No. No, not really. The way I look at it, it's just another two women in the universe that want nothing to do with me."

"Let's keep it that way. You know, I've always been impressed by how liberal you are when it comes to sexuality and race and religion and things like that."

"Hey, do I call you names?"

"What?"

"I'm not liberal. I'm selfish. The way I look at it, if it doesn't affect my life personally, I don't care what other people do. Seriously, why would I? Why should I give a damn what God they worship or books they read or people they sleep with or restrooms they use or music they listen to or what they study in school or geez, how they live their lives; the color of their skin or shape of their eyes or whether or not they wear a COVID mask in a grocery store? There are people out there who do nothing all day but search for something to be pissed off about when there is so much joy to be found. I refuse to be that guy."

I used my fork again, pointing at the sweet corn and roasted red pepper succotash Monica Meyer had prepared.

"For example, I never had this before," I said. "This is really good."

"Tell Monica."

While promising Nina that I would, my cell phone began vibrating on top of the small table where we were sitting. I turned it over and read the caller ID—Nevaeh Woods.

"Well, that didn't take long," I said.

"For what?" Nina asked.

"For pressure to build."

I rose from the table and stepped away until I was standing behind her desk, not because I didn't want Nina to hear the conversation but because I didn't want to distract her from her meal.

"Hi, Nevaeh," I said. "This is McKenzie."

"Why are you doing this?"

"Doing what?"

"I told you I didn't want you investigating my father's death anymore."

"Who told you I was?"

"You were at Mike Boland's funeral."

"I was invited to attend by friends of Mike's from the Potzmann-Schultz VFW post," I said. "I noticed that you weren't there. Neither was your stepmother."

"We sent flowers."

"Yes, I saw them. Very nice."

"Attending the services wasn't all that you did, though, was it?"

"Who told you that?"

"Enough, McKenzie. Enough is enough is enough. No more. I said to stop investigating Dad's death and I meant it. What more do I have to do?"

"Tell me why?"

"I told you why."

"Because you now believe that it was an accident that your father fell into the river."

"That's right. You said yourself that there wasn't any evidence to prove otherwise."

"And because the investigation is upsetting Bizzy and even though you're not related, you're family."

"It's true."

"I don't believe you."

I didn't know if Nevaeh had paused because she was surprised by my response or because she needed a moment to take a deep breath before screaming "Fuck you, McKenzie" into the phone and ending the call.

I turned to face Nina, who hadn't eaten a bite while I was talking to E. J. Woods's daughter.

"Pressure," I said.

FOURTEEN

It was during a bright, cloudless Tuesday afternoon that members of the Memorial Rifle Squad met the hearse carrying Mike Boland's casket as it slowly approached the pavilion that served the Fort Snelling National Cemetery. They snapped to attention as the black casket was removed from the hearse and carried by six strong men to a stand beneath the pavilion. The squad displayed the colors denoting all of the armed services of the United States, yet only the flag bearing the seal of the U.S. Army was dipped to salute Boland.

The cemetery was adjacent to the historic fort and the Minneapolis–St. Paul International Airport. It was the only national cemetery in Minnesota and provided the final resting place for more than 250,000 service members and some of their spouses; precise row after precise row of identical white headstones fanned out over 436 acres. It was very beautiful and very majestic and very sad all at the same time.

I can tell you the history of Fort Snelling. I learned it when they buried my father there a little more than a decade ago. Its original purpose was to keep the peace on the western frontier, except by 1855 the frontier had moved so far west that the garrison had been removed. It became an assembly ground and training center for Minnesota volunteers during the Civil War and continued to serve that purpose until 1946 when Fort Snel-

ling was deactivated as a post, although it remained the headquarters for the 88th Army Reserve Command.

The national cemetery was established in 1939 and now
boasted a population greater than every city in Minnesota save
Minneapolis and St. Paul. Because it was so sprawling, it was
difficult to locate a specific grave site even if you had been there
before unless you used the cemetery's grave finder. I had to use
it to find my dad even though I'd been there every Memorial
Day since he passed.

My old man had been a child serving underage with the
First Marines at the Chosin Reservoir in Korea; "The Forgot-
ten War" it was called. "At least I want to forget it," the old man
told me. He was forty-two when he married my mother. She
was twenty. I've always wondered how that happened only I
never got the chance to ask. That's because my mother died fifteen years later of cancer—"Such an emotional word," Nevaeh
called it. "Filled with fear and anger and grief and resignation."

I was twelve at the time. My father was fifty-seven. He was
a good man and kind. Also taciturn. He would go to all of my
baseball games, my hockey games. He would sit in the stands
and watch, yet rarely cheered and seldom had a comment beyond "Good game" when we won and "That's too bad" when
we lost. Most people who saw us together assumed he was my
grandfather.

I loved him more than I have words to say.

It was because of the old man that I took the price on
Thomas Teachwell, the enterprising embezzler I had tracked
nearly to the Canadian border on my own time. I wanted to
give him a more comfortable retirement, only Dad had passed
six months later.

I tried not to think about any of that, though, during the service honoring Mike Boland. I was there, after all, to observe the
crowd. It wasn't particularly large. There were a few people that

I recognized from the services I had attended the previous Friday in Red Wing and others from Potzmann-Schultz. Mostly I was wondering if the blonde Boland had met at the St. James Hotel in Red Wing would appear. I suspected that she had—Bizzy Woods was standing behind and off to the side from where Mrs. Boland sat on a bench facing her son's casket.

Nevaeh stood next to her. She gave her stepmother a nudge when she saw me among the other mourners. Bizzy waved her off with just a slight gesture of her hand as if my presence held no possible interest for her.

I continued to watch the Memorial Rifle Squad. It consisted of volunteers gathered from the various military branches that had been honorably discharged and were now members of veterans service organizations such as the American Legion, VFW, and DAV. They wore white shirts with the badge of the MRS stitched above their left pockets and garrison caps.

The squad accompanied Boland's casket to the pavilion, as it had done for every single veteran, over eighty thousand of them, since 1979 when the squad was formed. Words were spoken and seven members of the squad fired three rifle volleys; not an actual twenty-one-gun salute, oh no, that was only for dignitaries. "Taps" was played. The American flag was carefully folded and presented to Mrs. Boland just as it had been presented to me. I nearly lost it and might have if not for my inner voice telling me, *The old man would not approve.*

It all reminded me of a passage printed on the Fort Snelling Memorial Rifle Squad website entitled *The Last Duty Call.*

> I am a veteran and have served my country.
>
> I am here to receive military honors.
>
> I am here for my last earthly call to service.
>
> As I arrive at the cemetery pavilion, the color guard is called to attention. My branch of service flag dips and I am saluted.

Announcements state this ceremony consists of three distinct elements . . .

Three loud rifle volleys announce I have sacrificed for my country and can be laid honorably to rest.

A distant bugler plays the memorable twenty-four notes of Taps signifying my interment, and that God is nigh and all is well.

With precision and care, the flag of my country is folded. The folds slowly encase life's brilliant red and white stripes, which disappear into the dark blue with stars, a symbol of nightfall, a time for my rest and eternal peace.

The presenter gives my flag to a loved one as a lasting symbol of honorable service. Three shell casings from the rifle volleys are included to reflect . . .

DUTY, HONOR, and SACRIFICE.

The ceremony ends with one final salute honoring our country and my service.

This is a place of peace and lasting remembrance.

I am like all soldiers at this sacred place. Our tombstones remain as a symbol of the cost of freedom.

This is my new and our last duty call.

I had no idea who wrote it, yet it read to me like something out of Ralph Waldo Emerson.

After the service was concluded, the Memorial Rifle Squad marched off, followed in turn by the other mourners. Sheila and the other vets, Josh and Grant, gave me a nod as they passed yet said nothing, not to me or to each other. I heard Mrs. Boland say, "That was nice." Her friend Mary replied, "Yes, it was." I approached Mary. It was my intention to point Bizzy out to her and ask if she was, in fact, the woman Mary had seen with Boland at the St. James. I wasn't able to reach her side, however, because I was intercepted by Bizzy.

"Mr. McKenzie," she said. "It's a pleasure to see you again. I only wish it were under better circumstances."

I glanced over her shoulder. Nevaeh was moving slowly toward a car parked in the cemetery's lot. Her expression suggested that she was not happy and I could imagine her stepmother shooing her away with the words "I've got this."

"Mrs. Woods," I said.

"Please, call me Bizzy."

"May I ask where that name came from?"

"It was the best and last in a long succession of nicknames. I was born Elizabeth and that became Liz which became Lizzy which became Lizzy Bea—my last name was Beamon. Lizzy Bea became Bizzy Bea which became Bizzy. I must admit, I like it."

"So do I."

"Mr. McKenzie—"

"Just McKenzie is fine."

"I was told your first name is Rushmore."

I recited the joke that I kept in my pocket for just such occasions.

"My parents took a vacation to the Badlands of South Dakota," I said. "They told me that I was conceived in a motor lodge in the shadow of Mount Rushmore, so they named me after the monument. It could have been worse, though. It could have been Deadwood."

Bizzy thought that was funny. Most people did. She hooked her arm around mine.

"Come," she said.

We began strolling up the narrow road to another narrow road that led us deep into the cemetery. Bizzy was wearing a black summer sundress adorned with pink flowers; both her skirt and her hair rippled in the wind. I was in my funeral outfit—black shoes, black slacks, sports jacket, and white shirt. Together, with her arm linked in mine, I'm sure at a distance we appeared to be a romantic couple. Only her grip on my arm was stronger than it should have been and I was feeling the tension of a sprinter waiting for the gun to go off.

We were surrounded by white monuments and far removed from the other mourners when Bizzy said, "It's so quiet here," even as a passenger plane taking off from the airport passed overhead. "If it weren't for the planes . . . Do you think I should take a pic or a video?"

"I'm sure you'd get a lot of likes on your social media platforms."

"Do you follow me?"

"I've peeked at your posts from time to time. I especially liked the red dress you wore for International Women's Day."

"You don't think uploading a post from the cemetery would be in bad taste?"

"You're honoring a friend and employee; why would that be in bad taste?"

"Maybe later."

We walked some more.

"McKenzie, I will always be grateful you tried to help me that day at the marina when E. J. died," Bizzy said. "I'm also grateful that you made such an effort to help Nevaeh, too. You're a good man. A kind man. Believe me when I tell you that I know how rare that is. You must know, though, that none of this is any of your business. It was none of your business when Nevaeh asked you to become involved and it is certainly none of your business now that she's told you to please stop. It's between me and the insurance companies. It's between me and Heggstad Marina and don't tell me that the owner is a friend of yours because you already testified that he's not. So why, why, why are you doing this?"

"Mankind was my business," I quoted. *"The common welfare was my business; charity, mercy, forbearance, and benevolence*

were all my business. The dealings of my trade were but a drop of
water in the comprehensive ocean of my business!"

Bizzy stopped walking. She turned to face me.

"What the fuck?" she asked.

"Charles Dickens," I said. *"A Christmas Carol."*

She stared at me like I was nuts. Honestly, I couldn't blame
her.

"Here's the thing," I said. "You find a man in the water and
you ask yourself, how did he get there, and no one will tell you. A
curious mind might wonder why not."

"E. J. fell. It was an accident."

"If that's true, why are you here encouraging me to go away?"

"To keep you from turning it into something else."

"Ask your attorney; he'll tell you that if I can prove that your
husband was murdered or at least provide a convincing argument to that effect, the result would be the same. The insurance
companies would be compelled to honor their contracts. You'll
still get your four million dollars."

"Not if they think I murdered my husband."

"Did you?"

"Fuck no."

"Then what's the problem?"

"Fuck, fuck, fuck . . ."

Bizzy walked five long steps away from me, paused, and
slowly walked back.

"Please excuse my language," she said. "For years now I've
been trying to be a better person than I was, only sometimes the
past reaches out to me. McKenzie, I don't know what to tell you.
Twenty years ago, I would have known exactly what to say and
do, only now . . ."

She linked her arm with mine again and we kept strolling along
the narrow road until Bizzy veered off it onto the plush green lawn
and we found ourselves walking among the headstones.

"I didn't kill my husband," she said. "I loved E. J. He saved my life."

"Nevaeh told me that you saved each other."

"I suppose that's true."

"Bizzy, why were you at the marina that Saturday?"

"I already told you."

"I don't believe you."

"I hardly believe it myself. McKenzie, we were just driving around looking for a place to have breakfast. We did that a lot. If you knew E. J. and me, you'd know that we were both lousy cooks. We decided to go to Stillwater. There's a place called the Oasis Cafe that we'd been to before. They make breakfast sandwiches with buttermilk pancakes and it wasn't that far a drive from our house. While we were driving E. J. asked, 'Do you think the river is still frozen,' and I said, 'Does it matter?' He said, 'Let's take a look,' and I said, 'Are you crazy?' We kept driving and it became clear that E. J. was no longer looking for the cafe. Instead, he saw the marina and he said, 'Let's pull in here.' I didn't argue with him because you don't argue with E. J. when he gets something in his head. We parked and he said, 'Do you want to come with?' and I said, 'Heck, no. It's cold.' He went out onto the dock and I stayed in the car. I was swiping through my social media sites on my phone and after a while I looked up and asked myself, 'Where is he?' That's what happened and yes, I know it sounds stupid, but it happened just like that. I got out of the car and started looking for him and then you and your wife arrived."

The story sounds awfully plausible the way she told it, my inner voice informed me. *Well thought out; well-rehearsed. It might even be true.*

"Here we are," Bizzy said.

That's when I realized that we weren't just strolling; Bizzy was leading me to the grave of her husband. We stopped in front of his pearl-white granite headstone.

EARL JOHN
WOODS
MSG US ARMY
PERSIAN GULF
DESERT SHIELD/STORM
JUNE 10 1960
MARCH 25 2023
LOVING HUSBAND
AND FATHER

Woods had been buried seventy-six days ago according to my fuzzy math, yet the well-cared-for lawn above his grave gave the impression he had been there for a thousand years.

Bizzy stepped close to the headstone and ran her hand gently over the curved top.

"E. J.," she said. "None of us are perfect, McKenzie. Some of us are even less perfect than others. We can only do the best we can and hope it's good enough."

"Good enough for what?" I asked.

"Good enough to get into heaven."

Bizzy leaned down and kissed the top of the headstone.

"I'll meet you there," she whispered.

A moment later, Bizzy linked her arm around mine again.

"We should get back," she said. "Nevaeh is waiting."

A few minutes later we were on the narrow road and heading toward the parking lot. I still had questions.

"Bizzy," I said. "E. J. Woods Tree Care Services is an LLP."

"Yeah. So?"

"Who was E. J.'s business partner?"

"Me. I was."

"Why would you form a limited liability partnership instead of a limited liability company?"

"You're asking me? I don't know. Something to do with

taxes. It was Mike Boland's idea. You'll have to ask . . . Yeah. Poor Mike."

"I was told at his funeral service in Red Wing last week that Boland was spending time with a beautiful blonde; that they were seen entering the St. James Hotel together."

"Now what are you accusing me of?" Bizzy asked.

"This took place a month to six weeks ago; the witness was a little vague."

Bizzy took her time before she answered. I let her.

"Mike was very kind to me; a very good friend. Not just to me but to E. J., too. He helped us with our business. When E. J. died, Mike reached out to me. Tried to comfort me. He had always wanted to comfort me, if you get my meaning. This time I let him. I was grateful to him. I know you must think I'm some kind of a whore, spending a weekend with a man less than two months after my husband died. It didn't mean that I didn't love E. J. It didn't mean I wasn't still grieving. How long are you supposed to mourn, anyway?"

Your father mourned for the rest of his life.

"The problem was Mike wanted more than to just comfort me for a weekend," Bizzy added. "He wanted a relationship. A long-term relationship. I just wasn't ready for that. I didn't know if I would ever be ready for that. I told him so. I had to be honest with him. It was the very, very least I could do."

"Do you think that's why Mike was on the bluff?"

"Please God, I hope not."

We kept walking.

"It makes me look bad, though, doesn't it?" Bizzy said. "The insurance companies would use it against me if they knew."

"Probably."

"Do they have to know?"

"I'm not doing this to help the insurance companies."

"You will, though."

"Not necessarily."

"McKenzie, my attorney told me this morning that he received an email yesterday from the attorney for Heggstad Marina claiming that he, that we, had violated the rules by failing to disclose that E. J. had been seeing a therapist at the time of his death. I swear, McKenzie, I didn't know he was seeing a therapist until Nevaeh told me that you told her. Only you must have then told the lawyer or how else would she have known?"

"Yeah, that's on me. Only I didn't tell Heggstad's lawyer until three days after I told your lawyer, so . . ."

"So, now you know why I'm upset. McKenzie, how can I make you go away? I'd offer money. You can never have too much money."

Yes, you can.

"But you probably already have more than I do," Bizzy said. "I'd flirt with you shamelessly. You'd be surprised how often that works."

No, I wouldn't.

"On the other hand, I met your wife, remember? 'Course, you wouldn't be the first guy to cheat on a beautiful woman that he claims he loves, but with what Garrett Toomey dug up about you, what he told me and Nevaeh about the things you've done, the people you've helped, what do you think my chances are?"

Let's not find out.

"So, where does that leave me?" Bizzy asked.

"Threats."

"Garrett told me he tried that already."

"I meant physical threats against me and mine."

Bizzy turned her head until she could see my eyes and quickly looked away.

"I told you," she said. "I'm trying to be a better person than I was. Besides, I doubt that would work, either. You've killed people."

Don't remind me.

"I'm told that E. J. had a weakness for hot blondes," I said.

We stopped walking.

"So we're back to that again—a motive for killing my husband," Bizzy said. "McKenzie, E. J. and I understood each other. I think we understood each other better than any couple I've ever known. Blame it on my previous occupation. Do you know what I did? What I was convicted of doing?"

"Failure to pay your parking tickets?"

Bizzy was surprised by my answer. She actually chuckled and patted my arm as if I had done her a favor.

You sure weren't going to call her a prostitute to her face, were you?

"E. J. knew the truth, too," Bizzy said. "Of course he did. We met at the courthouse. The only time we ever spoke of it, though, was about a half hour before we were married. E. J. said, 'You're off the stroll for good, right?' and I said, 'Yes, sir.' Only I never asked him to give up his hot blondes. I knew he wouldn't. All I asked was that he remember who he was married to. Besides, do you honestly believe that I tried to kill my husband for cheating on me by pushing him off of a fucking dock?"

Which brings us back to where we started. I mean seriously—who in their right mind would think that was a good idea?

"So, are we good, McKenzie? Are you done with this now?"

"You knew him best—what would E. J. say?"

Bizzy laughed at that.

"Oh, honey, you really wouldn't want to know," she said. "If you think my language is bad . . ."

We continued walking. By the time we reached our cars, the other mourners had already departed. In the distance I could see the Memorial Rifle Squad forming up to honor yet another veteran.

Nevaeh was sitting behind the wheel of a BMW, the driver's side window rolled down. She smiled at me yet said nothing. Bizzy circled the car and opened the passenger door. She spoke to me over the roof.

"I like you, McKenzie," she said.

"Thank you."

"I wish you'd go away and leave me alone."

She climbed into the Beamer, Nevaeh started it up, and they drove off, leaving me standing alone in the parking lot.

"Well," I said. "So much for pressure."

I made a hands-free phone call while I drove my Mustang south on I-35 toward downtown Minneapolis. I was surprised by how pleasant H. B. Sutton sounded when she answered.

"Good afternoon, McKenzie," she said. "What can I do for you?"

What is going on?

"What is going on?" I repeated aloud.

"What do you mean?"

"You sound so happy."

"Why wouldn't I be?"

Okay.

"I have another LLP question for you if you don't mind?" I asked.

"Not at all. Shoot."

Who are you and what have you done with my friend?

"H, is it a good idea for a husband and wife to form a limited liability partnership?" I asked.

"Sure, if it's just the two of them, if there aren't any other partners. You organize the business that way for tax purposes, first. But also you can structure the partnership agreement in such a way that you can protect each other if things go south."

"Do you mean if the business fails?"

"No, I mean if the marriage fails. Normally a divorce could blow it all up or at least cripple the business. A well-designed partnership agreement, though, could keep it going even if the partners go their separate ways. Think of it as a prenup for a company."

"Switching from a limited liability company to an LLP— would that suggest that there might be trouble in paradise; that the spouses might be planning their divorce?"

"What a cynical individual you've become, McKenzie."

"I'm cynical?"

"It could simply be that the partners wanted to change the way they were compensated and taxed. Ask their accountant."

It was their accountant who suggested the change. Could Boland have done that because he was hoping to win Bizzy away from E. J.?

"You're right, H," I said aloud. "I'm becoming cynical. Say, I've been meaning to ask—how did your date go the other day?"

"Oh, McKenzie. I chickened out. I just couldn't force myself to leave the houseboat in my red dress so I switched to black. When I met Jamie—not Jim or James. His name is Jamie. When I met him at the restaurant he was wearing a black suit. So, there we were both wearing black. It was kind of awkward sitting across from each other in the booth. First date, you know. He was kind of yanking at his tie and collar looking uncomfortable. Then he said—Jamie said he was more of a jeans and sweatshirt guy but he wore a suit because he wanted to make a good first impression. And I said—God help me, I said I almost wore red because I wanted to make a *bad* impression. I just blurted it out. McKenzie, he stared at me for like a full minute and I'm thinking, Oh God, and then he leaned across the table and he kissed me. I'm still wearing that kiss, McKenzie. I've eaten, I've drank, I've washed my face, taken showers, yet I'm still wearing that kiss. Oh, and it was just a mess. Not the kiss, but to reach me Jamie had to lean way over the table—did I tell you we were in a booth? And he spilled our water glasses and my wineglass and oh, McKenzie, it was such a glorious mess, and the waitress came to help us mop it up and my lap was wet and so was the front of Jamie's shirt and suit jacket . . ."

Apparently, it wasn't too great a catastrophe considering the way she's laughing.

"What happened after that?" I asked.

"We had a pleasant meal and afterward we left the restaurant and he walked me to my car and I asked him if he remembered the kiss and he said of course he remembered the kiss, and I said that at the time I was afraid of tipping over the table otherwise I would have kissed you back and Jamie said, 'So what's stopping you now?' And we kissed again."

"And then?"

"And then we went our separate ways. It was our first date. Get your mind out of the gutter, geez."

"Was there a second date?" I asked.

"Yes. Saturday night. We met at Orchestra Hall to listen to the Minnesota Orchestra. Do you know that you're not allowed to bring drinks to your seats if you have ice in them? Apparently, the ice makes too much noise, so we drank wine."

"And then?"

"And then, and then—what are you? Sixteen? Okay, we kissed some more. In the parking ramp. Then we went home. I mean he went to his home and I went to my home. Stop it."

"What about a third date?" I asked.

"Tomorrow. We're going to the Guthrie Theater tomorrow night."

"What's on stage?"

"Heck, I don't know. Jamie asked me to meet him at the Guthrie and I said yes."

"You know what they say about third dates."

"Oh God, McKenzie."

"What?"

"I'm going to wear red. I mean it this time."

I drove back to the condominium. It was late in the afternoon yet there was plenty of time to get in my three miles before the paths along the Mississippi River became clogged with pedestrians. Afterward, I showered. It was while I was showering that Brad Heggstad called. I didn't realize it, though, until early evening when I picked up my cell from where I had left it on my desk. My plan was to head out to Rickie's and sponge a free dinner off my wife and listen to some tunes, except I felt the telltale vibration that told me someone had left a message. I drew the picture that allowed me to unlock my phone. The message told me to call Heggstad Marina, so I did.

"Hey," Brad said. "About a week ago you asked me to give you a heads-up when Rick Bennett came back to the marina. Well, he's back."

"Did you tell Sergeant Holmes?" I asked.

"I called the number he gave me. No one answered, though, so I left a message like I did for you only I haven't heard from him."

"Thanks, Brad. I'll see you in about an hour."

"Is there going to be a problem? I mean you and the deputies wanting to talk to this guy, is that going to be a problem?"

"No," I said. "I can't imagine why it would be."

FIFTEEN

It was nearly eight P.M. and the gates leading to Heggstad Marina hadn't been closed yet. Still, it wasn't nearly as busy as the last time I was there. While plenty of visitors lingered in the main building and loitered on the docks, more people seemed to be going than coming. Probably because it was a Tuesday evening, I told myself, although the party aboard the *Miss Behavin'*—I was beginning to think of it as a semipermanent party—was already in full swing. Knots of guests stood together talking and drinking while young couples in swimsuits danced, Meredith Brooks insisting that she was both a bitch and a lover. I wondered how many of the partiers had actually been invited and how many had just wandered over when the music began playing. As for Nelson LeMay, he was nowhere in sight.

I didn't see anyone aboard the *Maverick* as I approached, yet that didn't surprise me. Rick Bennett was probably hiding in his salon, I told myself. I veered off the main dock to the narrow wooden walkway that served both the *Maverick* and its neighbor. I called Bennett's name. That he didn't respond wasn't a surprise to me, either. I imagined him to be wearing headphones and listening to the blues. That's what I would have been doing. Nelson LeMay was playing his music awfully loud.

"Mr. Bennett," I called again.

Nothing.

Maybe he abandoned ship when the volume from LeMay's speakers became too great, my inner voice suggested.

Again, I was contemplating boat etiquette. Should I just climb aboard and knock on the salon door? I called Rick Bennett's name again. When he didn't answer I decided climbing aboard the thirty-six-foot Carver was my only option.

It was while I was settling my weight on the four-rung nautical ladder that led to the stern of the boat that I heard it—the sounds came to me during the low-volume bridge of Brooks's song—a voice growling, "I want my money," followed almost immediately by a single gunshot.

The voice and gunshot came from inside the salon.

What you need to remember is that there was never a decision moment, a point where I considered the consequences of my actions: the good and bad, right or wrong, the fact that I could get killed. I reacted, literally, without thinking, leaping quickly over the gunwale of the boat and dashing to the door of the salon simply because something in my genetic makeup or upbringing or life experiences wired me to be that guy—at least that's how I explained it to Nina later.

I was reaching for the handle of the door when it slid open in a rush.

There was a man standing on the other side.

He was Black, about my height.

I didn't see much of him, though.

I was concentrating on the gun.

It was a nine-millimeter Heckler and Koch—funny the things you notice when you're frightened out of your mind.

Something else you need to remember is that I never gave conscious thought to anything that happened next. It was all instinct and muscle memory.

The man brought the gun up. He would have been better off if he had just squeezed the trigger. Instead, he aimed it at my head.

I shifted my head away and swept my left arm up, striking his wrist with my wrist, pushing the gun hand away from my face. It went off.

Jesus, that was loud.

I brought my right hand up and hit the man solidly under the jaw with my heel.

He staggered slightly yet did not fall or drop the gun.

I took hold of his wrist with my left hand to keep the gun pointed away from me and attempted to drive my knee hard into his groin. He twisted his body, though, and instead I caught his upper thigh.

He pulled his wrist out of my grasp—the man was strong—and swung the gun toward my face. I turned my head and the gun caromed off my forehead just above my left eye. Swear to god, I didn't feel it until fifteen minutes later.

I swept my left arm up once more, again knocking the muzzle of the gun away, and followed up with a four-knuckle strike to his throat.

He felt that—he felt it immediately. He dropped the Heckler and Koch and brought his now empty hand to his neck.

I made a mistake then. I looked down for the gun, saw it, and attempted to sweep it across the stern of the boat with my foot. That gave the man plenty of time to hit me twice with his left fist behind my right ear. I staggered. He hit me again. I fell across the gunwale; nearly tumbled out of the boat.

That's when he screwed up. He bent down to retrieve the gun. That gave me time to roll my body off the boat.

I landed with a heavy thud on the narrow wooden walkway.

The Black man peered over the side of the boat.

He attempted to point the gun at me.

I rolled toward the hull of the *Maverick*.

That caused him to lean farther over the side of the boat.

It gave me enough time to slide between the hull of the boat and the dock.

I fell into the water just as he fired.

The bullet missed me, drilling through the dock into the river. Later I would wonder how that was possible. I mean, I'm sure I wouldn't have missed from that distance.

I managed to swim—if you want to call it that—under the wooden dock. I heard the Black man's weight bounce heavily on top of it. He fired twice more.

The bullets tore through the wood.

They missed me, but fragments of the wood sliced into my cheek below my right eye. I wouldn't feel that until later, either.

I heard a voice scream, "Motherfuck!"

I assumed it was the Black man, yet I was only guessing.

Next I heard the weight of his footsteps as he ran the length of the narrow dock away from me.

I gave it what I thought was a long time, yet only turned out to be about thirty seconds, before I swam under the narrow dock to a thick, round wooden piling that was used to help keep the main dock in place. I managed to climb up.

I glanced toward the entrance of the marina, don't ask me why, and saw people gathering near the gate. Instead of investigating, though, I turned toward the *Maverick*.

I shouldn't have climbed back aboard; the deputies would criticize me for that later. Hell, I would have, too, if I was still in harness. At least I was smart enough not to touch anything as I moved inside the salon, although I was dripping water on the floor. There was a small lamp burning. It was just bright enough to show me the body of Rick Bennett lying on the deck. My first thought was to check for a pulse, apply what little first aid I had been taught. Only I knew he was dead. He had been shot in the face. The bullet came out the back of his head. It was not a pretty sight. I turned away.

As I did, my eyes swept across the boat's galley. There was a laptop on the narrow counter, its screen open. I don't know what compelled me to do it, yet I tapped the touchpad and the screen lit up, showing me a map of the Mississippi River from Stillwater to St. Louis. The ports of a dozen cities were highlighted—Red Wing, Winona, Lacrosse, Prairie du Chien, Dubuque, Davenport, Burlington, and others.

Were these all your homes away from home, Rick? Did you have friends down there? Will they miss you?

I left the lounge and climbed off the boat.

The partiers on LeMay's yacht were no longer partying. Instead, they stood quietly murmuring to themselves, asking, "What's going on?" and "What does this mean?" They weren't sure what had happened, yet they all knew that it wasn't supposed to happen here. In the Cities, sure. On the North Side of Minneapolis or the Thomas Dale neighborhood in St. Paul, but not Stillwater. Not at the Heggstad Marina.

I spied Nelson LeMay standing on the bow of his yacht. He reached up and touched his face. For some reason, that compelled me to touch my face. My fingertips became wet with blood. I wiped them on my waterlogged clothes.

Nina is not going to like this.

I found the piling I had climbed and leaned against it. A few seconds later, I slid its length to the floor of the dock. I could hear the music spilling from the *Miss Behavin'*'s speakers; no one had thought to turn off the music system.

Amy Winehouse was singing "My tears dry on their own."

In the distance I could hear sirens.

Most murders are mistakes, errors in judgment committed spontaneously by completely rational people who in a moment of rage do completely irrational things. They'll confess later that they didn't mean to do it. A surprising number will confess the moment the cops walk through the door. They might as well. Often they'll be standing there covered in blood and surrounded by witnesses.

Only the murder of Richard Bennett was not a mistake. It was committed deliberately by a man who had no intention of confessing. It was committed, if I heard correctly, for money.

At least that was what I was thinking when the squad cars from the Stillwater Police Department arrived. There were three of them. One of the officers lingered at the entrance to the marina, surrounded by people who all seemed to be talking to him at once. The others climbed down to the docks and approached the *Maverick* as quickly as they could without running. I recognized one of them.

Officer Eden Stoll found me sitting on the dock, my back against the piling.

"McKenzie," she said. "We just received a 10-78."

I gestured at the *Maverick*.

"It's now a 10-79," I said.

"Make sure he isn't armed," the second officer said. His hand was resting on the butt of his piece.

"His name is McKenzie," Stoll said. "He was on the job in St. Paul."

"I don't care," the officer said.

I used the piling to help lift myself up and extended both of my arms. Stoll patted me down while her partner watched.

"The suspect is a Black man, about six feet, one-eighty," I said.

"If you say so," the second officer said.

"Murder victim is named Richard Bennett. He's inside the salon."

"Show us."

I sat back down.

"Wait for the detectives," I said. "The boat is clean. There's nothing you can do except contaminate the crime scene."

Stoll was inclined to listen to me. Her fellow officer was not. While Stoll used the microphone attached to her shoulder to inform dispatch that they were now at the scene of a murder instead of a shooting, he climbed the stairs onto the boat and slipped into the lounge. He returned less than a minute later.

"He's dead all right," the officer said.

"Is that your professional opinion?" I asked.

My response made him angry.

"Get up," he said.

"No."

He took a step closer to where I was sitting. Stoll intervened, putting herself between us. Her partner looked at her like she was a traitor.

"Washington County uses the Bureau of Criminal Apprehension, right?" I said. "Let the BCA's Crime Scene Team work the boat. You need to secure the crime scene." I gestured at the crowd on the *Miss Behavin'*. "Lots of witnesses. You should get their names, contact information—don't let anyone leave until the detectives arrive."

"Are you telling us how to do our job?"

"Apparently someone needs to."

Again, the officer was offended. He didn't like the way I was speaking to him. I wouldn't have liked it, either. Normally, I would have just sat there and kept my mouth shut, only I was in a bad mood.

Stoll bent to where I was sitting. She used the tip of her fingers to gently turn my face to the right and left. Blood stained my neck and the collar of my shirt; my clothes were wet and I was trembling from the cold despite the mid-seventies temperature.

Yeah, let's go with that—you were trembling because of the cold.

"That's an awful gash on your forehead," Stoll said. "There's a long sliver of wood imbedded in your cheek, too. Let me take it out."

"No," I said. "Leave it or it'll start bleeding again."

"McKenzie, you should be in a hospital. You might have a concussion. I know you're going to need stitches."

"We'll wait for the detectives. Edie"—*where did that come from?*—"you need to go to work."

She did. While her colleague hung around the dock, apparently convinced that I needed guarding, Stoll moved to the *Miss Behavin'*. People gathered around her, anxious to learn what she knew. I don't know if she told them. She did ask plenty of questions, though, and wrote the answers down in her notebook.

"She's wasting her time," the officer said. "The Sheriff's Investigative Division will take over when they get here, anyway. They always do."

Jealous much?

As if on cue, Sergeant Stephen Holmes and his people made their entrance. I might be giving the impression that this took a long time, yet it was only a few minutes after the Stillwater PD arrived. A couple of deputies stayed at the front gate and basically closed down the marina. No one was allowed in and no one was allowed out until they were carefully identified and questioned. I kept waiting for the owner of the marina to make an appearance, only he didn't.

"McKenzie, what are you doing here?" Holmes asked me.

"Brad Heggstad called and told me that Richard Bennett had returned. Heggstad said that he had also left a message for you, but I guess you didn't get it."

"I got it. I just thought it could wait until tomorrow."

"I drove to Stillwater to see Bennett. I arrived just in time to hear the gunshot that killed him. I'm afraid I allowed the suspect to escape. Sorry about that." I gestured toward the gate to the marina. "What happened over there?"

"According to witnesses, Heggstad was closing the front gate when a Black man hit him hard in the back of the head and ran through the opening into the parking lot. Heggstad might have broken his wrist when he fell. One of the witnesses transported him to Lakeview Hospital. I have a man heading over there right now."

"I'm sorry to hear that," I said.

"You look a little beaten up yourself."

"I hadn't noticed."

"Witnesses said that after hitting Heggstad, the suspect ran through the parking lot and up the street. If he drove, he didn't park in the lot."

"Probably knew about the surveillance cameras."

"We'll secure the footage after my man talks to Heggstad. Like I said, I was told that the suspect is Black."

"Yes."

"Can you ID him?"

"Only a general description, about six feet, one-eighty; I couldn't even tell you what clothes he was wearing except that they were dark. Sorry."

Behind Holmes, the Stillwater cop, who was still standing around like he had nothing better to do, smirked at me.

"The gash on your head, I'm surprised you know what clothes you're wearing," Holmes said. "I notice they're wet."

"I went into the river."

"Why did you go into the river?"

"Funny story."

"You're going to tell me, right?"

"Yes, sir."

"Start by telling me about Richard Bennett."

"He's inside the salon of his boat."

"Show me."

"No."

"No?"

"I'm not on the job anymore. There are things I don't have to stare at. I promise, Stephen"—*first Edie and now Stephen; suddenly everyone is your personal friend?*—"Bennett won't be hard to find."

"I better take a look," Holmes said.

I watched as he climbed the ladder into the boat and entered the lounge. Meanwhile, his deputies were busy interviewing not only the guests on the *Miss Behavin'*, but anyone they could find on the boats in the marina. I noticed that they didn't chase off Eden Stoll like her fellow officer had predicted. A few minutes later, Holmes returned. His face was visibly flushed. The Stillwater officer seemed amused by that.

"What the hell are you doing here?" Holmes barked at him.

The officer didn't answer. Holmes used his thumb to indicate that he wanted the officer gone. The officer walked up the dock toward the front entrance. He passed four men who were fast approaching from the opposite direction. The men wore windbreakers indicating that they were members of the BCA Crime Scene Team. I knew from experience that two of them were most likely forensic scientists and the other two were field agents. They were all toting suitcases that you would never see at an airport, two of them on wheels.

When they reached the *Maverick,* one of them said, "Evening, Sherlock," yet there was nothing derogatory in his voice.

"Watson," Holmes said in reply. He gestured at the boat. "It's all yours, boys."

"The ME should be here soon," Watson said.

Holmes nodded as the Crime Scene Team went to work, opening their suitcases and retrieving video cameras and other equipment, including yellow hard plastic tents with numbers printed on the sides that I knew they would use to mark the bullet holes in the dock and the ejected shell casings. *Jesus, how did he miss you?* Night was falling, so the team also set up lights while a field agent pulled out a roll of bright yellow tape.

Holmes squatted next to me on the dock; there was no place to sit.

"Touch anything when you were on the boat?" he asked.

"No. You?" Holmes didn't respond. "My prints might be on the stern of the boat; the hull, but not inside. I might have dripped water, though. Maybe some blood."

"I'll let the boys know your prints are on file anyway. McKenzie, talk to me."

I responded slowly and carefully, detailing everything that I had seen and done since receiving Heggstad's phone message even though I knew I would be giving my statement again—and again. While I was speaking, Stoll appeared. She stood quietly behind Holmes until I completed my story. Holmes didn't seem to mind.

"Witnesses partying on the boat corroborate McKenzie's statement," she said. "Most of them said they didn't hear the first gunshot, but they all heard the second, third, fourth, and fifth. A couple witnesses claim they saw McKenzie approach the boat. More claim they saw the suspect running away from it. One witness who was using her cell phone to film her partner while he danced has a few seconds of video showing the suspect running. I've recorded names and contact information."

Stoll held out her notebook. Holmes accepted it.

"Your investigators are re-interviewing the witnesses now," she added. "One of them secured the camera phone."

"We'll talk more later," Holmes said.

"I think we should get McKenzie to the hospital."

"I agree. You take him. I'll meet you there soon."

"Yes, Sergeant."

The two of them helped me to my feet and Stoll and I started off toward the direction of the front gate.

"Officer Stoll," Holmes said. "Good work."

"Thank you, Sergeant."

What about you? Don't you get any love?

Somehow Stoll and I managed to evade the media that had already gathered in the parking lot of the Heggstad Marina; the camera people seemed to be vying for position along the fence, wanting to get as much of the marina as possible in the background while the reporters did their live remotes. Apparently a killing on a boat in Stillwater was considered big news. But then, what is it they always say? "If it bleeds, it leads."

I sat in the front seat of Eden Stoll's patrol car as she drove to Lakeview Hospital less than ten minutes away. My clothes were still damp, but at least I had stopped trembling. I pulled out my cell phone. To my utter astonishment and delight, it still worked.

The children in China who put this together really know their stuff.

I called Nina.

"Hey, sweetie," I said. "Something came up and I'm going to be late."

I attempted to keep my voice light and carefree, only Nina had known me for a long time.

"What happened?" she asked. "Are you all right?"

"I'm fine."

"Are. You. All. Right?"

"Yes, Nina. I'm going to be fine. They're taking me to the hospital—"

"Hospital? If you're all right why are they taking you to the hospital?"

"A cut and a bruise—"

"Dammit, McKenzie."

"I'll be fine. I promise. I'll be home soon. You can kiss it and make it all better."

"That's not funny."

"I'm trying to tell you not to worry."

"Geez, why in the world would I worry? What hospital are you going to? I can drive down there."

"Nina, no. By the time you got here I'd be already driving home."

"You're able to drive?"

"I told you, it's only a cut and a bruise."

"If you say so."

"Nina, I'm really sorry about all of this."

"That's what you always tell me."

"I always mean it, too."

Nina paused for a long moment.

"We've had this discussion before," she said.

"Yes, we have."

"You are who you are. Wait, does this have anything to do with E. J. Woods? Is this because of me?"

"Okay, one—I don't know. And two—absolutely not."

"McKenzie—"

"I mean it, Nina. You're not responsible for anything someone else does, including me."

"I feel responsible."

"Please don't." By then Stoll had pulled her patrol car into Lakeview's parking lot. "Listen, I have to go. I'll see you soon."

"I love you."

"I love you more."

I hung up the phone just as Stoll turned off her engine.

"You love her more?" she said. "Is it a competition?"

"My wife has always given me much more than I could possibly give her."

The emergency personnel at Lakeview Hospital proved that they were both efficient and professional. In short order, they determined that I did not have a concussion; they treated the gash and bruise on my forehead with antiseptics and a bandage. However, it required eight stitches for them to close the wound after they removed what turned out to be a nearly two-inch-long sliver of wood imbedded in my cheek. They said the stitches should come out in three to five days to minimize scarring. I said a scar would only make me look more dashing. Stoll, who never left my side, said I could always hope.

After covering the stitches with petroleum jelly and a non-stick bandage, the physician in charge offered me a prescription for opioids to deal with the pain, only I turned him down. I figured I had enough problems.

Holmes arrived at the hospital along with a videographer and a Washington County assistant attorney named Nicholas Powell. They found an empty room where the videographer and I were installed. I spent nearly a full hour recording my statement. The assistant CA seemed to think that asking the same questions in a half dozen different ways would change my answers. They didn't. At the same time I nearly shouted at him, "Hey pal, even baseball games take less time than this."

Holmes wasn't pleased, either. He had remained interested in what I had to say for about twenty minutes, but checked out when Powell began repeating himself. Officer Eden Stoll had been in the room with us; Holmes had invited her and Powell seemed to enjoy having her for an audience. Maybe that was why he took his time. 'Course, he didn't see her yawning behind his back.

Afterward, Holmes said, "Now tell me that wasn't fun."

Stoll looked at him like he was nuts.

While at the hospital, I had the opportunity to speak with Brad Heggstad. He did indeed have a broken wrist that had been encased in plaster and while he didn't have a concussion, either, his head wound also required sutures. How the doctor managed that without shaving the hair around his wound remained a mystery to me.

I asked Heggstad what had happened to him. He told me that he never saw the man who hit him, although he was sure it would be on the video he directed his employees to turn over to the county deputies.

"I had turned on my cameras," he told me.

So, there's that.

I told him that I was sorry he was hurt. He told me that he was sorry that I was hurt. He then asked if I knew exactly what happened at the marina. The deputies had been somewhat vague when he asked them and the ACA was even less forthcoming when he filmed Heggstad's statement. Apparently, he didn't want to contaminate Heggstad's recollection of the evening's events. I explained.

"This is so bad," he said. "So very, very bad. Bad for the marina. Our reputation. If people don't feel safe . . . And Rick. Why would anyone do that to Rick?"

For money, my inner voice answered, only I didn't say so out loud.

"McKenzie, did this all happen because of you?" Heggstad asked. "I don't mean just you, I'm not blaming just you, but E. J. Woods; because of what happened to him; because of the lawsuit?"

"I don't know," I said.

God, I hated those three words.

Eventually, Stoll drove me back to the marina so I could

retrieve my Mustang. I asked her how much time was left in her shift.

"That ended hours ago," she told me.

"You're a good cop, Eden."

"Trying to be," she said.

After Stoll dropped me off, I lingered at the now locked gate to the marina. The media had departed and so too, apparently, had the BCA and Washington County deputies. All seemed quiet. I looked toward the *Deese and Dose*. From my perch it seemed empty; there were no lights. Of course, it was now nearing midnight.

Besides, it's not like Dave and Barbara actually live on their boat, my inner voice told me.

I gazed at the *Miss Behavin'*. LeMay's boat appeared empty, too.

Maybe he went back to New Hope. Unless he's shacking up with a twenty-year-old who views murder as an aphrodisiac.

I stood there for a few more minutes before walking to my car. Heggstad's question followed me there—"McKenzie, did this all happen because of you?"

My key fob unlocked the door; I opened it, and slid inside.

"You wanted to create pressure, didn't you?" I said aloud. "How's that working out so far?"

SIXTEEN

I was up before seven A.M., partly because, unlike Nina, I was an early riser. Mostly, though, it was because my face ached and resting on either side of it on a pillow just made it worse. After dosing myself with coffee and ibuprofen, I spent the early morning learning what the news media had to say. All four local TV stations reported the killing at the Heggstad Marina in as much detail as they could manage in thirty seconds. The newspapers—the *Stillwater Gazette* had the story on the front page; the *St. Paul Pioneer Press* and *Minneapolis Star Tribune* buried it inside—provided more information. Yet it all came down to the same thing: Stillwater native Richard Bennett was shot to death on his boat at the Heggstad Marina located on the St. Croix River, the Washington County Sheriff's Office was investigating, and no suspects had been identified. The only thing that made me happy about the coverage was that none of the media outlets mentioned my name, most likely because the sheriff's office hadn't released it.

That's why I was so surprised when I received the phone call.

"Stop it," Bizzy Woods told me. "McKenzie, you need to stop it."

"What are you talking about?" I asked, although I was pretty sure I already knew the answer.

"I heard what happened at the Heggstad Marina last night. I know Richard Bennett was killed. I know that you were involved."

How does she know you were involved? my inner voice wanted to know.

"Who told you that?" I asked.

"I know people, all right?"

What people?

"McKenzie, you can't believe that this has anything to do with me and E. J., yet I know that you do."

"How do you know?"

"From what you told my lawyer," Bizzy said. "You told Garrett Toomey that Mike Boland and Richard Bennett were friends and for some unknown reason you think they were involved in what happened to E. J."

"Actually, I never said that."

"Stop it, McKenzie, please God."

"Bizzy, you should be happy."

"Why should I be happy?"

"Doesn't what happened to Bennett strengthen your case against the marina? It helps prove that the place is unsafe."

Bizzy paused for what seemed like a long time.

"Fuck you, McKenzie," she said.

Like stepmother, like stepdaughter.

The bandages came off the next day. It was not a pretty sight. I looked a little like Frankenstein's monster. There was still redness around the eight stitches on my right cheek and a layer of crust had formed that needed to be carefully cleaned. A deep bruise covered most of my forehead above my left eye. It was black and blue and red and surrounded a soft scab and yes, it still hurt. I wanted to scratch the stitches and massage the bruise yet experience had taught me that neither was a good idea, so I resisted.

Nina surveyed my face as if it were a map, lightly brushing my cheek with her fingertips.

"You were so pretty when we first met," she said.

I'm sure she meant that in a manly way.

"When was that?" Nina asked. "Eight years ago, nine, when you followed that suspect into Rickie's? Now look at you. All beat up. Scars from guns and bombs and what else? Two weeks after we met you were in the ICU. They had to drill holes into your head to relieve an epidural hematoma from where that guy clubbed you. Remember?"

"Vividly."

"I should have known then what I was in for."

"Would you be happier if I was an accountant?"

Nina wrapped me in her arms and kissed my undamaged cheek.

"There are times when I could use a good accountant," she said. "McKenzie, we're not getting any younger."

"I'm not, but you . . ."

"Seriously."

"Yeah, I know," I said. "I've been wondering the same thing."

"Wondering what?"

"If it was time I started thinking about moving up to the senior league, the no-checking league. The thing is, Nina—I can still skate; I can still play hockey with the kids."

"Do you need to?"

"No, not really. I have nothing to prove. It's just that occasionally I'll get a call from someone looking for a guy to sub in."

"Like a whining female who asks, 'Can you do me a favor?'"

"Yeah."

"And then you're off."

"Depends on the female."

"I bet."

"It's always been hard for me to say no when someone asks for help. I blame my old man."

"So do I and I never even met him."

Nina broke the embrace and set the flat of her hand against my chest.

"I think I know him, though," she said. "Listen, I won't be the one to tell you to stop, only if I roll my eyes and sigh heavily when you answer the phone, promise me you won't be angry."

"Not even a little bit."

"Oh?"

"I mean I promise I won't be angry even a little bit."

Nina closed her eyes, shook her head, and grinned all at the same time, leaving me with the impression that she didn't believe a word I said.

"What happens now?" she asked.

"About what?"

"About Mr. Woods."

"Are you still having nightmares?"

"They're not nightmares, McKenzie. I don't wake up in a sweat or anything. They're just—there."

"I'm sorry to hear that. Nina, I don't know what more I can do. I had a long talk with Bizzy and while my suspicious nature forbids me from believing everything she told me, I have no reason beyond my suspicious nature to doubt her. As for Mike Boland—between what Bizzy and his therapist and his mother and the veterans at Potzmann-Schultz had to say, his story seems plausible, too; why he was on that damn bluff in Red Wing. If it wasn't for what happened in Stillwater Tuesday night . . .

"Besides," I said. "It's become a literal murder investigation and if I continue to poke around, I have no doubt the Washington County Sheriff's Office will take offense. I'm starting to think that Sergeant Holmes is more Sherlock than No Shit, anyway. Even if he isn't, the BCA is involved and they are very much Sherlock, so it looks like I'm out of it."

"In that case, I mean if you have nothing better to do . . ."

I would have kissed her then; I think Nina wanted me to kiss her then. Except my cell phone rang. I would have let it ring only Louis Armstrong's trumpet was pretty insistent. I picked it up off of my desk. Nina rolled her eyes and sighed dramatically; I doubt Cate Blanchett could have done it better.

"This is McKenzie," I said.

"McKenzie, Sergeant Stephen Holmes."

"Yes, Sergeant," I said.

"I need you to come down to the law enforcement center."

"Why?"

"Trust me; you'll want to be at this meeting."

"When?"

"How soon can you get here?"

"Thirty minutes."

"Do you know where we are?"

"I can find it."

"See you soon."

"Sure."

I turned off the phone.

"You're not out of it then," Nina said.

"Apparently not."

"Too bad. I was about to make a suggestion . . ."

"Please do."

"You told the man that you'll see him in thirty minutes. What I had in mind would take at least an hour."

I quickly called Holmes back.

The Washington County Law Enforcement Center looked as if it had been built yesterday, although it had actually been completed thirteen years ago. I had never been in a cop shop quite like it. The lobby had a marble floor. The high ceilings reminded me of a church. Plus, it appeared that the architects had never seen a window they didn't like.

In addition to the sheriff's office, the LEC also housed the county attorney's office as well as a 228-bed jail, which I thought was awfully convenient. After I identified myself at the desk, it took me and an escort a few minutes to find the correct conference room. Like the rest of the LEC, it was plush with a thick carpet and deep red wooden table surrounded by faux leather swivel chairs. The far wall was floor-to-ceiling glass with a spectacular view of the sprawling Washington County Government Center.

Sergeant Holmes stood when I entered the room. He didn't offer his hand, so I didn't offer mine.

"Good afternoon," I said. "Sorry to keep you waiting."

Only Holmes wasn't alone. He gestured at the woman sitting at the head of the conference room table, several files and a laptop scattered in front of her.

"You know Captain Follmer," he said.

"I do," I said.

Follmer nodded at me.

I nodded back.

What's going on?

"Sit," Holmes said.

I sat.

"McKenzie, you look like crap," Follmer said.

"You should see the other guy."

"About that," Holmes said.

The sergeant had an open laptop in front of him, too. He tapped a couple of keys and spun it around so I could view the screen. It displayed a video of a Black man dressed in dark clothes entering the marina through the front gate and navigating the maze of docks and slips directly to where the *Maverick* was parked. The scene had been filmed at a distance, though. I recognized the boat, yet the man was little more than a stick figure.

"He seems to know where he's going," I said.

"You mean like he's been there before?" Follmer asked.

"Yes, exactly."

Holmes tapped a couple more keys and the video moved ahead by twelve minutes. I watched myself entering the marina and negotiating the docks as if I also knew where I was heading. I recognized myself as I approached the *Maverick*, although I doubt that anyone else would have. Except Nina. Because of the position of the camera, though, I didn't see myself climbing aboard the boat or what happened next. Less than a minute later, the Black man was filmed scurrying over the docks toward the exit.

"Is this all you have?" I asked.

Holmes tapped more buttons and the camera angle shifted. I was able to see the back of the Black man as he came up behind Brad Heggstad while he was attempting to close and lock the gate. The Black man hit Heggstad on the head with the butt of his handgun, pushed past him, and dashed across the parking lot into the night. At no time did I see his face.

Holmes slid a photograph in front of me. It was too blurry to recognize the subject. You might have guessed it was a Black man wearing a black jacket, yet it could have been Michael Jordan. It could have been Michael B. Jordan. Hell, it could have been the actress Claudia Jordan, for that matter.

"Heggstad Marina's cameras aren't worth a damn," Holmes said. "There are eighty million cameras in this country recording our every move, people marching in the streets complaining about the invasion of privacy, yet when we need them the most, when they might actually be of some use, this is what we get. The video taken by the kid with her cell phone—the suspect was too far away to ID in that one, too. Blow up the image and you get what we already have."

"On the other hand," Follmer said.

She slid another photograph across the conference room table at me. This one was clean and sharp—a Black man, well dressed, in his early sixties I would guess. I glanced from that pic to the other and back again.

"Is this the same guy?" I asked.

"We think so," Follmer said.

"Who is he?"

"We have no idea."

"I'm sorry, guys," I said. "If you asked me here to give you a better ID than I did at the scene, a positive ID, you're wasting your time. I was too preoccupied to get a good look at the man's face. I can identify his gun, though."

"Funny," Follmer said. "You don't know him, yet he knows you."

That hit me. That hit me so hard I nearly lost my breath. I tried not to show it, though. Apparently, I didn't do a very good job.

"Something wrong, McKenzie?" Holmes asked. "You seem unhappy."

No shit, Sherlock—the way he slides back and forth between good cop and asshole, now we know how he got his nickname.

"I'm trying hard not to laugh," I said.

"I don't blame you," Follmer said.

"How does the suspect know my name? It wasn't in the newspapers or on TV."

"McKenzie, the reason we asked you here was to give you a heads-up," Holmes said.

Wait. Now he's the good cop again?

"We've been tracing Richard Bennett's movements," Holmes added. "Monday night, the night before he was killed, he was docked at Sunset Marina in Red Wing. Debra, you tell him."

"Stephen reached out to me early this morning," Follmer said. "I went over to the marina to ask if Bennett had been there. The two men behind the counter told me that they hadn't realized how popular he was. When I asked why they said that, they told me a story."

Captain Follmer recalled the story:

Red Wing has a population of about 16,500, yet less than two percent of its residents are Black. What's more, as far as the employees of the Sunset Marina knew, none of them owned luxury boats. That's why they were surprised late Tuesday morning to see a Black man approaching the high counter that they were standing behind.

"Hey," the first man said. "What can we do for ya?"

"Lookin' for a dude named Rick Bennett. Friend of mine."

The first man looked at the second man and waved his finger at him.

"Had no idea Rick was so popular," he said.

"Right?" the second man said.

"Whaddya mean?" the Black man asked.

"That woman sheriff deputy came looking for your friend, was it last week?" the second man said.

The first man waved his finger some more.

"Don't forget McKenzie," he said.

Shit, *my inner voice said.*

"Are you E. J.?" the second man asked.

"What?" the Black man said.

"E. J. Woods. McKenzie said you were pals with Rick."

"I am. Earl John is my real name. I'm just surprised that you know it is all."

"McKenzie told us."

"I don't know McKenzie. You say he's friends with Rick?"

"Yeah, both him and Mike Boland," the first man said.

"McKenzie knew Mike, too?"

Shit, shit, shit . . .

"Really sad what happened to Mike," the second man said.

"It was awful," the Black man said.

"Rick was really upset about it, Mike dying like that. He kept asking, 'What happened, what happened?' like we would know. We told him that McKenzie was looking into it."

"Was he?" the Black man asked.

"Yeah. Him and the lady sheriff's deputy. We saw both of them the day of the funeral, what we're trying to tell you. Rick was upset that he missed the funeral, too."

"Well, here." The first man rummaged through a drawer on the back of the high counter, found a card, and gave it to the Black man.

"His name and number," he said.

The Black man read the card.

"Oh, now I remember," he said. "Rushmore McKenzie."

Are you kidding me?!

"Only you're not having any better luck than he did," the second man said.

"What do you mean?"

"Bennett is gone, man. He left first thing this morning."

"Not first thing," the first man said. "He had an errand in town first thing."

"What I'm saying, Bennett left in a hurry."

The first man waved his finger at the Black man again.

"He's probably in Stillwater already."

"That was only a few hours before the suspect entered the Heggstad Marina," Holmes said.

"The boys at Sunset hadn't thought to ask the suspect for a

name," Follmer said. "They just assumed he was E. J. Woods. I don't know why."

You do. You gave up the name during your first visit. Said E. J. and Bennett were pals; made it seem as if E. J. was still alive.

"The photograph comes from the video filmed by Sunset Marina's security cameras," Follmer added. "We have the video, of course. Well, Washington County has it now. It's their case."

"Facial recognition technology?" I asked.

"We've reached out to Hennepin County," Holmes said. "They're the only law enforcement agency in Minnesota that has the technology. Only I'm not holding my breath."

"Neither would I," Follmer said. "The error rates are much too high for my peace of mind, especially among people of color, and the suspect—"

"Yeah," I said. "What about fingerprints?"

"The BCA lifted quite a few," Holmes said. "At best it takes one to two hours to run them through AFIS. At worst, I've known it to take as long as a week. In any case, I haven't heard from the BCA. If they had a match I'm sure they would have told me. The suspect wasn't wearing gloves, was he?"

"No."

"Didn't think so."

He could have been careful not to touch anything, like you.

"I appreciate that you reached out to me," I said.

"We're not done," Follmer said.

"Our tech guys were able to open Bennett's phones," Holmes said. "He had two of them. His business phone—that's what I call it—was a burner activated in mid-March. The first text he sent read, 'Boat in the water. Waiting for USACE to open river.'"

"USACE?" I repeated.

"U.S. Army Corps of Engineers. The St. Paul District opened the upper Mississippi to boat traffic on March 25."

The day E. J. Woods drowned.

"Bennett only used the business phone to send texts," Holmes added. "As far as the techs have been able to determine, he never once made an actual phone call."

Sounds like Nina's daughter.

"I have a transcript." Holmes searched through the sheets of paper in front of him, found the one he wanted. "Listen to this, and remember, these texts were all made this past week. Monday—sent 'ETA drop site 11:45 A.M.'; response 'I'll be there.' Monday night—sent 'Rendezvous at levee 6:15 P.M.'; response 'On site.' Tuesday—'Under the bridge 4:10 P.M.' There was this exchange on Wednesday—'You're late. I'm on my way. Leaving in two minutes. Please. I have the money.' And so on and so forth. The tech guys tried to trace the phone numbers to the owners—burner phones all."

Meaning their identities can't be traced; the owners remain anonymous.

"The home phone, that's what we labeled Bennett's second phone—it has GPS," Holmes said. "We were able to use it to track his movements. Bennett was always near a town when he sent his texts—Quincy, Fort Madison, Davenport, Dubuque."

"When I was in the lounge of the *Maverick,* I saw a laptop on the counter," I said. "There was a map on the screen."

"It wasn't a map," Holmes said. "It was a chart. Bennett used it to plot his course to specific landings on the Mississippi between St. Louis and Red Wing, none of them at actual marinas."

I found myself staring at the ceiling while I sighed heavily—both Nina and Cate Blanchett would have been proud.

"Rick was a smuggler," I said.

"The man who killed him," Follmer said. "We believe he was

Bennett's employer or partner. What you said you overheard—
the killer apparently thought that Bennett was holding out on
him."

"'I want my money,'" Holmes repeated.

"The way the boys at the Sunset Marina bandied your name
about, it's possible the suspect believes that you and Bennett
had something going on," Follmer said. "It's possible that he believes the money he obviously didn't get from Bennett is in your
pocket. He might reach out to you."

*He might do more than that. He might reach out to Nina
or someone else you care about. This guy knows who you are
by now, of course he does. A name—an uncommon name at
that—and a phone number? How long would it take for you
to turn that into a detailed biography and an address? Half an
afternoon?*

I picked up the photograph of the suspect.

"May I keep this?"

Holmes nodded his head in reply.

"What was Bennett smuggling?" I asked.

"We don't know. The BCA searched his boat as well as his
apartment in Stillwater. Apparently, he was very careful not to
get caught holding."

I stood.

"Like I said, I appreciate that you thought to reach out to
me."

"We're not being entirely altruistic," Follmer said.

"Quid pro quo," Holmes said. "Remember?"

I sat down again.

"What do you need from me?" I asked.

Holmes and Follmer wanted to know everything I had
learned about E. J. Woods and Mike Boland since we last
spoke. I gave them everything I had, including the contents of

the brief conversation I had with Bizzy over the phone yesterday morning.

"Hmm," Holmes said.

"What does 'Hmm' mean?"

"Bennett's second phone, his home phone, he sent a text on March 24 to Boland—the only contact he had with Boland that we could find."

Holmes found another sheet of paper in his pile and started reading.

"Sent 'What is E W doing here?'"

E W? Earl Woods? Elizabeth Woods?

"Response 'I don't know,'" Holmes continued. "Sent 'We're supposed to stay away from each other.' No response. Sent 'I'm leaving.' That was it; there was no reply to that text, either."

We talked it over and agreed that there was nothing connecting Richard Bennett to the death of E. J. Still, the text made us all go "hmm."

While I was thinking it over, Holmes again searched through the files in front of him, found what he wanted, and slid it in front of me.

"One more thing," he said.

The thick card was white and the exact same size as a driver's license. It bore the seal of the State of Minnesota with the words STATE OF MINNESOTA PERMIT TO CARRY A PISTOL printed above my name, address, and driver's license number.

"I took the liberty of making sure that it was valid," Holmes told me.

"I haven't carried in years," I said.

"I'd hate to see you get shot for want of shooting back."

He has a point.

I reached out, rested my palm on top of the card, and swept it across the conference room table toward me.

"If the suspect does reach out to you, you're going to contact us, right?" Holmes asked.

"Just as fast as I can dial 911," I said.

Schroeder Private Investigations was an interesting combination of cop shop and nerd HQ. It had a dozen men and women sitting at gray metal desks answering calls in short sleeves and shoulder holsters, their coats draped over the back of their chairs. These were the field agents; nearly every operative who worked there had been an investigator for one law enforcement agency or another—local police, sheriff's department, state cops, even the FBI. Yet it also had a dozen men and women, mostly younger, dressed as if they were about to either clean out their garages or attend a social event at Comic-Con. These were the computer geeks that ran skip traces, conducted background checks, hunted identity thieves, vetted jurors, uncovered hidden assets, and conducted cyber investigations without ever leaving the comfort of their workstations. I was impressed by how well the two groups seemed to get along.

I walked briskly into the office, made my way to the reception desk, and tapped the top of the desk to get the attention of the receptionist in case she didn't realize that I was in a hurry. The receptionist was named Gloria. I had met her before. She looked at me as if I were a complete stranger.

"How may I help you?" she asked.

"I need to see Greg Schroeder."

Gloria glanced at her computer screen.

"Do you have an appointment, Mr. . . . ?"

"McKenzie. No, I do not have an appointment."

Her head came up as if she remembered hearing my name yet couldn't place it.

"I'm afraid Mr. Schroeder is unavailable. I'm sure one of our other operatives would be happy—"

"Tell Greg that McKenzie is waiting. Give him this when you do."

I handed her the photograph of the suspect that I had received from Sergeant Holmes. She glanced at the pic and back at me, a quizzical expression on her face.

"Just a moment," she said.

Gloria left the reception area. I couldn't see where she went but I could guess. A moment later, she returned.

"This way," she said.

I followed her to Schroeder's corner office. He stood behind his desk while holding up the photograph. His tie was neatly knotted and pushed all the way up to his throat and he was wearing his suit coat, something he seldom did when we'd first met. Behind him was a splendid view of U.S. Bank Stadium in downtown Minneapolis.

"Who is he?" he asked.

"A suspect in a murder that occurred Tuesday evening at the Heggstad Marina in Stillwater. The Washington County Sheriff's Office produced the photograph, only it doesn't have a positive ID yet."

"You're bringing this to me because . . . ?"

"In case you should come across him while protecting Nina," I said. "My advice, shoot first and ask questions later."

Schroeder set the pic on his desk.

"Gloria!" he shouted.

Gloria stepped into the office; my guess was that Schroeder had positioned her outside to await instructions.

"Ron, Celeste, and Steve," he said. "Tell them I'll be out in a few minutes."

Gloria left. Schroeder spoke to me.

"That's the team we had on Nina the last time one of your projects went sideways," he said.

"I remember."

"Talk to me."

I would never work as a bodyguard myself. I could see myself doing it for Nina without hesitation. And Erica. And the family of my best friend Bobby Dunston—Shelby, Victoria, and Katie. I could even see myself doing it for Bobby, although I knew it would piss him off. Yet the idea of risking life and limb to guard a client, of taking a bullet to protect someone I didn't know personally for a paycheck, was far too much for me. Schroeder and his people, though, they were Professionals with a capital P. What's more, Greg and I knew each other long before Schroeder became a PI mogul, back when he was a one-man band; a traditional trench coat detective who drank his coffee black and his whiskey neat. I trusted him with my life. I trusted him with Nina's life.

I told Greg what I wanted. I told him why.

"Where is Nina now?" he asked.

"Rickie's."

"Do you want us to do this on the quiet?"

"No, I'll tell her you're coming."

"How long will we be providing protection?"

"I don't know yet. I'm not even sure if it's necessary. Greg—"

"We'll take good care of her," he said.

I called Nina on my way to the condo. She was not happy.

"Remember Greg Schroeder?" I asked.

"Yeah?" she said, making the word sound more like a question than an answer.

"He's sending some of his people over to Rickie's."

"Why?"

"Just to keep an eye on things."

"You mean to keep an eye on me, don't you?"

"I mean to keep an eye on anyone who comes near you, specifically six foot Black men weighing about one-eighty."

"What's going on, McKenzie?"

I explained.

"This is crazy," Nina said.

"Humor me. I know I'm probably overreacting, only we're pretty sure the suspect killed Rick Bennett for money that he thought was owed to him. Circumstances suggest that he might now believe that I have his money."

"Then Schroeder and his people should be guarding you, not me."

Good point.

"I'll be there in a little bit," I said.

It was Nina who first proposed that we buy our high-rise condominium in Minneapolis. At the time I was vehemently opposed to the idea.

"I will not live in Minneapolis," I told her.

"Why not?"

"Because I'm a St. Paul boy."

Outsiders might think that's a silly argument. Those who live here, though, know the truth. Whoever first called us the "Twin Cities" was being ironic if not downright insulting. Minneapolis and St. Paul were not twins. They were not brothers. Most of the time they weren't even friends. I knew people who refused to cross the Mississippi River in either direction, even to attend sporting events—the Vikings, Twins, Timberwolves, and Lynx in Minneapolis; the Wild, Loons, and Saints in St. Paul. My old man would only drive *through*

Minneapolis while on his way to somewhere else. You think I'm exaggerating.

What changed my mind about the condo, though, occurred during the walk-through when Nina crossed the living room area to what was then an empty bookcase between the fireplace and the south wall. She nudged the bookcase with her elbow. I heard a distinct click. The bookcase swung open to reveal an eight-by-ten carpeted chamber.

So yeah, I moved to Minneapolis. How many people do you know who have a secret room?

After I returned to the condo, I opened the secret room, although I've shown it to so many people it's not much of a secret anymore. I tripped a sensor when I entered and a ceiling light flicked on. There was hockey equipment in there, plus golf clubs, bats, balls, and a Paul Molitor autographed baseball glove that I hadn't worn in over two decades. I also had a safe filled with $40,000 worth of tens and twenties, plus various credit cards, a driver's license, and a passport with my picture and someone else's name—a few years ago I had to "disappear" and it was difficult because I wasn't prepared. Now I was.

Next to the safe was a gun cabinet with eight weapons—four of them registered. I retrieved a nine-millimeter SIG Sauer and holster, made sure the handgun was loaded, and positioned the gun and holster behind my right hip beneath my sports jacket. Next, I retrieved a miniature .25-caliber Colt automatic that I holstered to my ankle.

The secret room was among the reasons I wasn't concerned about keeping Nina safe at home. For one thing, it could be used as a panic room. The real estate agent explained that once the door was locked from the inside, the room was damn near impregnable. Plus, it was wired. I could easily contact the security desk downstairs even without my phone; the security desk was manned twenty-four-seven. It was just a matter of getting Nina from Rickie's to the underground parking garage and up to the condo.

I was concerned with only one person's safety—Nina's. It hadn't occurred to me that anyone else might be in danger, including myself, until the phone rang.

Barbara Deese was nearly breathless when she said, "McKenzie, will you help me, please?"

"Where are you?"

"On the *Deese and Dose* at the marina."

"Where's Dave?"

"He's in Chicago on business. I just spoke to him. He told me to call you."

"What's wrong, Barb? What do you need?"

"Dave was talking about moving to a different marina after what happened Tuesday night. Last thing he said when I dropped him off at the airport was to stay away from the place until we had a chance to figure it out."

"Barb—"

"I came down here because someone at the marina called. He said that a large package addressed to us had been delivered and we should come pick it up. McKenzie, I don't know what to do."

"I'm on my way."

SEVENTEEN

It took me longer to reach Heggstad Marina than usual. That's because I was careful to make sure I wasn't being followed; varying speeds, changing lanes, making a couple of unexpected turns. I was confident that there was no one behind me when I pulled into the half-filled parking lot. I moved quickly, yet not too quickly, to the entrance of the marina. It didn't seem as busy as the previous times I had been there. Most of the visitors wore shorts and T-shirts in contrast to my jeans, polo shirt, and sports jacket. I ignored them as I rapidly negotiated the maze of docks to the slip where the *Deese and Dose* was moored, the words of my old baseball coach ringing in my ears—*Hurry, but don't rush.*

When I reached the boat I didn't bother to ask for permission to come aboard or even knock on the closed salon door. Instead, I pulled it open, lowered my head, and stepped inside, my right hand resting on the butt of the SIG Sauer.

Barbara was sitting on the edge of the queen-size bed at the far end of the salon, her bare legs tucked beneath her, a worried expression on her face. Like the other visitors, she wore shorts and a sleeveless top.

"Are you okay?" I asked.

Barbara nodded.

"Are *you* okay?" she asked in return.

"I'm fine."

"What happened to your face?"

"Long story. Barb, you sounded upset on the phone."

"Does it hurt?"

"Barbara."

"I am upset," she said. "What with Mr. Woods dying and your so-called murder investigation and the fight last week and Mr. Bennett getting killed and now this."

"Now this what?"

Barbara pointed at the brown cardboard box sitting on top of the small folding table in the center of the salon. It was about fifteen-by-twelve-by-twelve inches in size with the large black-and-white mailing label of the United States Postal Service stuck to the side.

My first thought—is it a bomb?

I moved cautiously until I was hovering above the box and carefully unfolded the flaps. I didn't realize I was holding my breath until I gasped.

"Wow," I said.

The box was stuffed with cash: fives, tens, twenties, and fifties—no singles that I could see—tossed together like a salad. I grabbed a few of the bills, held them up to the light, and examined them closely just in case they were an optical illusion.

"Wow," I repeated. "Where did this come from?"

"Read the label," Barbara told me.

I did. The box had been mailed to: Barbara Deese, c/o Deese and Dose, Heggstad Marina, Stillwater, MN 55082.

It had been sent by: Richard Bennett, Sunset Marina, Red Wing, MN 55066.

"The postmark," Barbara said. "Mr. Bennett mailed this Tuesday. He mailed it the day he was killed."

I checked the postmark just because. She was correct.

"When I first opened the box and saw all that money . . . McKenzie, I thought it was some kind of a joke. Then I realized that the joke was on you; that the money was meant for you. Wasn't it? The box? Only why would Bennett send it to me if it was meant for you?"

"Bennett didn't have my address. He had yours, though."

"Because I gave it to him when we met that night. Only, McKenzie, why would he send this money to you?"

To keep it from the man who killed him, my inner voice answered.

I placed the bills back in the box and picked it up. I estimated that it weighed about ten pounds. I did the math. A single bill weighs one gram. There are 454 grams to a pound. I was holding at least 4,540 bills of various denominations.

"How much money is in here?" I asked. "Do you know?"

"Do you think I counted it? McKenzie, this frightens me. What should we do?"

I chuckled at the question. So many options danced in my head including taking it to the Grand Casino in Hinckley.

"My advice, we'll call the county sheriff's office," I said.

"No!" Barbara shouted.

My head snapped up and I saw her grab a small pillow and hold it over her chest like a shield.

Her unblinking eyes were pointing at something behind me. I spun toward it.

A Black man was standing silently in the doorway, a gun in his hand. I recognized the Heckler and Koch from personal experience. I recognized his face from the photograph Sergeant Holmes had given me. He was smiling, only I didn't think it was from happiness or joy. He smiled the way that Nelson LeMay smiled, out of habit.

"You're not calling anybody," he said.

I didn't have a response to that.

He gestured with his handgun.

"Move over there," he said. "Do it now."

I did, raising my hands to shoulder height as I circled the table. I took three backward steps until I was deliberately standing between Barbara and the Black man. That's when it occurred to me just how cramped the salon of the *Deese and Dose* actually was. Four adults of average height and weight might sit comfortably around a table about as large as an over-sized TV tray. Three people, though, two standing and one with an enormous nine-millimeter semiautomatic pistol—suddenly it seemed so very, very small.

The man pointed the Heckler and Koch at the box on the table.

"Is that what I think it is?" he asked.

"What do you think it is?"

"Don't move."

He brought his gun up and aimed it at my head.

"I mean it," he said.

The man drifted cautiously toward the table, all the while pointing the gun at me. For a moment, I was back at the academy, the instructor asking a group of recruits a simple question.

"What should you do if someone puts a gun to your head?"

"Whatever he tells you to do."

Yet that was only part of the answer. Most important, the instructor said, was to remain calm. He told us we would be incapable of thought or action if we slipped into an "Oh my God, oh my God, oh my God" mode. Plus, calm begets calm. If we panic, the person with the gun might panic. Stay calm and he'll stay calm. Oh, and establish eye contact. Looking into the assailant's eyes forces him to acknowledge your humanity and that might introduce a degree of hesitation. Hesitation is your friend.

I watched as calmly as I was able while the Black man moved to the edge of the table. His eyes flicked quickly back and forth from me to the box as he used his free hand to unfold the flaps. He spent less time studying the money than I had.

"This is mine," he said.

"Take it," I said.

"Is it all here?"

"Yes," Barbara said. "I didn't touch any of it."

"Bitch, you better not have."

Under normal circumstances I would have called him out for his misogynistic insult. Instead, I watched as he wrapped his free arm around the box and hugged it awkwardly to his side, all the while keeping the gun pointed at me. The heavy box began to slip from his grasp when he took a step backward, though, and he set it back on the table.

"Do you need help carrying that to your car?" I asked.

"You're fucking McKenzie, aren't you? Rushmore McKenzie. What kind of name is that?"

I came *this*close to telling him the joke.

"What's the deal you had with Rick Bennett?" he asked before I could.

"None."

"Don't give me that shit. He sent you my money."

"We don't know why he did that. We barely knew the man."

"Then what were you doing at his boat Tuesday night? Huh? You like what I did to your face?"

"No."

"You're lucky that's all I did."

Yes, you are. Don't push your luck.

I took a step forward, my hands still raised. If I was going to make a move I needed to get close; close enough to go for his wrist or the gun itself. He was at least fifteen years older than I was. That would be to my advantage. I hoped.

"I went to see Bennett—" I said.

"I told you not to move." The Black man waved his gun menacingly. "Get the fuck back."

I stepped back. I heard Barbara gasp for breath behind me.

Don't push your luck, I said. You never listen to me.

"I went to see Bennett to ask what he knew about Mike Boland's death," I said.

"He was pissed about Boland. They were friends; I didn't know that. We were all supposed to keep our distance; that was a rule from the start. Bennett figured I mighta had somethin' ta do with what happened to Mike. That's what he told me, anyway."

"Is that why you killed Bennett?"

"I had no choice." The Black man was yelling now. "This isn't my gun, it's his. He pulled it on me, accused me of pushin' Boland off that cliff. I took it away and shot him. What was I supposed to do? Then you showed up and I was forced to defend myself. All I wanted was my money. Bennett was supposed to give it to me in Red Wing. Instead he mailed it to you."

"Did he tell you that?"

"I knew from what they told me at the marina down there that him and you and Boland were all partners. Then you showin' up at his boat—Bennett didn't have my money which meant you must have it, that's what I figured. I staked out the marina here waiting for you to show up. I knew you would."

"Was Bennett right? Did you push Boland off that cliff?"

The Black man's eyes narrowed, his grip on the butt of the nine millimeter seemed to tighten, and his smile disappeared. I found it disconcerting.

Remember the part about keeping him calm?

"What's Boland to you, anyway?" he wanted to know.

"Nothing, except he was a friend to E. J. Woods; he worked for him."

"So fucking what?"

"I've been trying to find out what happened to E. J."

"You think I killed him, too, don't you? I didn't. Earl John was my friend . . ."

My friend?

"Me and him—everything was going great, had been going great for over five years until the accident. It coulda kept on being great even after Earl John drowned except people got greedy. Boland got greedy. I tried to make his death look like an accident, but you . . ."

The Black man waved the nine more or less at me.

"I've known shitheads like you my entire life," he said. "Assholes thinking they're allowed to fuck around in other people's shit. Rushmore McKenzie. You're nothing but a fucking monkey mouth."

And then I knew. Some of the details were still missing, yet I realized exactly what had happened and why. It was like opening a box of puzzle pieces only to discover that someone had already put them together. I was pretty sure I even knew the Black man's name.

Change the subject. Calm him down.

I used my chin to point at the box filled with cash.

"How much is in there, anyway?" I asked.

"One hundred and thirty-seven thousand, three hundred and fifty dollars. Maybe a little less. I don't worry if it's only a *little* less. Cost of doin' business."

"Drug smuggling must be pretty lucrative."

"Fuck drugs. I don't deal with no drugs. Me and Earl John would never do that."

"What was Bennett bringing up the river then?"

The Black man smiled some more, this time on purpose.

"Caviar," he said.

"Wait," I said. "What?"

"Russian caviar?" Barbara asked.

"Depends on which labels they put on the cans but sure, honey, why not Russian?" the Black man said.

"Labels they put on the cans?" I asked.

"The caviar comes from China. China produces like sixty

percent of the world's supply; they're tryin' to corner the market, you know? Some of it is pretty good. A lot of it is just cheap shit. Caviar for the masses. What we do, we buy the cheap Chinese for something like nine bucks a pound, ship it here from Hong Kong, stick a different label on the cans, call it Beluga, Almas, Ossetra, Kaluga, Sevruga; say it comes from Russia or Iran—restaurants, retail stores just buy that shit up, sell it for forty-five to two hundred and fifty bucks an ounce. An ounce. Sometimes they charge even more than that. They get away with it because the customer thinks that it's rare; that it's almost impossible to get because of government bans and embargoes and sanctions and shit. Russia and Iran, you know, they're the bad guys. Like China. 'Course, if they want 'guilt free' caviar, we can always say it comes from Italy, Germany, or France. Even Israel."

I didn't mean to say it out loud, the words just spilled out— "This is all about counterfeit caviar?"

"You don't like caviar, man?"

"I do," Barbara said.

I glanced at her.

At least she *seems calm.*

The Black man said, "Deal drugs, you got the DEA, FBI, fucking coast guard, cops all over the place not to mention other dealers who want what you got. Caviar, man; no one gives a shit about caviar. Bring it up the river from the Gulf of Mexico, through New Orleans—my territory is St. Louis up to the Cities."

"Richard Bennett would drive his boat down to St. Louis," I said. "He'd pick up the goods, and distribute them to your customers as he cruised back up the Mississippi."

"That's right. Eight times a year. Sometimes nine depending on the weather."

"When he reached Red Wing, Bennett would hand off the money he collected to Mike Boland. Boland would launder it through E. J. Woods Tree Care Services where he worked part-time as an accountant . . ."

That's the real reason why E. J. fired his daughter. He didn't want Nevaeh involved in this.

"E. J. would take his cut," I said. "And you, as a member of the limited liability partnership, would receive a clean check, with all federal and state taxes deducted, that you could deposit without fear in any bank in the country."

"I also got health insurance and a 401(k). You think you have it all figured out, huh, McKenzie?"

"Yes, Mr. Martin, I think I have it all figured out."

The way his eyes grew wide, I knew I had guessed right.

"Keith Martin," I said. "You and E. J. pulled a burglary of a tech store some years back and got caught. E. J. managed to get out from under the charge, but the state sent you to Oak Park Heights. That's where you met Richard Bennett."

Martin smiled—'course, he'd never really stopped smiling.

"That's where I met the dudes who put me onto the caviar gig, too," he said. "It's amazing the people you meet in prison."

There's only one question left to ask, my inner voice told me. *How fast can you draw the SIG Sauer nine-millimeter semiautomatic handgun holstered to your right hip, squeeze the trigger, and hit the mark? Martin will get a shot off, too. He missed you the other night. He won't miss now. The salon is so small it would be a miracle if he did and you've already used up your share. Yet if you could stop him from getting off a second round and shooting Barbara—forget all that crap about not wanting to be a bodyguard. You are her bodyguard now. She wouldn't be in this mess if it weren't for you.*

"I know what you're thinking," Martin said. "I see it on your face. You don't need to worry. I'm not going to shoot you or your woman."

Barbara is your woman from now until this is over. Don't forget.

"You shot Richard Bennett," I reminded him.

"I told you, I had no choice."

"What about Mike Boland?"

"I didn't have a choice about that, either. Like I told you, Boland got greedy."

"But not for money," I said.

"No. He got greedy for E. J.'s wife. For Bizzy. After E. J. died, he tried to make Bizzy his woman. Bizzy said no. He said he'd quit then, quit being our accountant. You know, a spurned lover and all that shit; we couldn't trust him to keep his mouth shut."

"So you lured him up that bluff and pushed him off."

"You gotta do what you gotta do."

"What's stoppin' you from doing the same to us?"

"You figured it all out, so will the cops if they haven't already," Martin said. "You don't think I knew this day was coming? You don't think I planned for it? Planned to disappear? All I need is a head start, man."

He pointed at the box filled with cash.

"This will help."

"Then take it and go," I said.

"When I say head start, I mean more than the five minutes I'm going to get carrying this to my car and driving off while you call the cops. What you're going to do is take me down the river."

"How far?"

"I'll tell you when we get there."

"No," Barbara said.

She moved out from behind me and stood at my side.

"No," Barbara repeated. "I will not."

Martin kept pointing his gun at me even as he spoke to her.

"You'll do what you're told, bitch," he said.

"No," Barbara said again.

Martin's eyes grew wide with anger.

"Tell your woman to keep her mouth shut," he said.

Keep him calm, keep him calm . . .

"Barbara," I said.

I attempted to place myself between her and the man with the gun again. She pushed me away. I'll repeat that—she pushed me away!

Who is this woman?

"No." Barbara was speaking to me but looking at Martin. "We're not going to help him escape. Why should we? So he can shoot us and dump our bodies in the St. Croix River? Or the Mississippi? I'd rather he shoot me here. Shoot me now. Get it over with."

"What is wrong with you?" Martin wanted to know. "I don't want to shoot anyone."

"You just admitted that you killed two people."

"That was business. This is—listen, sister, just take me where I want to go and you'll be fine."

"No."

"Fuck, I don't need this."

Martin swept his gun off me and aimed it at Barbara.

"Yeah?" she said. "Who's gonna drive the boat? You? McKenzie? This boat has two 375-horsepower engines; one starboard, one port. Do you even know how to start them? There are two gearshifts and two throttles. How do they work? You clowns wouldn't even be able to get out of the marina."

"See?" Martin said. "I need you. Why would I hurt you? C'mon now. Take me where I wanna go, everything be cool. McKenzie, tell her."

I lowered my hands and stepped between Barbara and Martin, my back to him.

"Put your hands where I can see them!" Martin said.

I raised my hands.

"Barbie." I used the hated nickname on purpose because I wanted her complete attention and to give the impression that I was in charge. "Barbie, we don't have a choice."

"Yeah, Barbie," Martin said.

I winked at her and smiled.

"Okay," she said.

Barbara spoke that single word as if she expected me to know what I was doing. I didn't. I only knew that we had a better chance on deck than below.

Martin was careful as he brought us up, sending me along the narrow companionway, up the stairs to the cockpit, and across from there to the stern of the *Deese and Dose*—after first pressing the muzzle of his nine millimeter against Barbara's spine.

"Do I have to tell you not to do anything stupid?" he asked.

Next came Barbara. He positioned her in the captain's chair, the boat's instrument panel and controls arrayed in front of her. The companionway was just off to the left of the helm. Martin was able to stand on the bottom rung of the stairs close to Barbara, a safe distance from me, and out of sight from everyone else at the marina.

"Take us out," he said.

Barbara started both engines and called to me to cast off first the bow lines and then the stern lines. Once I climbed back aboard, she backed the boat out of the slip at what I thought was a ridiculously slow pace. Once the *Deese and Dose* was clear of the dock, she spun the boat slowly like a top, without going either forward or backward, swinging the bow until it was pointing toward the St. Croix. She moved us along the narrow waterway at a careful speed, easing the Sundancer past dozens of other boats still in their slips. Finally, Barbara steered us clear of the docks and accelerated.

I heard Martin speaking to her.

"Good girl," he said. "How fast can you go?"

"About thirty-five miles per hour."

"Then get going."

"We're in a no-wake zone. If we go any faster than five miles per hour the river patrols will stop us."

"River patrols?"

Martin glanced forward and aft as if searching for a danger he hadn't anticipated. By then we were heading south on the St. Croix toward Stillwater. There were at least a dozen boats sharing the river with us. In the distance I could make out the city's famous vertical-lift bridge. We were about a hundred yards from the shoreline.

"Just keep going south," he said.

"Past Stillwater?" Barbara asked.

"Yes."

"How far past?"

"I'll tell you when to stop."

Martin climbed the rest of the way up the companionway onto the cockpit. I was standing in the stern of the *Deese and Dose,* resting against the transom, the boat's raised swimming platform on the other side of the transom directly behind me.

Martin moved closer while he tapped the muzzle of the Heckler and Koch against his thigh. He stopped when he was standing in the center of the deck between Barbara and me.

"It won't be long now," he said.

He's right, my inner voice told me. *If you're going to make a move, now's the time.*

Only I didn't get the chance.

That's because Barbara opened up the throttles.

The Sundancer shot forward like a dragster at the starting line.

At the same time, she swung the steering wheel hard right, nearly tipping the *Deese and Dose* on its side.

Martin toppled heavily to the deck, dropping his gun.

I nearly fell, too, yet remained upright because of my grip on the transom.

Barbara swung the steering wheel back and the boat righted itself.

It was now heading straight toward the rocky shoreline at its best possible speed.

Barbara slipped out from behind the controls, turned, and dashed across the small deck toward the stern.

"Jump," she said.

Jump she did, using the transom as a launching pad.

She hit the water well clear of the Sundancer as it sped away from her.

I glanced down and saw Martin searching the deck for his gun. He found it.

That was enough to convince me to roll myself over the transom onto the swimming platform.

I kept rolling until I fell off the platform into the St. Croix.

By the time my head came up out of the water, the Sundancer was slamming bow first into the rocks and sand of the shoreline. The boat's momentum caused the stern to come up out of the water and fall back again; I saw Martin's body hurling forward against the front of the cockpit. At the same time, the front of the boat seemed to leap up out of the water like a stone someone has skipped. It came crashing back down against the sand and rocks. Its fiberglass hull collapsed; it sounded like someone tearing a plastic shopping bag to shreds. The boat rolled onto its side. Martin tumbled out of the boat onto the shoreline and remained still. The engines of the *Deese and Dose* rumbled and shrieked and went silent.

My first thought—did Martin survive that?

My second—Barbara.

I turned in the water to find her. She was swimming smoothly toward me.

My third thought—damn the water is cold.

"Are you okay?" Barbara asked when she reached me.

"Yeah. You?"

"Sorry I didn't give you any warning about what I was going to do."

"Don't be sorry. You saved us."

We were both using sidestrokes as we slowly swam to shore. It wasn't far, about twenty yards before we were able to stand and start wading; the water came to my armpits. We were moving toward the boat, my eyes locked on the prone figure of Keith Martin.

"When we were in the salon and you winked, I thought you were sending me a message," Barbara said.

"What message?"

"I asked myself, what would McKenzie want me to do if I was Nina?"

Save yourself no matter what.

"You did well, Mrs. Deese," I said.

"Mrs. Deese? We're not friends anymore?"

"Your husband is going to kill me."

"Why? I'm the one who crashed his precious boat. Honestly, McKenzie—I never liked that damn thing."

A crowd started to gather even while we were still in the St. Croix River, if you want to call half a dozen boats a crowd. People shouted at us.

"Are you all right? What happened?"

I stopped wading when I saw Keith Martin slowly move to his knees. His eyes searched the sand and stones around him. He found his gun. Then he found us.

"Get behind me," I told Barbara. "Get low in the water."

Martin struggled to his feet yet managed only a step before he went back down to his knees again.

I reached beneath my waterlogged sports jacket, found the SIG Sauer, and brought it out.

Martin raised his gun with both hands.

I did the same, moving into a Weaver stance, my feet shoulder's width apart, knees bent, weight slightly forward, my gun hand pushing outward while my support hand pulled inward; water hugging my waist.

I let him fire first, just like they do in the movies.

A damn stupid thing to do!

When he did, I squeezed the trigger three times, hitting Martin twice.

People on the boats screamed.

I think Barbara did, too.

All I could hear, though, were the words of E. J. Woods's VFW buddies—*We all have PTSD, those of us who saw combat. We all have stories.*

JUST SO YOU KNOW

Washington County Assistant Attorney Nicholas Powell wanted to prosecute somebody, anybody. He held Barbara Deese and me in separate interrogation rooms long enough for our clothes to dry while he pondered possible charges. Unfortunately, circumstances worked against his ambitions. Circumstance one—the Heckler and Koch handgun that Keith Martin threatened us with was indeed registered to Richard Bennett and ballistics confirmed that it was used to kill him. Circumstance two—a dozen witnesses came forward to testify that Martin was attempting to kill us; that he had fired first. Circumstance three—the box filled with one hundred and thirty-seven thousand, three hundred and fifty dollars that was found in the wreckage of the *Deese and Dose* had somehow remained intact, mailing label and all. There was nothing for Powell to do but throw his arms in the air and call the FBI.

The FBI also interrogated us, except they treated us like witnesses to a smuggling and money-laundering scheme instead of suspects. We were actually allowed to make phone calls to our spouses. I had no idea what Dave Deese had to say about all of this. As for Nina, I'll let you guess.

Finally, Barbara and I were allowed to leave the LEC. Barbara hooked her arm around mine as we made our way from the cop shop into the lavish lobby.

"All that money Richard Bennett sent me; do I get to keep it?" Barbara asked.

"No," I said. "It's considered proceeds of a criminal activity, so . . ."

"Too bad. I was thinking of using it to replace Dave's boat."

She was smiling when she said it. The smile went away quickly, though, as she abruptly wrapped her arms around my shoulders, rested her face against my chest, and started weeping.

"What did we do?" she asked.

"It'll be okay," I said. "It'll be okay, I promise."

From your lips to God's ear.

Bizzy Woods denied everything, of course. She told anyone who would listen that she absolutely did not know that her beloved husband, his VFW buddy, and his childhood friend were involved in smuggling. She most certainly didn't know that they were using E. J.'s business to launder money, which was a federal crime punishable by up to twenty years in prison. Unfortunately, the Feds were unable to prove that she was lying. There were no witnesses left alive to contradict her, nor were they able to connect her directly to the "dirty money" or the accounting tricks that were used to scrub it clean.

Oh, the Feds could tell you how much ill-gotten gain had been laundered by E. J.'s company—approximately six million dollars over five and a half years. They could show the court how the money was disbursed and to whom. They could even pinpoint exactly when the crime began—three days after E. J. fired his daughter. Only they couldn't connect Bizzy directly to either the smuggling or the money laundering. Bizzy testified, under oath, that she had nothing to do with the company's bookkeeping, a claim that was confirmed by the employees of the business, by Marilyn Staples and Jack Matachek. She was not a partner except by marriage, despite what she told me. She was not a salaried employee. She never once received a paycheck from the company; they were all made out to E. J. And E. J. had never told her a thing about his activities—or so she claimed.

As for the testimony that Barbara Deese and I provided, we had to admit that Keith Martin never actually said that he and Bizzy were partners, that they were working together. He said "me and Earl John," yet he never said "me and Bizzy." He used the words "our" and "we," yet he never explained exactly who he meant by "our" and "we." What's more, the FBI had been unable to uncover a shred of evidence to prove that Bizzy and Keith Martin had ever met. No phone calls, no texts, emails, photographs, social media posts; no witnesses coming forward to say, "Yeah, him and her were seen together in such and such a place at such and such a time."

That Bizzy profited from the long-running criminal activities, there was no doubt. But was she complicit? And if she wasn't, could she be made to suffer for her husband's crimes?

"I am heartbroken by these events," Bizzy announced to the media, her loyal attorney Garrett Toomey at her side. "I cannot believe the man I loved had deceived me all these years."

Once the Feds realized they couldn't prove either knowledge or intent, they dropped all charges.

Sergeant Stephen Holmes of the Washington County Sheriff's Office was despondent. He actually quoted his namesake at me—*"When you have eliminated all which is impossible then whatever remains, however improbable, must be the truth."*

"Did you tell that to the FBI?" I asked.

"Once they got the case, they couldn't be bothered with the ruminations of a poor sheriff's deputy."

"Isn't that always the way?"

"What do you want, McKenzie?" Holmes asked.

"I am vexed by the turn of events."

"Please tell me you didn't come here just to give me crap?"

We were sitting in a conference room at the Washington County LEC. I had asked to see him. He'd brought his laptop, which could access the case file, at my request.

"Bear with me," I said. "Keith Martin told Barbara Deese and me when he was holding us on the boat, he said that he didn't know that Bennett and Boland were friends, that the people involved in the smuggling and money laundering scheme were supposed to keep their distance. Okay, now remember what you told me about the text that Richard Bennett sent to Michael Boland back in March? He wrote, 'What is E W doing here?'"

"You told all that to the Feds," Holmes reminded me. "They didn't care."

"I'm not talking about the Feds' smuggling or money laundering case. I'm talking about the murder of Earl John Woods."

That caught his attention.

"Keep talking," Holmes said.

"At the time, we didn't know if Bennett was texting about Earl Woods or Elizabeth Woods."

"Go on."

"What was the time stamped on the text that Bennett sent to Boland?"

The sergeant fired up his laptop and accessed the case file. It took a few minutes.

"Eight forty P.M., Friday, March 24," he said. "The day before Woods drowned."

"No, no, no, listen—I was told by his friends at the Potzmann-Schultz VFW post that E. J. was eating ribs on Friday. It was a tradition. BBQ Ribs Friday. They also said that E. J. left the VFW at approximately nine P.M. *after* having a private conversation with Mike Boland. His friends said that E. J. told them he was going to see what Bizzy was up to. That means the 'E.W.' that Bennett saw at the marina had to be Elizabeth Woods."

"What are you telling me?" Holmes wanted to know.

"E. J. Woods was a jealous man."

"Tell me more."

"Bizzy's attorney, a man named Garrett Toomey, said that E. J. was in the process of gaining a fifth insurance policy to bring his total up to an even five million bucks. He told me E. J. was talking to a financial advisor when he was killed, someone Bizzy knew. Nelson LeMay is a financial advisor."

"Who is Nelson LeMay?"

I explained before adding, "I believe that Bizzy decided she wanted a little bit of what E. J. was getting throughout their marriage and went to visit LeMay on his boat; LeMay is pretty persuasive when it comes to that sort of thing. Bennett sees them together and contacts Boland, who, for reasons of his own, tells E. J."

Holmes completed the story.

"Woods goes to the marina and discovers LeMay and his wife together," he said. "There's a scuffle, Woods somehow falls into the river; maybe he trips or maybe he's pushed. The thing is—he doesn't come out."

"It fits the timeline. The Ramsey County Medical Examiner concluded that the victim drowned from one to sixteen hours before his body was discovered."

"And afterward?"

"LeMay is a smart guy. So is Bizzy. Neither of them want to go to jail. Plus, there's all that cash Bizzy stands to gain. So, LeMay leaves the marina while Bizzy remains, holed up in E. J.'s SUV. Maybe she fell asleep; that's why she didn't see my friends Dave and Barbara Deese. But we know she was wide awake to see Nina and I arrive. It explains why she was dressed for the warm Friday afternoon instead of the freezing Saturday morning. It explains why there was a fourth car in the parking lot."

"McKenzie, you can sing and dance with the best of them," Holmes said. "Only there is no way on God's green earth that we can prove any of this in court."

"What makes you think we have to?"

Nelson LeMay was both annoyed and confused. Stillwater Police Officer Eden Stoll had arrested him on his yacht "for the murder of Earl John Woods," she said, slapped the cuffs on him, and drove him to the Washington County Law Enforcement Center, where he was enshrined in an interrogation room. There he sat alone on a metal chair that was bolted to the floor and facing a one-way mirror for a good half hour without explanation. Probably it seemed longer to him.

When we thought it was long enough, I walked into the interrogation room.

"What are you doing here?" LeMay wanted to know.

I tried to appear as confused as he was, turning my head to read the number on the door.

"They told me to wait in here," I said. "The deputies. So, they arrested you already."

"What are you talking about?"

"Did they read you your rights?" I wasn't speaking to LeMay so much as the camera that was rolling on the other side of the mirror. "Did they tell you that you can call a lawyer?"

"McKenzie—"

"Seriously, Nelson. You should call an attorney. Don't answer any questions until you do."

"I don't need an attorney. I didn't do anything wrong."

"Famous last words. Did they read you your rights?"

"Yes, they read me my rights. They didn't tell me why I'm here, though."

"For the murder of E. J. Woods. I thought that was understood."

"That's crazy."

"I just saw Bizzy down the hall. She doesn't think it's crazy."

LeMay's eyes grew wide. His expression shifted from confusion and annoyance to fear.

"Why would they arrest her?" he asked.

I rolled the dice.

"Remember I told you about the fourth car in the parking lot when E. J. died?" I asked. "It was Bizzy's. They brought me down here to identify it."

"What does that have to do with me?"

I shrugged my reply and sat in the chair across from him.

"Why isn't anyone talking to me?" LeMay wanted to know.

"Prisoner's dilemma," I said.

"What the hell is that?"

"Don't you watch TV? *Law and Order? Bosch?* Those *CSI* shows? Two prisoners are accused of a crime. They're each put in separate rooms. If neither of them confesses, maybe the charges go away or they only spend a little time in jail. But if one confesses, goes State's evidence, and the other does not, the one who speaks first will get a lighter sentence or might even be released while the other prisoner goes to jail forever. *The Closer* with Kyra Sedgwick; that was my favorite."

LeMay shook his head vigorously.

"No, no, no, no, no," he chanted.

"Call a lawyer, Nelson."

"If what you're saying is true, why aren't they also talking to me, asking me questions?"

"Bizzy," I said. "My guess is that they like her more than you. She's a babe."

We sat in silence after that, waiting. I like to believe that LeMay spent the passing minutes contemplating every woman he had ever screwed in his life and the very real possibility that one of them was now going to screw him—even though Bizzy had not been arrested and she was not in an interrogation room down the hall. I kinda made that up.

Finally, Sergeant Stephen Holmes entered the room followed by Officer Eden Stoll. Holmes was speaking almost absent-mindedly.

"Mr. LeMay, you have the right to remain silent. Anything you say can and will be used against you—"

"I know my rights," LeMay said.

"Mr. LeMay—"

LeMay stood and gazed directly at Stoll. Maybe he thought she'd be more likely to give him a break.

"It was an accident," he said.

Elizabeth Woods and Nelson LeMay were both convicted of involuntary manslaughter in the second degree. They both received sentences of five years with the expectation that they'd be out in thirty-eight months if not sooner.

The wrongful death lawsuit filed against Heggstad Marina was subsequently dropped. So were the breach-of-contract lawsuits Bizzy had filed against the life insurance companies. That's because, since it was proven that Earl John Woods did not commit suicide, they were forced to honor their policies. However, citing the "slayer rules," the insurance companies refused to pay Bizzy. Instead, the four million dollars went to E. J.'s contingent beneficiary—his daughter, Nevaeh. I heard that Nevaeh had promised to share the money with her step-mother when she was released from prison. I'll believe it when I see it.

I called several times to check on Barbara Deese. She always seemed cheerful during our conversations. Finally, I spoke to

Dave Deese. He was not cheerful. More to the point, he said that his wife wasn't nearly as carefree as she wanted people to believe.

"She's having a hard time getting past the fact that she helped kill that man," Dave told me.

"She didn't kill him, I did."

"Barbara doesn't see it that way."

"Your wife saved our lives."

"Only she's not sure if that's true, anymore. She's wondering if that Martin guy would have let you go like he promised."

"No," I said.

"She's having bad dreams about it. We got her into therapy. She says it's helping."

"I am so sorry about all of this, Dave."

"You did such a big favor for me and then this happened . . . Barbara won't let me beat the hell out of you."

"Thank her for me."

"I'm still tempted, though."

"About your boat," I said.

"Forget the damn boat. We're done with the river."

"If there's anything I can do to make it up to you . . ."

"You can pick up the tab at Rickie's forever."

"That might cost more than the boat."

While Barbara was now suffering from bad dreams, Nina told me that hers had ceased. She seemed disappointed.

"I thought there might be one last dream, and in it Mr. Woods would smile or wink at me; say thank you," she said. "Only there wasn't a last dream. They just stopped."

I gave her a hug and said, "That's a good thing." At the same time I wished that all of my bad dreams would stop, too.

ABOUT THE AUTHOR

DAVID HOUSEWRIGHT is the author of numerous novels featuring Rushmore McKenzie, most recently *In a Hard Wind*. He has won the Edgar Award and is the three-time winner of the Minnesota Book Award for his crime fiction. He is a past president of the Private Eye Writers of America (PWA). He lives in St. Paul, Minnesota.